Deirdre's fingers traced Indy's brow, cheekbones, jaw. "Indy, I've wanted this to happen. I wasn't sure you did, not until last night at the pub."

He ran his hands lightly along her sides, his thumbs grazing lightly over the swell of her breasts. "Your heart's pounding," he whispered.

He pulled her to him, felt her thighs pressed against his. They moved against each other, and suddenly, the world exploded; the earth shuddered. It moved; it really did.

For an instant, the rumble and vibration under their feet seemed natural, a part of them, self-created by the sudden fury and hunger of their passion. Then a concussion hurtled them to the ground and a sound like a thousand claps of thunder pounded his eardrums. Dust filled the cave. He heard Deirdre coughing.

"What happened?" she gasped.

An earthquake, a cave-in, an explosion. "I don't know."

Indy helped her to her feet. They'd taken three or four steps when another blast rocked the cave. They dropped to the floor, and covered their heads as dirt rained over them.

Deirdre coughed. "I can hardly breathe. What's going on?"

Slowly, he lifted his head; he smelled the answer. "Gunpowder. Someone dynamited the entrance."

THE INDIANA JONES SERIES
Ask your bookseller for the books you have missed

AND THE

DANCE OF THE GIANTS

ROB MacGREGOR

BANTAM BOOKS
NEW YORK   TORONTO   LONDON   SYDNEY   AUCKLAND

INDIANA JONES AND THE DANCE OF THE GIANTS
A Bantam Book

PUBLISHING HISTORY
Bantam mass market edition published June 1991
Bantam reissue / June 2008

Published by
Bantam Dell
A Division of Random House, Inc.
New York, New York

Bantam Books and the rooster colophon are registered trademarks of Random House, Inc.

ISBN 978-0-553-29035-6

Printed in the United States of America
Published simultaneously in Canada

www.bantamdell.com

OPM   18 17 16 15 14 13 12 11 10

*If thou be fain to grace the burial-place of these
men with a work that shall endure forever, send
for the Dance of the Giants...*

— GEOFFREY OF MONMOUTH,
HISTORIES OF THE KINGS OF BRITAIN

*Behind Merlin in a misty past one may glimpse
the hierarchy of the druids, and behind that lie
shamanist cults of the Upper Palaeolithic, ex-
tending twenty and thirty millennia into the
darkness. Nor is that the beginning, though in
truth it seems there is neither beginning nor end,
but a Mystery.*

— NIKOLAI TOLSTOY,
THE QUEST FOR MERLIN

1

SURPRISE PACKAGE

Summer 1925

Everywhere he looked, he saw figures draped in billowy black robes, their heads covered with cowls. They chanted, a monotonous, rhythmic drone, over and over. It was endless, maddening.

He peered through the gray haze, trying to get his bearings. It was either dawn or dusk; he wasn't sure and it disturbed him that he didn't know. He could see that he was inside some sort of temple. It was circular and roofless with immense stone pillars arching toward the leaden sky.

He didn't belong here; he was out of place. His head protruded above everyone else's, and he was the only person who wasn't wearing a robe. He looked down at himself and saw that he wasn't wearing anything. Then he realized that he was standing on a flat rock and that was why he was taller than everyone else.

What was he doing here? How had he gotten here?

They were looking at him now. Every head was turned toward him. The droning grew louder; it pounded against him. Why were they moving toward him? Why wouldn't his feet move? Why did his body feel like lead?

One man stood in front of all the others. He pointed at him. "Jones, we know you're coming. Know you're coming."

That was it—the chant.

Now they were rushing at him, a sea of black, their robes flapping at their ankles. He looked around frantically for an escape route. His arms pumped at his sides, his feet blurred beneath him, but he didn't seem to be getting anywhere. They must have drugged him; but who were they?

His head snapped around. They were almost on top of him. *Move. Move. Fast.* Air exploded from his lungs. A grinning face leered at him. The sky tilted. The pillars were toppling toward him. And suddenly he was awake, his arms twitching, his feet jerking, a scream poised at the edge of his tongue.

He sucked in his breath and looked around. But he could still hear the incessant chanting. He blinked his eyes, orienting himself. The train. Of course. The cars rumbled over the rails, the sound of the chanting, and someone was pounding on the door of his compartment. He sat forward, and ran his hands across his perspiration-soaked brow.

"Who is it?"

The pounding stopped. The door opened and a slender, gray-haired Englishman wearing a conductor's uniform peered in at him. "Mr. Jones? Sorry if I disturbed you."

Indy rubbed his face. "That's all right. What is it?"

The conductor held up a package. "It was waiting for you at the last stop."

"You sure it's for me?" Indy took the flat, rectangular box. It was wrapped in white paper, with an envelope taped to it that said *Indy Jones.* "Probably only one of us aboard." He thanked the conductor, who smiled thinly, nodded, and retreated.

He turned the package over in his hand. It looked like a candy box. It rattled when he shook it. He held it to his nose; it smelled faintly of chocolate. Who would send chocolates? he wondered as he slipped a card out of the envelope. The message was typewritten: *Have an enjoyable trip, and good luck on your new job. Henry Jones, Sr.*

He blinked and reread it. Now how the hell did his father know he would be on this train? And since when did *he* wire him boxes of candy? They hadn't even spoken for more than two years, not since Indy had informed him of his switch in studies from linguistics to archaeology, a move his father had described as foolhardy and perfidious.

Then his frown vanished, and a smile curled on his lips. It was Shannon; it had to be. Jack Shannon knew all about his relationship with his father. The package was a goddamn joke, at least to someone with Shannon's jaded sense of humor. He shook his head, and set the card down on the box.

He stared out the window at the unbroken grayness of the countryside, and thought about his last night in Paris. A cloud of blue haze had hung in the air of the nightclub as the black woman on stage swayed and sang, her voice deep and sonorous, a perfect accompaniment to the soulful sounds of the cornet being played in the shadows behind her. As the last notes of the song had slowly faded away to the applause of the crowd, the tall, gangly cornet player with the goatee and unruly hair had walked off the stage. He shook hands, nodded, and smiled as he wove his way through the tables. Finally, he lowered himself into a chair at a table near the corner farthest from the stage.

"You're sounding real good, Jack. You *and* Louise," Indy said.

"Thanks. It's really come together in the last six months."

"I'll miss it."

Shannon studied his face. "I don't blame you for leaving. It's getting too hectic. The scene's changed." He leaned forward and lit a cigarette from the burning candle on the table. "Sometimes, I look around and there's hardly a Parisian in the Jungle anymore. All tourists. Every night a new crowd. The regulars never show up until the last set, anymore. If they show up at all."

Indy put on his fedora. "You know you're welcome to come and visit anytime you like."

"I may take you up on that. I'd like to see London again."

Indy shook off his daydream, and focused on his surroundings. The rural countryside had given way to sooty brick factories and spewing smokestacks; he would be at Victoria Station in another half hour. After leaving Paris earlier in the week, he'd spent a couple of days in Brittany, where he'd examined some of the megalithic ruins in the region. Then this morning he'd taken a ferry across the channel and boarded the train.

He ripped the paper from the package. French chocolates from Paris. "Nice going, Shannon."

He was about to remove the cover and sample a chocolate when the train suddenly braked for another station and a book slid off the seat. He leaned over and picked it up. The cover had flopped open to an epigraph on the first page of the eighteenth-century tome, which read: *Felix qui potuit rerum cognoscere causas.*

"Fortunate is he who can know the inner meaning of things," he said.

He closed the cover. The book was called *Choir Gaur, The Grand Orrery of the Ancient Druids, Commonly Called Stonehenge.* He laughed to himself. He didn't have to look any further for the meaning of his dream. He'd been reading the book before he'd fallen asleep. *Why black robes, though?* he wondered. He was sure druids wore white. But who said dreams made sense?

The train started up again. He tapped his fingers on the package, then lifted the cover, and reached inside for a chocolate. It took a moment before he comprehended what he was seeing and feeling. Something black and hairy was crawling up his fingers, and it wasn't made of chocolate. He uttered a short cry, shook his hand, and gaped at the box. There were a few chocolates, but the rest of the compartments were filled with walnut-size spiders.

His knees jerked, kicking the box into the air. Chocolates and spiders spewed over him. He brushed them off and leaped to his feet. He stomped on spiders and squashed chocolates, sweeping his arms and legs and body clean of the crawling creatures, and trying not to think about how close he had come to taking a bite out of one of them.

Finally, he examined his seat and sat down again, but as he did felt one creeping inside his pants leg, and another on the inside of his collar. He nearly jumped out of his clothes. He shook his leg until the spider fell to the floor, and crushed it under his shoe. Then, carefully, he reached up to his collar and brushed at his neck.

He laughed nervously as a chocolate dropped to the floor. Relieved, he sat down, but immediately felt a tingling on his calf, and pulled up his pants leg. Dozens of tiny, newly hatched spiders wisped over his leg. "*Aw . . . aw . . .*" His teeth chattered; he shuddered.

He brushed them off, swatting them with a rolled-up newspaper. Then, he inspected his leg to make sure none was left.

He picked up the box and examined it. It hadn't been a matter of spiders invading the chocolate box. Someone had planted them.

"Shannon?" he said aloud. Would he go to all the trouble for a practical joke that he wouldn't even see carried out? Maybe, but this was no joke.

He looked at the card again. Maybe it *was* his father? No, couldn't be. He wouldn't. Besides, it was addressed to Indy Jones, and his father never called him that. But Shannon knew that. If this was his idea of playing a joke, why wouldn't he have addressed it to Henry Jones, Jr., as his father's letters had always read when they were college roommates back in Chicago?

He heard a tap on the door. "Yes?"

The conductor opened it. "I need to check your ticket, please."

Indy reached cautiously into his coat pocket, and handed his ticket to the conductor. "Mind if I switch compartments for the rest of the trip? This one has spiders."

"Spiders?" The conductor's eyes shifted about the compartment; his shoulders twitched. Indy understood perfectly. He pointed at a spider crawling along the window frame.

The conductor handed Indy his ticket, and backed out of the compartment. "Right this way, sir."

Indy quickly gathered up his books, and the conductor carried his luggage. At the last moment, he grabbed the empty box and wrapper, hoping they held some clue to the source of the so-called gift. When he was settled in his new seat, he asked the conductor how he might find out where the package he'd received had come from.

"That's easy. Just look at the number in the corner of the wrapper."

Indy flattened it out. "Twelve."

"That's it. They always put a number on the packages so the telegraph office can notify the sender that the package was delivered, if they request the service."

"So where's twelve?"

The conductor smiled. "That's easy. It was sent from London."

2

CLASS ACT

Indy glanced over his shoulder as he passed through the gate of the university and caught sight of a tall, dark-haired man moving behind him. The man had been following him for the last three mornings. He looked back again, but the man had vanished into a crowd of students. Maybe it was just someone who was walking the same route.

Even though six weeks had passed since his first day of classes, he hadn't been able to put the incident with the spiders behind him. He wanted to think it was all a mistake, that the candy box hadn't been intended for him. But he knew it had. He just didn't know why. He'd been expecting something to happen, some indication of what the box had meant, but there'd been nothing.

Despite his efforts, he'd had no luck tracing the source of the package. Shannon had sworn that he knew nothing about it, and Indy believed him. Whoever had sent it had been careful not to leave a trail.

But he was too busy to spend much time dwelling on it. He arrived on campus each day by eight, read over his notes in his office, and taught a two-hour class at nine, and another at one. Although his classes were over at three, his work had just begun. He went back to his office or to the library, where he took out his class syllabus, opened his books, and began preparations for the next class.

He yawned as he entered Petrie Hall. Much of the material he was teaching was new to him, so he was a student as well as a teacher. At best, he was a week ahead of his students, and some days even less. Most of the time he was thankful for the syllabus, which provided him with a general outline of topics to be discussed for the week. But other times, he felt restricted by it. Already he could see ways of improving the class, if he taught it again, but there was no guarantee of that. He wouldn't know for another couple of weeks, when the summer session ended, whether he would be teaching here this fall.

Landing the job so soon after being awarded his Ph.D. had been a surprise. In fact, he would have been content to remain in Paris, and look for a position at one of the city's universities while he continued his part-time job in the archaeology lab at the Sorbonne. But Marcus Brody, an old family friend and a curator of a New York museum, had given him the lead for the job. The native Londoner had wired him that one of his contacts at the University of London had informed him about an opening for a summer teaching job in archaeology that could become full time in the fall.

He hadn't thought he had much of a chance, but

he'd applied, mainly to show Brody he appreciated the help. While the position was for an introductory course, its emphasis was on Britain's megalithic monuments, a topic which he'd examined only superficially in his studies. A week later he was asked to come to London for an interview, and a few days later he received a letter informing him that he'd been hired. Although the interview had gone well, he was convinced that Brody had more influence in professional circles than he'd imagined.

As he entered the classroom, he walked over to the blackboard, and wrote two words in large letters: FIELD WALKING, then moved to the podium and laid down his notebook. The walls of the room were lined with wooden cases containing neatly arranged displays of pottery shards, bone fragments, and a few skulls. A table next to the podium was stacked with reference books and field manuals, and behind it was the blackboard and a wall cluttered with photographs from digs, which documented discoveries or detailed technical procedures.

He greeted the students, noticing the blonde who always snapped her gum, the serious young men in wool suits and ties, and the girls in sweaters with ponytails and ribbons in their hair. His eyes fell for a moment on the good-looking redhead who sat in the center of the front row. Of all the students, she was the one who most interested him, but she also kept him on edge. She spoke up often, too often, interrupting him with a question or comment, or answering questions he posed to the class as if she were the only one present. But that wasn't the only reason he was wary of her. Her name was Deirdre Campbell, and she was the daughter of Dr. Joanna Campbell, the head of the department and his boss.

He opened his notebook to the lesson he'd prepared the day before yesterday. "Archaeology is one profession where you can take pleasant jaunts in the countryside," he began, "and still be working. We even have a name for it. It's called field walking."

Indy looked over the rows of bowed heads of students taking notes. Deirdre, however, sat back in her chair watching him. He explained that field walking involved looking for deviations in the landscape. Slight undulations could indicate the remains of an ancient ditch or the site of a medieval village. Change in the color of the soil or the density of the vegetation was another indicator. If the boundary of a field shifted for no apparent reason or the shoreline of a body of water followed a peculiarly straight line, it might mean the presence of an ancient wall.

He looked up to see a hand raised. It didn't take her long to get started. "Yes, Miss Campbell?"

"What about Stonehenge?"

She spoke with a Scottish lilt, pronouncing it "Stoonheenge." Indy looked blankly at her. "What about it?"

"Well, field walking" (field-wooking, she said) "didn't do much good there. People have walked all over Stonehenge and the surrounding area and didn't see any changes in the landscape because they were too close to them."

Thank God he knew what she was talking about. There was nothing in the syllabus about the use of aerial photography, but he'd been preparing for an upcoming lecture on Stonehenge and had read about the photos taken of the ruins.

"Good point," he said, and quickly explained what she meant. Near the end of the war, a military airport was built a short distance from the ruins, and photographs taken by a squadron of the Royal Air Force in the summer of 1921 revealed some surprising details. It was discovered that the grain in an area leading away from the monument grew in darker colors than the surrounding grain. Yet, it was impossible to see the difference from ground level.

"Does anyone know what would cause this to happen?" he asked.

Of course Deirdre did.

"It shows that the ground had been dug up in those darker areas, and the roots of the plants were able to penetrate the tough layer of chalk that's just beneath the topsoil."

"That's right," Indy said. "In September of twenty-three, Crawford and Passamore began studying these darker areas, using the pictures as their only guide. They discovered the exact entrance to the ruin and a straight road which reached nearly to Salisbury, eight miles to the north. Stonehenge may be the first archaeological site anywhere that has taken advantage of aerial photography. I'm sure we'll see a lot more of its use in years to come. But we can thank the Royal Air Force for furthering our knowledge of Stonehenge."

Indy looked up to see Deirdre's hand again. He knew most teachers would love to have a dozen bright students like Deirdre in class, but she was getting on his nerves.

"What about the controversy with the military authorities?" she asked.

Even when she posed a question, she phrased it in a way that showed she already knew the answer. What the hell was she doing, testing him for her mother? This time he was at a loss. In spite of all the time he spent preparing his lectures, he knew there were gaps in his knowledge, and this must be one of them. "Sorry. I'm not sure what you mean."

"That's understandable," she said in a knowing voice. "You haven't been in England long, and I hear they don't report our British doings very thoroughly in your newspapers. But it was quite a controversy here. Near the end of the war, the authorities wanted to knock down Stonehenge, because they felt the stones might be dangerous to low-flying airplanes."

"You're kidding."

"Not at all. It was quite a stink."

Indy noticed several heads bobbing in agreement. "Well, I'll have to look into it." He cleared his throat again. He was embarrassed, and angry with Deirdre. She was acting as if this were her class. He needed to straighten her out, and quickly.

She must have sensed his unease, because she only spoke up a couple of more times during the remainder of his lecture. As the class came to an end, Indy said that next time he would be talking about Stonehenge. "We've already discussed menhirs and dolmens, and now you can add trilithons to your vocabulary. Your assignment is to read all the articles titled 'Excavations at Stonehenge' by Colonel William Hawley that have been published in the *Antiquaries Journal* since 1920. Hawley, as you know, is the archaeologist in charge of the current digging at Stonehenge. We'll talk about what he's found so far and the implications. By the way, does anyone know what he found under the so-called slaughter stone?"

After a few seconds, Deirdre raised her hand, but this time only to shoulder level. Indy waited a moment longer for other hands, but there were no others. "Go ahead, Miss Campbell."

"He's found some flint tools and pottery shards and deer-antler picks, but I think the item you're referring to is a bottle of port left by another archaeologist, William Cunnington, a hundred and twenty years ago."

Everyone laughed.

"Very good. You stole my joke. See me after class, will you, Miss Campbell? Class dismissed. And don't forget, for those who have waited, and there's a lot of you, tomorrow's the deadline for getting your topic approved for your term paper."

As the students filed out of the room, Indy gathered up his notes and thought about what he would say. When everyone but Deirdre had left, he remained behind his podium as if he were about to continue his lecture for a class of one. She approached the podium with her hands folded in front of her over a notebook. She was a petite woman, an inch or two over five feet. Her long auburn hair had curls that twirled down over her shoulders. Her skin was pale, and her eyes were the violet of heather. She wore just a touch of makeup. There was something contradictory about her appearance. She was frail, but savvy; innocent, but sophisticated. Looking at her for some reason made him think of an oxymoron his father used to quote when his mother was agitated about something he found trivial: " 'O heavy lightness, serious vanity!' "

"You're Scottish, aren't you, Miss Campbell?" he began.

"Yes, I am."

"So am I. Well, I mean my father is, or was. He was born in Scotland." Bad start.

She stared directly into his eyes, challenging him, a slight smile on her lips. "Is that why you asked me to stay after class, so we could discuss our ancestors?"

He cleared his throat. He was nervous. She was the one who should be, but wasn't. "I want to ask you if you..."

"Yes?"

He looked down at the podium. "...If you would mind...Miss Campbell, why are you taking this class? I mean you seem to know the material, and your mother is certainly more knowledgeable about British archaeology than I am."

"But you're the one teaching the class. She's not. I can't get credits through heredity."

He knew that if he angered her it might get back to her mother and it could be the end of his chances for being rehired for the fall, but he had to say something.

"Miss Campbell—"

"You can call me Deirdre."

He met her gaze. "Deirdre, listen, I'd appreciate it if you would give the others in the class a chance to talk."

Her eyes blinked rapidly. "What do you mean?"

"I think you might be intimidating them."

"Oh? No reason for it. They're certainly free to say anything they like."

"Yeah." Indy looked down at the podium again as if his notes would give him an idea of what to say.

"Can I make an observation, Professor?"

Now what? "Go ahead."

"It seems to me that you are the one who is intimidated."

He shrugged. "Not intimidated, just a bit irritated."

"Why?"

"Look, this is my first teaching job. I've never been involved in any fieldwork here. I'm not English."

"You don't have to apologize to *me* for not being English. Remember, I'm not either."

Indy didn't join her laughter. "And your mother is my boss."

"You don't have to make an accusation out of that fact. If you want to know, I'm enjoying your class. I think you're doing a terrific job, and I've told Joanna, my mum."

"Oh, well, thank you."

"She keeps teasing me about you." She smiled awkwardly, her face reddened. "I'd better go."

He watched her leave. He smiled to himself. A real oddball, that one. He liked her, he decided. But then he'd known that from the first day of class.

3

ROOMMATES

"I know it's around here. I just ate here last week," Indy said as he stopped midway down a block in the heart of Soho.

Jack Shannon jammed his hands in his pockets and looked around. "Don't worry about it. I could eat anywhere right now. I'm starved."

Shannon had arrived unexpectedly a couple of days earlier, taking up the offer Indy had made before he left Paris. But Indy's busy schedule had meant they'd hardly seen each other. Tonight would be the first time they'd talked for more than a few minutes.

"There it is across the street," Indy said. "C'mon."

"Doesn't look like much," Shannon sniffed as they crossed the street.

"So what? The food's as good as anything in Paris. Well, almost."

The fact that Indy had found a French restaurant which reminded him of the bistros in Paris wasn't surprising. Not in Soho. Thousands of Huguenots from France had settled in the neighborhood near the end of the seventeenth century, followed by Swiss, Italians, Chinese, Indians, and others. The streets were a clamorous hodgepodge with open markets and shops offering everything Marco Polo had encountered on his distant journey, and much more. While the variety of inexpensive foreign cuisine was a main attraction, late at night the offerings along some of the streets were aimed at satisfying other cravings.

A waiter led them to a table, and Indy ordered a bottle of wine. "Dinner's on me, tonight. This is going to be a celebration."

Shannon smiled, and stroked his red goatee. "I'm glad you look at it that way. I hope it's not an imposition. I mean, I can find a room somewhere."

"Don't worry about it. I'm hardly ever home, and if you get in the way I'll let you know. Now tell me how you got this job."

"I was just walking down Oxford Street with my horn and saw the basement door of this club propped open. I thought what the hell, and walked in. I gave the owner a little down-home South Side Chicago sweet talk, and blew a couple of tunes for him. Before I could catch my breath, I was sitting in with a couple guys from the house band, and that was it. They told me to start tonight."

"Great. But what about Paris and the Jungle?"

"What about it? I'm ready for a change, Indy. The band's doing fine without me. Anyhow, I'm giving someone else a chance to play horn. Louise's man from New Orleans. He's played with King Oliver, and been around. He's hot."

The wine arrived and they toasted to their future, and to London. Indy spoke hopefully of his chances of remaining in London for another year. He was getting comfortable with the city, and from here he could travel anywhere. The English were actively involved in archaeological digs from Guatemala to Egypt. "It's really the center of things, you know."

Shannon sipped his wine, and scrutinized Indy, his expression sour. "Sounds like these Brits are brainwashing you. Next thing, you'll be talking about growing up in the jolly old colonies."

"Jack, I'm just making a point. London is a hub, it's cosmopolitan."

"Don't think I know that word. How do you say it in French?"

Indy laughed. "You sure you want to work here?"

Shannon shrugged. "For a while. I think I'll improve my playing. Everything was getting too pat for me at the Jungle. I need some variations on the theme."

Shannon seemed just as disenchanted as ever, Indy thought. The same as he'd been in Chicago, the same as he'd been most of the time in Paris. It was as if the jazz culture demanded a certain mordacious perspective on life. Dissonance. Syncopated rhythm, the accent intentionally out of place.

They finished their hors d'oeuvres, and their dinners had arrived when Shannon brought up a topic that Indy had been trying to blot from his mind. "You ever hear anything more from the sucker who sent you that box of spiders?"

"No. Not that I know of."

"When I got your letter, I thought it was a joke at first."

Indy took a bite of his broiled cod. "I thought it was one, too, until I opened the box."

Shannon made a face and shook his head. "Spiders. I would've gone nuts if that had happened to me. But who the hell could have done it?"

"No idea. But whoever it was had a lousy sense of humor. Those spiders were black widows, and if even one had bitten me, I probably wouldn't be here now."

Shannon stabbed at his green beans, piled high next to his roast beef. "How do you know they were black widows?"

"From pictures in an encyclopedia."

"I wonder where someone in London would get black widow spiders?" Shannon mused.

"Don't know. If I had any time, I'd look into it."

Shannon nodded thoughtfully. "Helluva welcome. If Belecamus was still around, I'd guess that she was behind it."

"Well, she's not," Indy said curtly, cutting off the topic. Dorian Belecamus had been his first archaeology professor at the Sorbonne in Paris, and she had lured him into accompanying her to Delphi, Greece, to work with her as an assistant. She'd given him a taste not only of field experience, but also of treachery. She'd schemed against him, using him in a plot against the king of Greece that had nearly cost Indy his life.

But Indy had made a significant discovery at Delphi. He had found and recovered an ancient, sacred relic, known as the Omphalos, which was now in New York on display in Marcus Brody's archaeology museum. In spite of Belecamus's perfidy, her violent death, and his narrow escape from the same fate, the experience had convinced him that archaeology was the career he would pursue.

"How's the fish?" Shannon asked.

"Fine. What about your dinner? You haven't said a word about it."

"It's acceptable. This beef is raw, but the sauce is good."

"Jack, the beef is supposed to be like that. If it was overcooked, it wouldn't have any flavor. Anyhow, since when are you a connoisseur of fine foods?"

Shannon set his fork down. "What the hell's wrong with you? You haven't been here all evening. Now you blow up at me."

"It's nothing."

"Something's on your mind. Let me guess, it's a woman, right?"

Indy sipped from his glass of water. "I got a letter from Leeland Milford today."

"God, that crazy old coot? How's he doing?"

"Good, I suppose, and he's not crazy. Just a bit eccentric."

Shannon laughed. "Yeah. A bit."

Milford was a retired professor, a noted authority on medieval England, and a friend of Indy's father. Shannon had met him when he and Indy were college roommates and Milford was in town to give a lecture. He had struck Shannon as odd because during dinner Milford had twice forgotten who Shannon was, once when Shannon had returned to the table with coffee and later when he'd taken out his cornet. Each time, Indy had had to reintroduce him.

"What did he have to say, or haven't you interpreted his pig Latin yet?" Shannon asked.

"It's Middle English, not pig Latin, and he didn't write his letter in it." Besides his forgetfulness, Milford also had the disturbing habit of shifting into Middle English during conversations, even when the topic had nothing to do with his expertise. "He says Dad is still angry about my going into archaeology. He thinks I'm wasting my life, and everything he taught me. In other words, nothing's new."

"So what can you do? You've got your own life to lead."

"Try telling my father that. Anyhow, I got the letter just in time. Milford is arriving here tomorrow and wants to see me."

"Lucky you," Shannon said. "Mind if I skip that one?"

Indy laughed. "I figured you would. I'm going to meet him at the train station, and we'll go out to lunch or something."

"Better brush up on your Middle English for the professor emeritus."

Indy didn't answer. He was staring toward the entrance of the restaurant as two women were escorted to a corner table. It was Joanna Campbell and Deirdre. His eyes were drawn to the younger woman. Even from across the room she looked radiant. She wore a navy blue flapper dress with a large, white sailor collar, and a bow in front. The dress was tight around her hips and fell to midcalf with a white fringe at the bottom. A matching floppy hat with a down-turned rim covered her head, and her auburn hair curled over her shoulders.

Shannon peered across the room, following his gaze. "You know her?"

"Both of them. It's my boss and her daughter. I better go over and say hi."

"Meet you outside."

Deirdre spotted him first. "Professor Jones. What a surprise." She extended a hand and he took it for a moment. There was a mystique about her that he couldn't quite define, something hidden that added to her beauty, the source of her strength. It was almost an effort to shift his gaze as she gave his hand a quick squeeze.

Dr. Campbell extended a limp, elegant hand. Her black hair was glazed with silver threads. Her features, like her daughter's, were finely chiseled. She looked distinguished as ever, and a bit mysterious tonight in a black dress, a cape, and a red silk scarf that fell to her thighs.

As they exchanged small talk about the restaurant and neighborhood, Indy had to concentrate on appearing interested in what Dr. Campbell was saying. It was as if there was a magnetic attraction that pulled his eyes, and his thoughts, to Deirdre. He wondered what she was thinking, and what she was going to say to him next.

"Well?" Dr. Campbell asked.

"I'm sorry. I missed something."

The professor smiled, and glanced at her daughter, then back to Indy. "I asked you how you were finding British archaeology compared to Greek."

"I guess it's a bit like the difference in the languages. But once you're fluent you can easily go back and forth between the two."

"And are you fluent, as you say, in the British form?"

He wondered how much Deirdre had told her mother about the class, and if she had mentioned the admonition he'd given her for dominating classroom discussion. "I'm working on it."

"That's a fair answer to an unfair question, at least unfair coming from me," Dr. Campbell said.

"Not at all," Indy said, and tried to think of something to say so he could gracefully take his leave.

"By the way," Dr. Campbell said, leaning toward him, "I've heard rumors that some peculiar things have happened to people who hold the Omphalos. So much so that they don't allow it to be touched, anymore. Did anything like that happen to you when you found it at Delphi?"

Indy smiled, and shrugged. "People's imaginations run wild, you know. They think they're touching the Oracle at Delphi, or something, and it goes to their heads."

He gazed across the room, looking at nothing in particular. From his own experience with the Omphalos and those of others, he knew that the person holding the stone underwent some sort of transformation in thoughts and feelings. In his case, he'd seen his future as if he were living it in fast motion, and some of what he'd seen had already come to pass.

In spite of the wonder of it all, he never wanted to hold the Omphalos again. Things like that were not supposed to happen, and besides, when the experience was taking place and immediately afterwards, he'd felt as if he were losing his mind. He certainly wasn't about to talk about any of that with Joanna Campbell.

"Professor Jones, are you all right?" Deirdre asked.

He snapped out of his reverie. "I'm sorry. I was trying to remember how it affected me, and to be honest I can't recall much of anything."

"Well, I can understand that," Dr. Campbell said, "considering the circumstances." She turned to Deirdre. "There was an attempt to overthrow the king of Greece right there at Delphi, I understand, and one of the Greek archaeologists was somehow involved. Isn't that right?"

"There were a couple of harrowing moments. Well, my friend is waiting. I should be going now." He stood, and nodded to Dr. Campbell, then Deirdre.

"Professor Jones," Dr. Campbell said before he could get away, "one more thing. Do you know of the connection between the Greeks and the ancients of this island?"

Indy smiled uneasily. "I'm not sure what you mean, Dr. Campbell."

She regarded him a moment. "Think about it, Jones. I'm sure you know. It's part of your background. Nice to see you."

"I'll see you tomorrow," Deirdre said and flashed a brilliant smile.

"You will? Oh, in class. Of course." He nodded to both women again, backed away, and headed to the door.

Shannon was waiting outside. "Thought you were going to stay for another dinner."

"Sorry. Let's get out of here."

They headed down the wide avenue, making their way past a crowd on the corner where everyone spoke Italian. No matter what the hour, the streets of Soho bustled with crowds, and it seemed the languages varied from street to street. They crossed Greek Street a minute later, and Indy was actually surprised when he didn't hear anyone speaking Greek.

Shannon, meanwhile, was lost in another world. He snapped his fingers every other step as if he were hearing some tune inside his head. "She's a real looker, that one."

Indy looked around. "Who?"

"Who'd ya think? The redhead."

"Oh, Deirdre. She's more than that, Jack. She's one of my students, the brightest of the bunch. In fact, it's almost as if she's competing with me in class."

"What do you mean?"

"I don't know. She acts like she knows as much as me, if not more."

"Maybe she does."

"Thanks a lot, ol' pal."

Shannon tapped him on the shoulder with his fist. "Just kidding. But if she knows so much, why is she taking the class?"

"That's what I asked her. Says she needs the credit. But I wonder if she's spying on me."

"Spying, for whom?" Shannon sidestepped a man wearing a topcoat and bowler hat who was making furtive gestures toward a woman who was leaning against a wall. She wore a short, frilly dress, and her eyes were painted so boldly that they seemed to cover half her face.

Nearby, another Soho prostitute motioned to Indy. He glanced momentarily at her, looked away. "Her mother, of course. I'm on probation. I won't know if I've got a full-time job until September."

"I think you're letting your imagination get the best

of you. The girl's probably just a good student. Ever since you had that run-in with Dorian Belecamus, you don't trust any women you meet."

"That's not true. And stop throwing out her name like you're waving a red flag in front of me."

"You know what you ought to do?" Shannon said, ignoring Indy's burst of anger.

"What?"

"Take her out. Get to know her better. She can put in a good word for you. Hell, if she's going out to dinner with her mother, she's probably not seeing anyone."

"Jack, for God's sake, that's probably the worst thing I could do. Going out with a student is no way to prove anything, except that I'm willing to gamble my chances at a job."

Shannon seemed unconvinced. They walked on in silence, each with his own thoughts. Indy intentionally tried not to think about Deirdre. Instead, he puzzled a moment over the question Dr. Campbell had asked as he'd left. He wasn't even sure whether she was referring to the Celts, or the ancients before them, and he had no idea how they were connected with the Greeks. Another gap in his knowledge. But what was the point of her question? To test him? Maybe it was something important he should know. He'd better find out.

He wondered if Dr. Campbell was the professor Marcus Brody knew, the one who had told Marcus about the teaching job. She, in fact, had made the final decision to hire him. The turning point in the interview, oddly enough, had been related to his name.

"Indy Jones," she'd said, and smiled. The two

other professors had chuckled, and one asked if he was any relation to In-e-go.

In-e-go who? he'd almost asked, but caught himself. In the days before the interview, he'd spent hours immersed in the study of texts on the ancient ruins of Britain, and remembered reading about Inigo Jones, architect general to King James I and Charles I.

"Oh, I don't think so. There're lots of us Joneses, and no relative of mine would think that Stonehenge was built by the Romans. Of course, that was three hundred years ago, and so much has changed in what we know of the ancients." The comment, he thought, must have pleased Dr. Campbell, and sealed her decision.

Finally, they reached the club. An evening of jazz was just what he needed. It would be his first night out since he'd arrived in London. How he'd changed since he and Shannon were in their last year at the University of Chicago. They'd been so caught up in their discovery of the underground world of jazz that had suddenly blossomed in Chicago that they'd both nearly dropped out. For Indy, the experience had filled a craving for adventure; for Shannon, it had been a more serious endeavor that had changed him forever, and eventually altered his future. He'd given up a secure job as an accountant in a growing trucking company for the uncertainty of a life as a jazz musician.

As they descended the stairs to the basement nightclub, Indy sensed someone watching him and glanced over his shoulder. He saw a man on the sidewalk moving toward him. He was tall and slender, with dark hair neatly combed back, and narrow eyes, and he was about Indy's age. It was the man he thought had been following him to the university. The man walked past the club, and down the street without a glance back.

"Did you see that guy?" Shannon asked, opening the door.

The smell of stale beer and smoke wafted over him as they stopped in the doorway. Indy heard a clatter of glasses, the babble of voices. "What about him?"

"I saw him on the street outside the restaurant while I was waiting for you, and I'm sure I've seen him hanging around Russell Square outside the flat."

Indy stared after the man who'd disappeared from sight. "It's probably nothing, just a coincidence," he said with a shrug.

But he didn't believe it.

4

BETWEEN THE SHELVES

All morning Indy cursed himself for staying out too late. Even though he didn't have any classes today, he was holding court in his office. According to the guidelines of the course, he was required to approve each student's term paper topic in advance, and he'd listened to one after another for nearly two hours. He felt drained, and it wasn't over yet. Although he'd been encouraging students for the past three weeks to see him as soon as possible, nearly half had waited until the final day.

He looked up at the lanky kid standing in front of him. "Stonehenge."

"What about it?" Indy asked.

"That's my topic."

"Sit down. You can't just write about Stonehenge. You've got to be more specific."

"Okay." He stared at Indy. "I'll write about the early investigators."

"Still too general. Pick a century."

"Seventeenth."

"Okay. Now select two researchers from that century and compare and contrast what they deducted."

"Do I have to select them now?" he whined. "I'd rather wait and think about it."

Indy smiled, and rubbed the back of his neck. Obviously, the kid didn't have any names in mind. "Just make sure that the two you pick did their work during the same century."

"Got it." He stood and hurried out of the office.

Indy massaged his temples as he waited for another student. "Next," he called out, then leaned over and craned his neck as he looked toward the outer room. When no one appeared, he leaned back in his chair. "Hooray," he said softly.

He glanced at the clock on the wall. Just enough time. He would take the underground to King's Cross Station and meet Leeland Milford's train. He zipped his briefcase, stood up, and was about to walk out when Deirdre Campbell appeared in the doorway.

She beamed a smile. "Hope I'm not too late to talk to you about my paper."

He dropped back in his chair. He was disappointed that he hadn't gotten away. Yet, he was pleased to see that it was Deirdre who was holding him up. "Sit down, and tell me about it."

Her presence seemed to brighten the room; it was as if her pale skin or her shiny, auburn curls gave off a light of their own. Or maybe it was her intelligence. After listening to several students like the last one, who were content to do the least they could to pass the course, Deirdre was a refreshing change. He appreciated her enthusiasm, and was already sorry he'd told her to control herself.

"Thank you," she said, and lowered herself into the chair across from his desk. "It was a surprise seeing you last night."

"Yeah. A surprise," Indy said.

Deirdre looked down at her hands. "I told my mother what you said to me after class yesterday, and she agreed with you. I guess I have been sort of showing off" *(shooing off)*. "She told me I should be a wee bit more blate in class."

"Blate?"

"That's a Scottish word, means 'shy.' "

Indy looked over his wire-rimmed spectacles at her. "I see."

"Maybe I talk so much because some of the English look down on the Scottish as if those of us from the north are ignorant." She raised her eyes, and smiled. "Then again maybe I just wanted to impress you." Her soft-spoken confession was so disarming Indy couldn't take his eyes off her. She was like a flower opening her blossoms and apologizing for her radiance.

"Don't worry about trying to impress me," he answered. "I'm impressed."

She gazed back, and their eyes locked. He had an urge to reach for her hand and lift her up from her chair. He wondered how her lips would taste, how she would feel in his arms. *Down, boy,* a voice inside ordered. *You want to keep this job or not?*

"So let me guess." He cleared his throat, turning businesslike. "You're writing about Stonehenge like almost everyone else."

"No. Ninian's Cave in Scotland."

Indy repeated the name. "Don't think we've talked about it in class. What's there that interests you?"

"It's where Merlin was buried."

Indy clasped his hands behind his neck, and smiled. "Really?"

"Yes." She didn't seem to be joking.

"Merlin, as in King Arthur's counselor?"

"That's right."

"Merlin's a legend, Deirdre. This is an archaeology course, not mythology."

"I've got evidence."

"You do? What kind of evidence?"

She smiled coyly. "You'll have to read my paper. I think you'll find it interesting."

"If what you say is true, I'll find it more than interesting. Astonishing is more like it."

"So you approve of the idea?"

Indy grinned. "What you're proposing is more than a term paper, Deirdre. It's the springboard for a career. If you can prove that Merlin actually lived, you'll achieve more recognition than most archaeologists do in their entire careers."

She rose gracefully from her chair. "I'll get to work on it right away."

Indy watched her leave his office. Maybe she wasn't as bright as he had thought. With any other student, he would have disapproved of the idea immediately. It was far beyond the scope of a term paper for a beginning course. It was a topic for a Ph.D. thesis, and an ambitious one at that. If no one had yet proven Merlin's existence, what could she possibly know that would be sufficient to change minds? He was curious to find out.

As he left his office and hurried toward the underground, a sour thought occurred to him. Deirdre must have told her mother about this so-called evidence of Merlin's existence. Whatever it was, Joanna Campbell probably didn't agree with her daughter. He had the sudden, nauseating feeling he might find himself in the middle of a mother-daughter squabble. Swell. Just what he needed.

The train from Portsmouth, where Leeland Milford's ship had docked, was on time, but Indy wasn't. As he reached the platform, most of the passengers had already disembarked. He glanced past a young couple with two children, a man in a kilt, and a group of schoolgirls in uniforms. Then he saw Milford moving along the platform, a leather bag in either hand.

He wore a long dark overcoat that was distinctly out of season. His head was bald save for a bushy white fringe above each ear, and a mustache that was a thick, white brush drooping over his lips. His eyes were pale blue and watery.

Although he didn't know Milford well, Indy knew he could be unpredictable. He could be open and friendly one moment, cross the next. He grinned as he saw Milford's lips moving, probably in some exclamation about Indy being late. As he neared him, Indy heard him clearly say: "Damn train. Faster on a bicycle. *So whylome wont.*" And then Milford was past him. He'd just kept walking.

"Dr. Milford." Indy hurried after him. "Hello. Dr. Milford. It's me, Indy."

Milford stopped and slowly turned, a frown forming on his forehead. "Ah, Indy. What a surprise." He shook Indy's hand, but without any sign of enthusiasm. "What are you doing here?"

"I got your letter."

"You did?"

"Remember, you wrote that you wanted to meet me at the station."

Milford looked perplexed. "Well, if you say so."

Indy offered to take one his bags, but Milford refused.

"I'm fine, young man. Ye shewd neuer tyke to sea or road wid more than ye can handle. Or *so whylome wont*."

"I'll remember that." *So whylome wont* was a pet Middle English phrase that Milford used. Indy had learned long ago that it meant "so they say," but Milford used it freely in conversation and never explained its meaning.

When they reached the street, Indy waved down a taxi, and they climbed into the backseat. "What are you going to do in London, Dr. Milford? Your letter wasn't really clear on that."

"I have certain matters to attend to." He leaned forward, and tapped the driver on the shoulder. "To the British Museum Library, good man. Forward, e'er forward wid thee wind."

The driver turned, and looked between Indy and Milford. "Whereya from, sir, Newfoundland?"

"Just hoist your sails, mate," Indy said, then turned to Milford. "You sure you wouldn't like to eat something before you go to the museum?"

"I ate already. Besides, my true hunger, as always, is for knowledge."

Indy nodded. "It's a good library."

"The best library of its kind in the world, by God," Milford proclaimed. "Everything that has been published in Britain since 1757 is there. Several million volumes, and tens of thousands of manuscripts and ancient papyri. Best collection of writings from the Middle Ages. Virtually anything you want to know on the history of Britain is there."

His description of the library made Indy think again of the comment Joanna Campbell had made at the restaurant. "Dr. Milford, do you know of any connection between the ancient Greeks and the ancients of the British Isles?"

Milford was silent a moment. "That was before my time."

Indy smiled. "I suppose so." In spite of what he seemed to be saying, Indy knew that to Milford "before his time" meant before the Middle Ages, the period of his expertise.

"However, I do remember a colleague of mine talking about that very topic, oh, maybe twenty years ago." He scratched his bald head with his index finger. "It's funny the things you remember, but not so funny the things you forget."

"What did he tell you?"

"Who?"

Indy chuckled. "Your colleague. The one who told you about the connection between ancient Greeks and Britons."

The taxi driver pulled over to the curb in front of the library. "Oh, well, if you want to know, you can find it right inside these doors."

Indy paid for the taxi when Milford walked off,

then hurried after the old professor as he climbed the steps of the library. "Can you give me a hint?"

"You're always better off finding your own answers rather than having them handed to you," the older man said as he climbed the steps.

"That's what Dad always said, too," Indy replied glumly.

Milford stopped at the top of the steps and set his bags down. His gaze met Indy's. "He was always a bit harsh on you," he said gently. "I'll give you your hint. Look up the writings of Hecataeus." He picked up his bags again as Indy opened the door for him. "But keep in mind that nothing he wrote has survived."

Indy frowned, and watched Milford hobble into the foyer. "Then how can I look anything up?"

Milford looked over his shoulder. "Think, my boy, think. We know about Hecataeus's writings because others have quoted him. So he becomes the subject rather than the author."

A lesson in using a library catalog. Indy forced a smile. "Okay, I'll take a look."

"Where are you going to be?" Indy asked as he followed Milford into a huge bowl-shaped room with aisles like spokes leading away from the center.

Milford frowned, placed a finger to his lips, then turned away.

Indy shook his head, and moved off to begin his search in the vast warehouse of knowledge. Maybe Milford was just babbling, and threw out a name. Maybe it wasn't the right name.

What did he know about Hecataeus? He'd memorized the name as part of his studies by associating it with Hecate, a goddess of the earth, the moon, and

the underworld, who was associated with sorcery.
Hecataeus had written about the ancient Greeks and
their relationship with a mysterious people known as
the Hyperboreans, a term from Greek mythology relating to a "northerly people." Some scholars thought
it was a reference to the people of Atlantis. But that
was about all he could remember.

The general catalog was located at the base of the
bowl-shaped room. The catalog listed everything in
the library, and took up dozens of volumes, each five
hundred pages long. But finally he found the name in
the subject category, and was directed to a book
called, ironically, *Historical Library,* by Diodorus
Siculus, a Greek historian who lived much of his life
in Rome and was a contemporary of Caesar and
Augustus. *Historical Library* took Diodorus thirty
years to write and consisted of forty volumes.
Fortunately, since Indy had looked up Hecataeus, he
was referred to the appropriate volume number and
pages.

He moved to a reference desk nearby, and was directed to another room. There, a second librarian
found the ancient book for him. The man frowned at
Indy, and warned him that the book was ancient and
valuable and that he was to handle it with extreme
care.

As he read the writings of Hecataeus, paraphrased
from his now nonexistent book, *Circuit of the Earth,*
Indy realized that his description of the Hyperborean
island was more specific than he'd imagined. It was a
country larger than Sicily, lying opposite Gaul. It
sounded like Britain, but feasibly it could be any of
the Scandinavian islands. Then he read that on the is-

land was a vast temple in a circular form, and he changed his mind. The temple sounded too much like Stonehenge. He decided that "Hyperboreans" must be an ancient name for the inhabitants of the British Isles.

Hecataeus also told of the goodwill between the Hyperboreans and Greeks, and explained that certain Greeks visited the Hyperborean island and left votives bearing Greek inscriptions. And there was more. The Hyperborean island was supposedly the birthplace of Leto, the daughter of giants, and she became the mother of Apollo. For that reason, the Hyperboreans worshipped Apollo, and their circular temple was consecrated to him. He was said to visit the temple every nineteen years, in a grand festival in which he danced among his worshippers and played a harp. His appearance also coincided with a nineteen-year cycle in which the stars returned to their point of origin in the heavens.

Apollo was the connection, Indy thought. As he closed the book, he recalled Joanna Campbell's words: "I'm sure you know. It's part of your background." The myth of Apollo, particularly its association with Delphi, was indeed that. He just hadn't connected the Hyperborean island with the British Isles. But it made sense. Apollo was known as an interloper on the Greek Olympus, and was said to spend part of each year "beyond the north wind." Now that he'd puzzled through her question, he wondered if Dr. Campbell was just testing his knowledge, or if she had some particular reason in mind.

He rubbed his face. He should go home, and take a nap. He was about to get up from the table when he

spotted a pair of eyes watching him through a bookcase. He tried to act as if he didn't know he was being
watched. He leafed through the book again, stretched
his arms. The eyes were still there.

Maybe it was a librarian, watching to see that he
didn't damage the book. But something was familiar
about the close-set eyes. They were like those of the
man he thought had been following him.

Suddenly, like a sprinter at the sound of the gun, he
bolted out of his chair and rushed to the end of the
bookcase. As he rounded it, he saw a tall man hurrying down an aisle, and moving between another row
of bookcases. Narrow Eyes was definitely trying to
evade him, and Indy followed his winding trail
through the maze of shelves.

He moved stealthily along, peering between bookcases until he came upon another aisle. He looked in
either direction, and turned right. Then he saw him
just as the man slipped out a door and into the hallway. Indy loped across the room, and spotted him
again as he ducked into the huge, bowl-shaped reading room.

From the doorway of the room, Indy could see the
entire room, but Narrow Eyes was nowhere in sight.
Indy was puzzling over where the man might have
gone, when he heard a noise, someone trying to sup-
press a cough. He jerked his head to the right, and
there he was, pressed against the wall just ten feet
from the door.

As soon as Indy spotted him, Narrow Eyes rushed
at him, driving him down one of the aisles. They fell
to the floor, tumbling over and over. Halfway down
the aisle, Narrow Eyes decided he'd had enough. He

wriggled out of Indy's grasp, scrambled to his feet, and dashed back up the aisle. Now everyone in the room was following the silent chase.

Narrow Eyes had almost reached the door when Indy grabbed him by the shirt and pulled him to the floor. They tumbled over several times until they struck a desk. The man behind it bolted up from his chair. "Why this wretchedness of outlawry? Have I been wandering with madness and a madman?"

Indy let go of Narrow Eyes's shirt at the sound of the familiar voice. "Dr. Milford, I—I can't talk now." Narrow Eyes crawled under Milford's desk and into another aisle.

"Excuse me," Indy said, and vaulted the desk, but the man was nowhere in sight. Then he saw him crawling under desks toward a third aisle. Indy dropped to his knees and crawled after him. Someone kicked him in the side; people shouted, calling for help.

God, what had he started? He'd only meant to catch the man back in the bookshelves of the other room and demand to know why he was watching him. Indy cut off Narrow Eyes's escape route so the man raced down toward the central axis, dodging desks and librarians. Indy gave chase, and finally saw his chance. He dove belly-first across a desk and caught Narrow Eyes by the belt. "That's my desk you're lying on, sonny," an old woman said. She swatted him twice on the head with a rolled-up newspaper, and Narrow Eyes broke free.

Indy was up in an instant, and hurrying after Narrow Eyes. But the man was already more than halfway up the bowl, headed toward the door. Indy was about to give up the chase when a leg shot out, and Narrow Eyes sprawled on his face.

"Down ye on your filthy face, friendless foe," Milford shouted.

Indy piled on the prone figure, pinning him to the floor. Then grabbing him by the collar, he jerked back his fist. "Okay, who the hell are you? Why are you following me?"

The man snarled at him; his narrow-spaced, dark eyes were two black coals. They shifted, focusing on something beyond Indy. Just then Indy was struck on the head with a book. Narrow Eyes pushed him off, and raced away.

Indy turned to see the old woman whose desk he'd slid across. "You don't understand, ma'am."

"You're damn right I don't, sonny," she said, and she gouged his eye with the eraser end of a pencil.

Indy yelled in pain and covered his face. Then he heard Narrow Eyes's voice for the first time. "Jones, listen to me."

Indy raised his head and with his good eye saw the man standing in the doorway. "I warn you. Stay away from Deirdre Campbell."

"That's right. You stay away from her," the old lady said, and she raised the book again.

Milford was suddenly at his side. "Stop hitting him. I'll handle this. He's with me."

Swell, Indy thought. *Just swell. Beat up by an old lady. Saved by Dr. Milford. And all because of Deirdre, and a jealous boyfriend.*

5

TOWER OF LONDON

In class, a day later: "If we want to understand what kind of precision the ancients aimed at, our errors in examining their work must be so small as to be insignificant by the side of their errors," Indy said, reading from his notes. "If they went to the nearest hundredth of an inch, we must go to the nearest thousandth, in order to know what their ideas of accuracy were."

Indy stopped to take a sip of water. His left eye was swollen shut from the jab he'd taken in his tussle at the library, and he wore a black patch over it. He'd told the class that he'd had an accident and that a doctor had recommended he wear the patch for a few days.

His good eye roamed over the faces. Some peered earnestly ahead, awaiting his next word; others scribbled furiously in their notebooks. In the front row, Deirdre sat back in her chair, threading and unthreading her fingers. She wore a long dress today that reached to her ankles, which were pulled under the seat. It was as if the dress were a metaphor for the lies she was covering up. Her notebook was closed, and her lips were pursed in a pout. Before class, she'd asked what had happened and in a gruff voice he'd asked her to sit down. Maybe he'd treated her rudely, but he was only returning the favor. She must have said something to her boyfriend, or whoever Narrow Eyes was, to make him jealous. She was using him; probably using both of them for her own manipulative purposes. He wanted no part of her schemes.

"Don't credit me with that statement, by the way," Indy continued. "Those were the words of Sir Flinders Petrie, the renowned Egyptologist, who also studied some of the nine hundred stone circles in the British Isles, including Stonehenge. In his research conducted in 1877, he took extraordinarily accurate measurements of the monument and drew an exact plan, which was published on a one-to-two-hundred scale. Some of you who are writing your papers on Stonehenge may already be familiar with Petrie's book, *Stonehenge: Plans, Description, and Theories.*"

Indy explained that Petrie remained one of the most respected investigators of Stonehenge because he had avoided wild speculation. That, he explained, was the trap of Stonehenge, and he was now going to address some of the outlandish theories put forth over the past few hundred years.

"Take a look at the work of the eighteenth-century investigator John Smith. He was the first to notice that if you stood at the center of Stonehenge at dawn on the summer solstice, the sun rose directly above the heel stone located outside the inner ring of stones.

Fine enough. But he also thought that Stonehenge had been built by druids.

"That belief, in fact, is probably the most widespread delusion about Stonehenge. Druids were Celts, and the Celtic culture did not rise until nearly two thousand years after the earliest phase of Stonehenge was built around 1900 B.C. Even the later phase, which includes the Sarsen Circle and the five freestanding archways or trilithons inside the circle, was finished about 1550 B.C. Still far too early for the druids."

Deirdre raised her hand for the first time. Indy glanced briefly at her, then looked down at his notes. "However, for a couple of centuries, antiquarians—as archaeologists used to be called—believed that—"

"Professor Jones?"

"Miss Campbell, I'll take questions at the end," he snapped. "If I stop every time you or someone else raises a hand, I won't get through my material today."

"Sorry." She sank down in her seat. Indy noticed some of the other students snickering as if they thought it was about time he told her to stop interrupting him.

"As I was saying, for centuries antiquarians believed that Stonehenge was built by the druids. But that's not really surprising. The fact is, the best-kept secret about archaeology is that we are almost always wrong. Look back a century, and virtually everything we thought was true is now baloney. The history of archaeology is one of misinformation compounded with romantic, far-fetched hypotheses, and nowhere is that more true than in the exploration of Stonehenge, this country's most famous monument of antiquity."

He hoped he sounded authoritative. He was actually repeating a statement of one of his French professors, an Egyptologist who had worked with Flinders Petrie. "What we know about Stonehenge is that it ranks with the Great Pyramid of Egypt as the most spectacular undertaking that has survived from antiquity. It has been a subject of learned debate since the sixteenth century, and has been interpreted as a burial chamber, a memorial, and a temple associated with human sacrifice. Some said it was built by druids, others said the Romans, still others said the Vikings."

A student raised his hand. "Can I ask a question or should I wait?"

"You just did. Go ahead." Indy sighed.

"What about all these druids who gather at Stonehenge every now and then like they own the bloody place?"

Indy laughed. "They're misguided mystics. They claim the site as their own, and they're wrong."

As the class came to an end, Indy picked up his pocket watch, which he kept on the podium, and dropped it into his pocket. "Remember those papers are due on Monday."

He gathered his books and notes together as he prepared to leave. He'd promised to meet Milford at the Tower of London in an hour. In the aftermath of the incident in the library, he had accompanied the old professor to the club where he was staying, and the resident physician had examined his sore eye. Milford had been both appalled and amazed that Indy had gotten into a fight with a stranger, and in a library of all places. In spite of Indy's efforts to ease his friend's concern, Milford was convinced that Indy was suffering from emotional problems, and he was sure it must have something to do with the breach between father and son. Finally, the old professor had suggested they meet at the tower to continue their talk.

"Professor Jones?"

He looked up; Deirdre was standing in front of him. Her violet eyes sought an explanation. "How can I help you?" he said sharply. "I'm in a hurry."

"Why are you angry with me? I didn't ask a lot of questions today, and you were mad before class even started."

"It has nothing to do with your questions. It's your behavior outside of class."

She shook her head. "What're you talking about?" she stammered.

"Ask your boyfriend."

She was taken back. Her savviness was gone. She looked innocent, frail. "I don't know what you're talking about, Professor Jones."

"What I mean is this: Some guy has been following me around, and yesterday after we got into a little spat he told me to stay away from you. Now why would he say that? I don't have any idea, do you?"

"I'm sorry. I really am. But I don't have a boyfriend." She abruptly turned, and hurried out of the room.

"Yeah, sure." Indy glanced at his pocket watch. "Late again."

Indy walked out of the Tower Hill underground station five minutes after he was to meet Milford. The

Tower of London dated back to the eleventh century when William the Conqueror built it after the Battle of Hastings, and as Indy approached it, he felt as if he were walking back into time. Towers spiraled skyward; banners fluttered in the wind. An ancient moat now kept tourists, rather than enemies, from scaling the walls, and a drawbridge offered passage to the interior.

Milford was nowhere in sight, so Indy eavesdropped on a guide who was addressing a group of tourists. The White Tower, the man explained, was built not only to protect the city from attack, but to keep a watch on the shipping traffic on the Thames and to hold its citizens in awe of William the Conqueror's power. The construction began in 1078 and was finished in 1100 by Rannulf Flambard, the Bishop of Durham, who ironically was the first prisoner incarcerated behind its walls.

Many more followed, and the list of prominent prisoners was an impressive one, the guide continued, ticking off the names of royalty: King David II of Scotland, King John the Good of France, King James I of Scotland, Charles, Duke of Orléans, and Princess Elizabeth, who later became Queen Elizabeth I. Among those executed or murdered in the tower were: Henry VI, Edward V and his brother the Duke of York, Sir Thomas More, Henry VIII's queens Anne Boleyn and Catherine Howard, Thomas Cromwell, and the Duke of Monmouth. As the notoriety of the tower grew, so did its size. Over the centuries additional towers were added until they numbered thirteen. They were later ringed by a wall with six more towers.

"I always come here when I'm in London," Milford said as he came up behind Indy. "It's a place of concrete history, where royalty met their demise, where dark deeds were plotted. Concrete history."

"Afternoon, Dr. Milford." Even though the temperature was moderate and the day relatively sunny, Milford was wearing his black overcoat.

"How is your eye today?" the professor asked, stroking his mustache as he assessed Indy. "You look like you're playing pirate."

"That was your doctor's idea. It'll be better in no time."

"That's the spirit," Milford said as they crossed the moat and passed one of the towers. "You seem to be rebounding well from this mental condition."

Indy knew there was no point in arguing about his mental stability. "Things just got out of hand at the library. But I'm fine."

"Hm, I hope so."

"What exactly did you mean by concrete history?" Indy asked, changing the topic as they reached the far side of the moat and approached the tour group, which was huddled around the guide below one of the towers.

"Listen to him," Milford said, nodding toward the guide.

"This is the Bell Tower, planned by Richard I around 1190 and completed in the thirteenth century. On the ramparts running north to the Beauchamp Tower is Princess Elizabeth's Walk. Her Highness was one of the tower's success stories. Even though she was held prisoner for several months, she later became Queen Elizabeth I.

"Now let's take a look at the Bloody Tower, begun
by Henry III, where the prisoners did not have the
luck of Princess Elizabeth. Edward V and the Duke of
York were murdered there, among others. After that,
we'll go into Wakefield Tower where Henry VI was
murdered, and on the brighter side, the place where
the Crown Jewels are still kept."

"Concrete history, Indy," Milford said as the group
moved on. "We know those people lived and died. It
is recorded. No one disputes the facts. That's what I
like. But we go back another five centuries or so before this tower was built and concrete history turns
soft and mushy. Legend and history freely mix.
Reality and fantasy are a blur. Treacherous territory."
He paused a moment watching Indy. "As Samuel
Johnson said two centuries ago: 'All that is really
known of the ancient state of Britain is contained in a
few pages.'"

Indy nodded. "Very true." Milford seemed relaxed
and rested today, and consequently more coherent.
There were fewer memory glitches, and less slippage
into Middle English. "Too bad we don't have a catalog of history for places like Stonehenge like we do for
the Tower of London."

Milford laughed. "Then the archaeologists would
have no prehistory to create. They would have nothing to do but hunt treasure, which I don't suppose
would bother most of them in the least."

"Now you sound like Dad. You got something
against archaeology, too?"

Milford stopped and gazed up at the White Tower,
the original structure at the center of the tower com-
plex. "Maybe I'm slow to change, Indy, but when I

was your age, the true scholars felt their time was best spent studying the ancient writings we already possess in our libraries. The task of hunting for new ones was left to the second-rate scholars, the ones who couldn't match the demands of true scholarship. They were the ones who were relegated to dirtying their hands and hearts in mere adventuristic endeavors."

"Things have changed, Dr. Milford. Archaeology is no longer in the nineteenth century."

"*So whylome wont.* Maybe you're right. Our friend Marcus Brody would agree." Milford gestured toward the entrance to the tower.

"Have you seen Marcus lately?" Indy asked.

Milford stopped just outside the door of the tower. His watery blue eyes met Indy's, his mustache twitched. "I did, before I left, and you know, there was something he wanted me to tell you." He shrugged and opened the door. "It'll come to me."

They followed a stairway up into the interior of the four-story Norman structure. On the second floor, Milford examined a collection of weapons and armor dating back to the early Middle Ages.

"Too bad they don't have Excalibur here," Indy said, hoping to provoke Milford into expressing his thoughts on the Arthurian legend.

"Legends are deceptive, Indy." Milford ran his hand over the blade of a sword.

"There's one that says Merlin built Stonehenge."

Milford pointed the sword at Indy. " 'If thou be fain to grace the burial-place of these men with a work that shall endure forever, send for the—' "

"Geoffrey of Monmouth," Indy interrupted. "*Historia Regum Britanniae.*"

"Very good," Milford said. "You know your literature of the Middle Ages."

"A bit." *Histories of the British Kings* had been required reading in Indy's childhood. It was the primary source of many of the Arthurian legends, and in spite of the archaic language, his father had insisted he read and understand it.

Milford laid down the sword. "Do you know this one?" He cleared his throat and said:

" 'For he by wordes could call out of the sky
Both sunne and moone, and make them him obay,
The land to sea, and sea to maineland dry,
And darksom night he eke could turne to day.' "

Indy shook his head. "Don't think so."

Milford smiled. "Edmund Spenser, from the sixteenth century."

"You think Merlin actually lived, Dr. Milford?"

"If he did, he worshipped the sun god, not the son of God, and of course by the sixth century in Britain that was not acceptable. The pagans were a dying force. Their time was over. Legend or fact, the Christians called Merlin the son of the devil."

They slowly descended the stone stairway, and Indy's voice echoed eerily. "Do you think it's possible to prove that Merlin was a historical person?"

"Indy, scholars have spent lifetimes attempting to prove just that. But they've failed to present a convincing argument. I'm afraid it'll always be speculation."

"Maybe archaeologists could find the proof."

They stepped outside the White Tower. Milford

tilted his head back and gazed toward the peak of the tower. "If that ever happened, I'd have to reassess my ideas on archaeology, as well as Merlin. I'd probably have to start believing in dragons, too."

Indy laughed. He was glad that he'd agreed to meet with Milford. When the old professor was rested, he was still as charming and witty as he remembered him. He thought back to an evening several years ago that he'd spent with his father, Milford, and Marcus Brody, when he was visiting New York on a Christmas break from college. They were celebrating Brody's appointment as director of the museum, and his move from Chicago to New York.

Milford had suggested that Brody should inaugurate his tenure by displaying the skeletons of America's early presidents. He had added in a hushed tone that he knew where several of them were, and they weren't in graves. Brody gave Milford an odd look as if he wasn't quite sure if he was serious or not. Then he mumbled something about how he strongly doubted that the American public would accept such a display.

"It would be different, of course, if they were Indian leaders," Indy's father had added with a snort. "Right, Marcus?"

Brody hadn't answered. He was still thinking about what Milford had said, and asked in a matter-of-fact voice where these skeletons might be hidden. Milford had leaned forward in his chair, cupped one hand over his mouth, and whispered: "In the closets of the White House. Every president had his skeletons there."

Indy was suddenly jolted from his thoughts by the

sight of a young woman gazing their way from up on Princess Elizabeth's Walk. She wore a long dress, and her hair fell over her shoulders. From a distance, she could have been the princess, a spectral figure returning for a visit to her place of confinement. As they moved closer, the woman stepped into the shadows and seemed to literally glide through the open tower door.

"Did you see her, Indy?"

"Yes, I did."

"They say there are ghosts here," Milford said in a hushed voice. "It's the first one I've seen, though."

Indy nodded in agreement. Maybe there were ghosts in the tower, but that wasn't one of them. He'd recognized the dress, and the woman in it. He had no doubt who it was. Deirdre had followed him, and he wondered why.

6

DEIRDRE'S MISTAKE

Deirdre climbed the familiar steps from the street, opened the iron gate, and followed the walk to her mother's house in Notting Hill. She thought of the old family house as her mother's, even though she'd always lived here. It was just that her mother's presence was so overpowering that she sometimes felt more like a guest than a family member.

The house was filled with Oriental furnishings, most of which had been purchased by Deirdre's grandfather, who had been the English ambassador to China. Low tables, tall vases, high-backed chairs made of mahogany, folding room dividers, oversized paper fans. Everything was black or red, satin-covered or highly polished. Deirdre hated it, but Joanna had spent the first twelve years of her life in China and the furniture was her past. There was something mysterious about the Orient to Deirdre. Mysterious and forbidding. And, even though she loved her mother, there was a side of her that was enigmatic as the furniture.

Deirdre's room was her only sanctuary, and she did what she liked with it. Her paintings of quiet English countryside scenes, still life watercolors, and ancient ruins covered the walls. But none found space on the walls beyond the room. They were too modern, Joanna said. They wouldn't match the Oriental decor.

"Deirdre, is that you?" Joanna called out from her study.

"Of course it is." She headed upstairs. One day she would have her own flat, and she would arrange things the way she wanted them, and if she decided to leave her coat on the sofa or the dining room table for an hour or a day, she would. She walked into her room and flopped down on the bed. But right now something more than trifling home-life problems had put her in an ill-tempered mood.

It was Adrian. She didn't know what to do about him. He was sapping her strength, her will. He was controlling her life, ruining it.

She heard a tap on her door. "Deirdre, honey, what's wrong?"

"Nothing." She rolled over and buried her head in a pillow.

The door creaked open. "You didn't even say hello to me. Did you have a bad day, dear?"

She didn't answer.

The springs squeaked as Joanna sat on the edge of the bed. "What happened? Please tell me."

"Oh, Mother Joanna." Ever since her father had died when she was fifteen, her mother had encouraged her to call her by her first name, to be her friend, as well as her mother. At first, it had seemed awkward and she'd called her Mother Joanna. Now she used the phrase only as an endearment, when something personal was involved.

"It's Adrian."

"What about him?" Joanna's voice tensed. Adrian was not a topic that either of them liked to discuss. "What did he do?"

"He won't leave me alone. I was going to tell you, but I didn't want to upset you."

"What did he do?" Joanna repeated.

"He's had someone watching me, and now the creep has started following Professor Jones," she said.

"How do you know?" Joanna asked, her voice terse.

"Because after class today he told me someone warned him to stay away from me. I think they got into a fight, because Professor Jones is wearing an eye patch now."

Joanna hesitated before she answered. "I'm not really surprised, Deirdre. You don't know Adrian as I do."

"I wish I'd never known him at all."

She'd met Adrian accidentally when she'd returned early from a trip home to Scotland and found Joanna entertaining several guests at a dinner party. Adrian was among them. He was older, more worldly than she, and she was awed by his suaveness, his knowledge, and the people he knew. When he'd asked to see her again, she'd felt honored more than anything. He offered her ingress to a world of wealth and power that surpassed anything she'd imagined, and she'd wanted a peek.

"Well..." Joanna said evenly. She was rarely critical

of Deirdre, and typically responded to her shortcomings with that one word.

"Okay, I admit it, you were right about him from the beginning." Joanna had discouraged her from seeing Adrian when she found out that he had asked her to lunch. "But you know I only saw him three times, and nothing happened between us."

Nothing much, she thought.

"Three times too many," Joanna said.

"I had no idea he'd be this way. He knows I don't want to see him. Why can't he just leave me alone?"

"With age you'll grow more sensitive and be able to quickly distinguish between sincere, honorable people and those whose thoughts are only of themselves and their whims."

Deirdre admired Joanna's patience. If she'd done as her mother had told her over the years, she probably would have saved herself considerable pain. But she was stubborn. She needed to find out things for herself. To her credit, Joanna had never faulted her for that.

"What else did Professor Jones say?"

"He won't even talk to me."

Neither of them said anything for so long that Deirdre looked up to see if her mother had left the room. She saw for the first time that Joanna was wearing one of her silk Oriental robes, and that her hair fell loosely over her shoulders. She was gazing at one of Deirdre's paintings, a seascape she had painted when she was fifteen. Water crashed against a rock at the base of a cliff, and above the spray was the black oval entrance to a cave. If you looked closely, you could see that the spray formed the face of a bearded man. The painting was called Merlin's Cave, and it was Joanna's favorite.

Deirdre stood up, straightening the wrinkles in her long dress. "Well, I'd better get to work. I've got a paper due Monday."

"For Professor Jones?"

"Yes, and I'm following through on your suggestion, too."

"Oh? What was his reaction?" Joanna asked curiously.

Deirdre shrugged, then allowed a smile. "Interest. A lot of interest."

"I'm not surprised," Joanna responded.

Deirdre hugged her. "Thanks for listening, Mother Joanna."

"Don't fret about Adrian. It won't do any good. Just forget you ever met him."

"I'll try."

Joanna started to leave, then stopped. "If you need any help with your paper, just let me know."

Deirdre gave her mother an assessing look. "That doesn't sound like you." Joanna had never given her any answers or helped her write papers. She'd advised her, but always made her do everything on her own.

Joanna smiled, took Deirdre's hand in her own, and patted it. "Maybe I want you to impress Professor Jones."

Deirdre looked glumly at her. "I think I've already done that, thanks to Adrian."

Joanna squeezed her hand. "Don't worry. It'll all work out."

For the first time since the course had begun, Deirdre didn't sit in the center of the front row. She took a seat three rows back and to one side. It was her way of letting Jones know that she was abiding by his wish that she stay away from him. But she hoped he would also sense the hurt she felt, and the injustice of his accusation.

A man in the row in front of her turned around and grinned. "Why you sitting over here today, Scottie? Teacher's pet in the doghouse?"

"Shut up, and turn around."

"My, aren't we short with our fellow students," he said and turned away.

She certainly hadn't made any friends in this class, but she didn't care. At least she hadn't cared before Professor Jones turned against her.

"Don't listen to him," the girl next to her said, and smiled.

"Thanks, I won't." At least they all didn't hate her.

Just then Jones entered the room and greeted the class. He was still wearing an eye patch, and his single eye stopped for a fraction of a second on the empty front row seat, then he searched the room until he found her. Instantly, he shifted his gaze, but not quickly enough. Good. He'd noticed.

She felt an emptiness as she watched him begin his lecture. She found everything about him appealing, from his easygoing manner, his openness, and his verve to his rugged good looks and savvy hazel eyes.

She was angry with herself for showing off in class. Why hadn't she held back, and just let her knowledge of the field slowly seep into Jones's awareness rather than pushing it on him? She should've realized that a young professor teaching his first course would be more wary than pleased with a student who showed superior knowledge.

Before allowing Deirdre to join her at digs each summer, Joanna had required her to study the same textbooks as her graduate students. She'd wanted to prove herself to the older students, and with Joanna's help had become as knowledgeable as the best of her mother's pupils. She'd taken Jones's course both to please Joanna, who'd recommended it, and for the easy credits it would give her.

"I'm going to divert from my planned lesson today," Jones began, "and talk about a subject related to archaeology that inspires some archaeologists, and angers others." He always started off slowly, warming to his subject. Gradually, his enthusiasm grew until he spoke with such ardor that she couldn't help but join with a question or a comment. Oddly, no one else in class seemed to react as she did. They acted as if they were in Dr. Mahoney's beginning psychology lecture listening to him drone on about case studies and Freudian analysis. It was as if the class consisted of the two of them, Indy and Deirdre. At least, that was how it had been until Adrian had interfered.

"What I'm referring to is mythology and legend, two related and sometimes interchangeable terms for pseudohistory. At worst, myths and legends are gossip and lies, folk tale ignorance and superstition. That's why many archaeologists keep an arm's length or two away from them, even when they relate to their own work."

His eye roved the class, but avoided her. She wondered if he had seen her at the Tower of London. She'd followed him hoping to find the creep Adrian had hired to follow her. She wanted to give him a message for Adrian: that she would notify the police if anyone followed her or Jones again. But the creep had been nowhere in sight.

"While myths should never be blindly accepted as an explanation of what happened at some time in the past, it is not only logical for archaeologists to study those which relate to the particular culture they are investigating, but relevant and necessary. Virtually every myth contains a nugget of truth, a hidden meaning, or a lead for an archaeologist to pursue."

A student raised her hand. "I don't see this topic in the syllabus, Professor Jones."

"It's not. It's my own addition."

"Will we be tested on it?" someone else asked.

Jones looked off to the side of the room as if distracted by a noise in the hall. Deirdre could tell he was annoyed by such banal questions, and she sympathized with him. She guessed he hadn't even considered what they were asking.

"You'll be given an optional essay question on your final test," he said. "Now, if I can continue, I'd like to tell you a story. A very old one."

Deirdre sat back in her chair and listened as Jones related a Greek legend about a people who lived "beyond the north wind." She knew the story well, but she was curious what he would make of it.

"Hecataeus's description of the island is almost certainly of the British Isles," he said when finishing the tale. "While we certainly have to question whether a woman named Leto was ever born to giants on the island or whether she later gave birth to an immortal god, the story does indicate that ancient Greeks and the distant predecessors of the Celts knew of each other. So what can we surmise about these legendary Hyperboreans?"

Deirdre saw him glance expectantly in her direction. She had a good answer for the question, but she kept her hands folded on the desk. Finally, Jones pointed to a man in the back row.

"The Hyperboreans may have traveled south and possibly visited Delphi where Apollo reigned," the student said. "Later, they brought home stories of the god which were passed from generation to generation."

"Okay," Jones said. "But remember the myth is Greek in origin. How would the Greeks know that Apollo visited the island of the Hyperboreans every nineteen years?"

Someone else raised a hand. "Maybe one day Greeks showed up on the shores of Britain and discovered that a sun god was worshipped here as well as in their homeland. So they just made up the story that it was Apollo, and that he visited the island and his mother was born there."

Jones nodded. "That's possible. But the Greeks, for all their glories in architecture and sculpture, mathematics and astronomy, were not much on geography. They weren't known as great travelers, like the Phoenicians, Egyptians, and the Celts themselves. But individual Greeks may have set off on their own, and traveled along the trade routes established by other peoples."

Jones's gaze paused on Deirdre again. She knew he was literally asking for her to enter the discussion. She demurred. "Now, let's take a look at the legend of Stonehenge."

Deirdre listened as Jones related the tale which was even more familiar to her than the story of the Hyperboreans. The story took place around the year 460, after the departure of the Roman legions from Britain. It was a period of great instability when the Saxons, led by Hengist, made repeated attacks against the Britons, ruled by Vortigern.

Finally, a peace conference was held between the rivals, and those attending were told to come unarmed. But Hengist told his men to hide daggers in their clothes and the peace conference turned into a slaughter as hundreds of British nobles were murdered. Soon after, Aurelius Ambrosius, who had been reared in exile in Brittany, succeeded the slain Vortigern as king of England, and Hengist was driven from power. Ambrosius decided to commemorate the mass murder by erecting a monument at the site of the massacre.

"He wanted the monument to last for all time, so he called upon the magician Merlin for help," Jones continued. He glanced at his notes. "And Merlin replied: 'If thou be fain to grace the burial-place of these men with a work that shall endure forever, send for the Dance of the Giants that is in Killaraus, a mountain in Ireland. For a structure of stones is there that none of this age could raise ... For the stones be big, nor is there stone anywhere of more virtue, and, so they be set up round this plot in a circle, even as they be now there set up, here shall they stand for ever.' "

"Excuse me, Professor Jones," a student said. "But how is this story related to archaeology? I mean we all know that Stonehenge was built long before the time you're talking about."

"You're right, of course. But let me finish, and

hopefully you'll see the connection between the myth and science.

"Ambrosius gathered an army which sailed to Ireland under the command of Uther of Pendragron with Merlin at his side. They defeated an Irish army, which defended the great stones, but were unable to move the great blocks until Merlin worked magic upon them. Then, the soldiers were easily able to transport them to their ships and return to England. Still under the guidance of Merlin, the stones were erected in the same form as they had been at Killaraus."

Jones paused and looked in the direction of the student who'd asked the last question. "Granted, this is fantasy. The structure is far older than the fifth century, and scientists have assumed the stones originated from nearby the site."

It was obvious that he was setting up the class for something. Deirdre was captivated; she had no idea what he was leading up to.

"Now, let me refer you to an article which appeared not long ago in the *Antiquaries Journal,* the July 1923 issue to be precise. The article is by Dr. Herbert Thomas and is entitled 'The Source of the Stones of Stonehenge.' Thomas provides convincing evidence that the bluestones—the ones used in the early construction—could not have originated in the area beyond the Salisbury Plain, the site most often attributed as their source. Instead, the eminent geologist offers convincing evidence that they came from the Prescelly Mountains in South Wales, one hundred and thirty-five miles from Stonehenge."

Jones moved away from the podium and paced in front of the class. "Now of course Wales is a fair distance from Ireland. Yet, the new information seems to partially confirm Geoffrey of Monmouth's tale that the builders of Stonehenge transported the stones a great distance and over water. The myth, you see, apparently contained a nugget of truth, and it's all the more astonishing when you consider the true age of Stonehenge, because the wheel, as far as we know, was not in use four thousand years ago."

Deirdre was not only impressed by the story's relevance, but pleased that Jones had brought up Merlin. He'd soon be finding out much more about the ancient enchanter.

When class ended, the students filed by Jones's desk and dropped off their papers. He promised that he would return them at the end of the week when the final exam was given. As Deirdre turned in hers, Jones spoke up. "Thank you, Miss Campbell. I'm looking forward to reading it."

She smiled, but didn't say anything for a moment. Maybe her silence was as foolish as her garrulous behavior had been. "I'm looking forward to your reaction," she answered, then quickly left the room.

SCORPIONS IN LONDON

Clutching a stack of papers under one arm, Indy reached into his jacket pocket for the keys to his Russell Square flat. He stabbed at the lock and missed. He stabbed again, then a third time. The keys slipped from his grip, and clattered onto the wooden floor.

"Damn it." He bent down and balanced the papers on one knee. He patted the floor, feeling dust and grit, but no keys. "C'mon. Where are ya?"

If he'd pressed himself earlier in the week, he would've finished grading the papers by now. But he'd managed to get through fewer than half of them, and now they were due back tomorrow in time for the final exam.

He peered around the pile of papers in the dim hallway light, and spotted the keys behind his heel. He pressed his chin against the papers, and reached between his legs. He grasped the keys with his fingertips, but the papers bulged in the middle, threatening to spill over the hallway. He adjusted the pile as best he could, and stood up. He fumbled with the keys until he found the right one. But just as he reached for the lock again, the knob turned from the inside, and the door creaked open a couple of inches.

"Jack, grab some of these papers, will ya?" Indy had hardly seen Shannon since his friend had gotten the job at the club. Shannon was asleep when Indy left in the morning, and by the time Indy came home Shannon had gone out for the evening. But this morning Shannon had been awake, and said he'd be home this evening.

"Jack?" Indy backed into the room. Just as he turned his legs were kicked out from beneath him. He dropped to the floor. Papers spewed from his hands.

"Damn you, Shannon," he yelled, pushing off from the floor. "What the hell are you—"

Something heavy struck him across the back of the neck. The pain was bright, brief; then he slumped to the floor.

He twitched his nose. Something was tickling him. As he came awake, his first thought was that he must be late for class. Then he realized he was on the floor, lying on sheets of papers. A pair of spats was inches from his face.

"Don't move," a voice said. Shannon's voice.

Indy felt a tickling sensation against his cheek. He shifted his good eye to the side, but couldn't see what was tickling him. He raised his head slightly, and looked up just as Shannon squatted down.

"Don't move!" Shannon hissed again.

Shannon's arm was raised and it looked as if he were about to slap Indy with the back of his hand.

Then with a flick of his wrist, he knocked something off Indy's shoulder. Two quick steps. A foot slammed against the floor, and Indy heard a crackling sound, like dry twigs snapping.

"What was it?" Indy lifted his head.

"Scorpion."

"What?"

"You heard me. Its tail was twitching against your cheek like it was going to strike."

Indy stood up, and looked at the four-inch-long carcass lying next to Shannon's foot. It was crushed against the title page of a term paper. He walked across the paper-covered floor, and prodded the thing with his toe. A shiver flared across his back as if an icy finger had run down his spine.

"God." It was all he could say.

"You okay?" Shannon asked.

Indy touched his neck. "Yeah. I think so."

"What happened?" Shannon scrutinized him as if he expected to see more scorpions on him.

"I don't know." Indy looked at the papers strewn across the floor, shook his head, then winced as a shot of pain radiated from his neck to his right shoulder. "Look at this mess."

Shannon moved about the room looking in the corners, between stacks of books, behind furniture. "Let's see. You came home, and before you closed the door, you tripped, dropped your papers, and knocked yourself out. Then, somehow, a scorpion crawled on your shoulder."

"Not exactly."

"Didn't think so."

"Someone was here. Nailed me on the neck before

I got a look at him." He pulled out his pocket watch and saw that about twenty minutes had elapsed since he'd arrived at the flat.

"I don't see anything missing right off. Everything looks in order. No sign of ransacking."

"Not much to take." Indy stepped over the papers. He walked into the bathroom, wet a cloth, and placed it against his neck. Then he saw it. "Hey, Jack. Come here."

Another scorpion was perched on the edge of the toilet. Indy grabbed a towel and carefully nudged it forward until it dropped into the bowl. He jerked the cord, flushing the creature into the sewer.

He looked over at Shannon. "What do you make of it?"

"Don't know. But if I had to guess, I'd say that there was some connection between the black widows and the scorpions. In fact, I'd put money on it."

"I don't get it."

"Why don't you lie down. I'll take a look around. Where there's two, there might be more."

Indy walked into the bedroom, and cautiously pulled back the sheets. Seeing that it was clean of scorpions, he eased down and closed his eyes.

He was just starting to drift off when he felt something moving under his ear. Slowly, he turned and raised the pillow off the bed. "Aw—" He choked back a yell. "Stay right there," he murmured, then slowly rolled out of the bed.

Shannon walked into the room. "You say something?"

"Four of them, under the pillow. You better check your bed."

"Let's get those guys first." Shannon disappeared, and returned a few seconds later with a box and a broom. He quickly swept the scorpions into the box as Indy held it, and slammed the cover shut.

"Hey, we're getting good at this. Maybe we should go into business exterminating scorpions." Shannon laughed. "Seems to be quite a problem around here."

"Very funny, Jack. Let's search the place before we do anything."

They spent the next half hour scouring the apartment, from the tops of the bookshelves and the ledges above the window frames to the corners and underneath the furniture. Shannon discovered two more scorpions nestled together in one of Indy's shoes. They were tossed into the box with the others.

"I think we've looked everywhere," Indy said as he carried a stack of papers over to his rolltop desk. He was about to set them down when he saw another scorpion poking its head out of a cubbyhole in the desk. He dropped the papers. "That's it. I'm not staying here, and I'm calling the cops."

"No, we can't." Shannon squashed the scorpion with a book. "I don't have work papers. I'll be kicked out."

"I'll say you're a tourist."

"No. If someone sees me at the club, you'll be booted out, too, for harboring me."

Indy looked at the desk. "We can't just ignore the whole thing like it didn't happen. We've got the proof right here," he said, pointing at the box.

Shannon carried the box into the kitchen where he opened a window that faced a brick wall. He pushed it open with one hand, and dumped the scorpions out the window.

"Hey, what did you do that for?" Indy looked out the window, but the scorpions had disappeared into the dark alley two stories below.

"Leave it to me. I'm going to find out what's going on."

"How are you going to do that?" Indy snapped.

Shannon looked away. "I've got contacts. I'll get to the bottom of it."

Indy knew Shannon, and yet he didn't know him. There was a side to him they rarely talked about. Shannon's father, uncles, and brothers were involved in the Irish Mafia in Chicago, and although Shannon had spurned that life, it seemed as if he could never completely escape it, no matter where he was. The family had kept tabs on him through contacts in Europe, and Indy knew that he was not above calling upon those contacts for help.

"I don't know," Indy said uneasily. "I don't want to start any more trouble."

"Relax. I didn't say anything about breaking any fingers or arms, or anything like that. We'll just find out who our connoisseur of poisonous creatures is, and see just what his problem is with you. My guess is that it's got everything to do with this boyfriend of your boss's daughter."

Indy sat on the floor and gathered together all the term papers into one pile. "No. Couldn't be."

"Why not?"

"Because the spiders in the candy box were sent before I even met Deirdre."

Shannon was silent, mulling it over. "Good point. But you know what?"

"What?"

"I still think there's some sort of connection. My gut feeling."

"Yeah, well, I'm going to my office for the night. My predecessor left a cot in the closet."

"Christ, Indy, why don't you stay at a hotel?"

He picked up the stack of papers. "No, this way I'll get my work done."

8

ESPLUMOIR

It was almost two A.M., and Indy had spent the last three hours grading papers. His feet were propped up on his desk, and he yawned as he jotted a note on the cover page of the one he'd just finished. He scrawled a B minus at the end of the note, then dropped it on the pile.

He rubbed the ache in the back of his neck. The paper, like nearly every other one he'd read, had not contained a single original thought. No speculation, no drawing of a thoughtful conclusion, no questioning of the authorities unless some other more recent authority had already done it. Mostly, it was repetition of what had been said. Learning by rote. But what could he expect? This was an introductory course, and the idea was to learn the foundations, not to create something new.

He'd intentionally put off reading Deirdre's paper, saving it for last. Hers would be different; he knew that much. That she would speculate seemed reasonable enough. But that she would actually attempt to prove that Merlin had lived seemed so far beyond the realm of the course that he now doubted what she'd told him in the conference.

He held the paper in his hands, feeling its weight. It was twenty-five pages, about three times the length of any of the others. The title was a mouthful: "Merlin and the Esplumoir: Evidence Suggesting that the Fabled Enchanter Was an Historical Personage." The paper began by saying that while it was virtually impossible to separate the life of Merlin from the myth, it might soon be possible to prove that Merlin was more than a myth. Then, without elucidating further on the so-called evidence, she launched into a biographical sketch.

Whether he was a mythical or historical figure, he lived in the latter part of the sixth century in the Lowlands of Scotland, at the time when Christianity was taking firm root in Britain and paganism was waning. He was a druid, a prophet, and a trickster living in a pagan enclave, she said. All of what she wrote was based on writings centuries later, and Indy knew the stories well. He read over it quickly, and made one note suggesting there was also evidence that the legend of Merlin might have been derived from a Welsh bard called Myrddin Embreis from a century earlier.

Next she moved to the tale of Merlin's death, saying that the story was relevant to her purpose. While Merlin was best known as the counselor of Arthur and two other British kings before him, the story of what happened to the great conjurer in later years was one of the most mysterious aspects of the legend. It was said that he met Vivien, a virgin, and fell in love.

She swore to be his wife, but only if he would teach her the secret of how to trap someone permanently, by words, so he could never get out.

Merlin was so captivated by the young woman that he granted her wish. However, all along Vivien was scheming to defend herself. She immediately used the spell to trap Merlin in a grotto. From that time on, Merlin was never seen again, but he cried out from his tomb, and his cry was often heard in the forest.

However, in another version of the story from an ancient text called Didot-*Perceval,* the enchanter voluntarily retreated from life, and his last words were these: "Now I will retire into my *esplumoir* and never be seen again."

"Maybe Merlin knew all along that Vivien was scheming against him," Deirdre speculated. "He was an accomplished enchanter, who knew well the ways of men and women. Heartbroken and disappointed, he simply played out her wishes. That leads us to the question: What was the *esplumoir,* and where was it?"

Indy paused in his reading, and leaned back in his chair. Deirdre was already ahead of most of the other students, because of the mere fact that she'd brought in two varying sources on the myth, and then speculated on the meaning of the variations. Of course, what she'd written wouldn't get far as a premise for a Ph.D. thesis. He could hear his old professors attacking her from all sides. First of all, she had made a great leap of faith in assuming the myth was a true-life experience that had merely been misinterpreted. She'd also glazed over an important part of the myth. If

Merlin had decided to depart this world on his own, why had he cried out from his tomb?

He turned the page, hoping that her evidence would be something besides another myth. She next gave a detailed explanation of the source and meaning of the word *esplumoir*. In effect, she said the word was of mysterious origin, but apparently its roots appeared to be *plumae* (feathers) and *mutare* (to mutate). The word literally referred to the molting process of a bird. However, seen symbolically, it meant to transform oneself.

Indy picked up his red pencil, circled *mutare*, and made a question mark in the margin. He had more than a passing knowledge of word roots, and doubted the derivation. He also saw another explanation of the word's meaning, and wrote: "It could be from a Latin verb: *ex-plumae*—to remove feathers." It was a minor distinction, but one he couldn't pass by without comment.

Scholars who had pondered the meaning of *esplumoir*, she continued, invariably saw it as symbolic of transformation from life to death. "But the *esplumoir* may actually be a physical place, a place where Merlin retired to chronicle his life with a plumed feather. It is my contention that this place, the *esplumoir*, is a cave located near Whithorn in western Scotland. This assertion is supported by new evidence in the form of a letter written by a monk in the fifteenth century. The letter was found in the archives of Priory Church in Whithorn, and is here translated from its original Latin."

Here we go, thought Indy. *Let's see what she's*

come up with. The letter was dated April 7, 1496, and was addressed to Pope Alexander VI.

I write on a matter of most urgent concern. Nine months ago, I was assigned to explore the ruins of Candida Casa, the first Christian church in Scotland, which was founded in the village of Whithorn, by Saint Ninian in the final years of the fourth century of our Lord. There I have recently made a discovery of a very unusual nature. It is a gold leaf scroll and on it is writing which portends to be the words of the legendary wizard known as Merlin. That itself is disturbing considering where it was found, but even more disconcerting is the nature of what is written on the scroll. Rather than place the unholy words to paper, I am sending this scroll to your attention.

You should also know that there is a cave near Whithorn, which not only bears the name of the founder of Candida Casa, but in the local folklore is also called Merlin's Cave, and it is said that the man who many say was the son of the devil may have spent his last years in its residence, thus befouling the holy nature of the cave. I bring this to your attention because I believe not only that it supports the veracity of the authorship claimed upon the scroll, but that there may be reason to exorcise the cave of the presence of the demonman, who many say still lurks in spirit in its recesses.

Your most humble servant,
Fr. James Thomas Mathers

Indy was fascinated by the letter, and wanted to find out more about it. But there was little else. Deirdre reiterated her conclusions, but made no mention of who had found the letter, when it had been found, or whether it had been authenticated. For all he knew, the letter was a hoax. Hell, maybe Deirdre had made it up. Maybe her mother had put her up to it just to see if he would swallow it without further evidence. Anything was possible when an undergraduate wrote a paper like this one in an entry-level course.

He didn't know whether to give her an A or an F or both. The letter probably was a fraud, but maybe she wasn't responsible. He was considering the note he would write when he heard a noise, like a door creaking. He looked up, cocking his head. He was sure he was the only one on the floor. The archaeology department offices had been dark and locked when he arrived.

Footsteps. Someone was here. He waited. The footsteps grew louder, stopped. Whoever it was must have seen the light from under his door. He imagined Narrow Eyes standing in the hallway with a bucket of scorpions or black widows, or maybe a few rattlesnakes destined for his office. Now he wished he'd reacted more quickly and turned off the light.

He heard a tapping at the door. *Do something,* he told himself. "Who's there?" he barked.

"It's Joanna Campbell. Is that you, Professor Jones?"

Indy leaped up, wishing he hadn't sounded so gruff. He hurried over to the door. "Come in. Sorry, I didn't know who it was."

It was the first time he'd seen Dr. Campbell with her hair loose, and the sight of her long, silvery hair cascading over the shoulders of her black cape struck him oddly. She looked more like a sorceress than an archaeologist. But maybe his recent reading material was affecting his thoughts.

"I saw your light," she said, stepping into the office and looking quickly around, her eyes stopping a moment on the cot. "You're working late."

"Grading term papers." He expected her to respond with a judgmental remark about his waiting until the last minute. Maybe she was thinking it, but she didn't say it.

"I have trouble sleeping some nights, and come in to handle administrative details. I find I can get much more done when no one's here."

"I can understand that." Indy nervously tapped his fingers on Deirdre's paper and wondered if he should say anything about it. "I hope I'm not disturbing you by being here."

Joanna Campbell moved farther into the office and turned her back to him as she examined the books on his shelf. "No, not at all. In fact, it's time we talked." She looked over her shoulder at him. "This seems as good a place and time as any. That is, if it's all right with you."

"No problem at all." *What did she want to talk about?* "You can have my chair, if you like." Indy gestured toward it. "Or would you prefer going to your office?"

She turned and smiled. "Nonsense. Sit. This chair is fine." She placed her hands on the back of the straight-backed wooden chair across from his desk, but didn't sit down.

Indy lowered himself into his chair, and sat back uneasily. He waited for her to begin.

"How do you like it here?"

"I'm enjoying it."

She nodded. "I'm told that you don't always follow the syllabus with which I provided you."

Here it was: the very thing he had feared. Deirdre had told her everything. There was no way for him to hide anything that had taken place in class. "Well, I've tried, but there were times when I felt it was important to expand on certain themes."

"It's unusual for a beginning instructor at this university to divert from the syllabus, especially an instructor with so little practical experience in British archaeology."

"I know, but sometimes it's important to put forth your own ideas. I think that's true for a beginning professor as well as a more experienced one."

"Granted, and I understand you are an engaging lecturer, certainly an improvement over your pedantic predecessor." She glanced at the cot again, and looked amused. "Everyone thought he was so dedicated because he spent so much time in his office. The truth was he kept a bottle of bourbon in one of his drawers and read pulp novels until he passed out. And not from the reading material, either. Although that may have been a contributing factor."

"I've heard rumors about his reading habits." She was confiding in him and Indy felt reassured, but only for a moment.

"Now, I must tell you that I'm a bit uncomfortable

with anyone on our teaching staff who lacks field experience in the British Isles, especially someone like yourself who is teaching a course focusing on our ancient monuments."

"That's understandable, but it is a beginning course," he added quickly, "and as soon as there's an opportunity I would like to be involved in fieldwork. In fact, I was talking with Professor Stottlemire about his upcoming excavation along the rampart of the Herefordshire Beacon hillfort. He seemed very interested in my joining him."

"It's an interesting site, and a nice place to take a walk, but you wouldn't want to work with Stottlemire. He'll take credit for any new ideas and anything you might uncover. The Beacon hillfort is definitely *his* territory."

Indy shrugged. "Well, I was just looking for an opening, and—"

"That's fine, Jones. But you should have asked me weeks ago."

"I didn't want to be presumptuous since there was no guarantee that I'd be here in the fall."

She waved a hand. "Not to worry. You're doing a commendable job. Your position is safe. That is, if you want it."

"Yes, of course, I do."

"Good. Then the matter we have to discuss right now is your fieldwork."

He suddenly felt light-headed with relief. He was staying in England, and all the spiders and scorpions in London couldn't stop him. What's more, Dr. Campbell wanted to talk about fieldwork. "Do you have any suggestions, any new excavations starting?"

"Yes, as a matter of fact. I'm going to be leading a dig myself at Whithorn, Scotland."

"Whithorn?" Indy looked down at Deirdre's paper, then back up at Dr. Campbell. "I was just reading your daughter's paper on—"

"I know all about it. Deirdre is going along as my assistant. I hope you'll join us."

"Yes. Certainly, but..." He picked up Deirdre's paper. "Does this paper about Merlin have anything to do with your excavation plans?"

"Of course. It has everything to do with it."

9

THE "CRUC"

A distinguished, decidedly upper-class British voice was speaking over the airwaves. "It is imperative that the thinking members of Parliament join together to fight this menace known as the Commonwealth. If this plan ever came into being, it would be the first step in the dissolution of the British Empire, and we can never allow that to happen in our lifetime."

"Thank you, Mr. Powell," another radio voice said. "Now, before we go any further I want to ask you—"

"Jack, turn that damn thing off, will you?" Indy called out.

He heard a click as Shannon shut off the radio in the living room.

"Need any help?" Shannon asked.

Indy's clothes were spread out on the bed as he packed his duffel bag. "No, I think I can pack my own bag."

"Hey, maybe you ought to put your eye patch back on," Shannon said.

"What for?"

"It makes you look meaner. Fits your cranky mood."

"Sorry, but I haven't slept well for three nights now. I keep waking up thinking there's a goddamn scorpion crawling on my neck."

"The place is clean, Indy. I guarantee it."

"I know. But still ..."

Shannon leaned against the dresser, resting a long, lanky arm on the top of it. "So when are you coming back?"

"Fall classes start in three weeks. I should be here at least a couple of days ahead of time."

"If I hear anything on the bug man, I'll send you a note. Check general delivery."

Indy stuffed a pair of socks in the bag. "I'd just like to forget the whole thing happened. Maybe they were going after someone else, and got the wrong flat."

"Could be. I doubt it, though. I still think those spiders and scorpions are connected, somehow."

Indy didn't answer. He folded a pair of khaki pants and a sweatshirt into the duffel bag and zippered it shut.

"Have you mentioned the scorpions to your girlfriend?"

"No, I didn't say anything to her, and she's not my girlfriend. She's my student."

"That's right." Shannon moved away from the dresser, and clasped Indy on the shoulder. "I bet you'll be singing a different tune when you come back from Scotland."

"Jack, I'll be with her mother, too."

"You better watch out for both of them."

"Cut it out, will ya?"

"Sorry. Just kidding. But you do like the girl, don't you?"

Indy shrugged. "Sure I do. But just don't bring up Dorian Belecamus, because Deirdre's nothing like her. They're worlds apart. And I am going to talk to her about her boyfriend, or old boyfriend, whoever he is. I just haven't had the opportunity yet."

"Right, worlds apart," Shannon mused. "She's good-looking, intelligent, a bit mysterious. Nothing like Belecamus was."

He had a point. But Deirdre had an entirely different attitude. "She may not have told me her life story, but she's not deceptive. There's a freshness, an innocence about her. I know I can trust her."

"Love is blind, Indy."

Indy folded an undershirt. "Shannon, you know something? You're the most suspicious person I've ever met."

"Gotta be. But then I'm not making my living in some ivory tower."

Indy flung the undershirt against the bed, and turned to face his roommate. "You got some problem with what I do? Is that it?"

Shannon raised his hands. "Nope. No problem at all with what you do. It's your attitude. You're gullible. You need more street savvy."

"You'd think some of yours might've rubbed off on me by now."

Shannon grinned. "You would think so, wouldn't you?"

"I'll tell you one thing. I may not be the greatest judge of women, but Deirdre is on the level. I'm sure of it."

"You may be surprised to hear this, but I agree with you. She's as naive as you are."

As if he even knew her, Indy thought, but he wasn't going to argue. He looked up at the clock on the wall. "Okay, I'm going to say good-bye to Milford. You sure you don't want to join me?"

Shannon laughed. "Positive. He wouldn't remember me."

"Actually, you'd be surprised. He might. He only seems to forget recent things. He has a wonderful memory of past events."

"I'll take your word for it." Shannon followed him to the door. "You're going to be back by four then, right?"

"That's what I said. Four o'clock." He opened the door and turned. "Since when are you so concerned about my coming and going?"

Shannon threw up his hands. "Hey, I just want to say good-bye before I leave for the club. That's all."

"Tell you what, if I don't see you, I'll stop by for a drink."

"Just be here by four, will ya?"

Indy padded across the thick carpeting of the lobby to the reception desk of the Empire Club, where Leeland Milford was staying. Ornate gold-framed portraits of men, several with monocles, hung on the walls, and heavy mahogany furniture filled the room. A thin, angular man sat behind the desk. He had a mustache that looked as if it had been penciled in. When Indy asked him where he would find Milford's room, he combed it with his fingernails, and in a voice as stuffy as his surroundings said: "Dr. Milford. Was he expecting you?"

"Yes, and he's waiting."

The clerk's expression turned blatantly smug. "Sorry, sir, but he's left. Said something about going to Madame Tussaud's, I believe."

"Did he now?" Indy said, mimicking the man's tone. "Guess I'll be on my jolly way then."

Indy turned on his heels and headed to the nearest underground. Ten minutes later, he found Milford at the wax museum standing motionless to one side of Henry VIII and his six wives. He was gripping the lapels of his overcoat and looked like a wax figure himself that had been stuck in the wrong century.

"Authentic, isn't it?" Indy said.

Milford slowly turned his head. His watery blue eyes gazed at Indy, and his thick mustache twitched. "Yes, but let me show you something else."

Indy shook his head as he followed the older man into another room. Not even a hint of surprise that he was here. Not a good sign, he thought. He was hoping Milford would be on an even keel today. On Friday morning, final exam day, Indy had found him waiting in his office when he'd arrived. Milford had acted befuddled, insisting he had something important to tell Indy, but then when he couldn't remember what it was, he'd insisted that he must have already told him.

They'd bantered inanely for a couple of minutes until it was time for Indy's class. He'd quickly set a date for lunch at the club, hoping that Milford would recall whatever it was he considered so important. The conversation had so abraded his nerves that he'd forgotten the students' graded papers in his office and had to go back for them.

"Look here at Robespierre and Marat," Milford said, stepping up to the wax figures of the French Revolutionary leaders. "Now these two are especially authentic in appearance."

"Why is that?" Indy asked.

"Because their heads were used as models by Madame Tussaud immediately after they were guillotined."

Indy cleared his throat. "That was handy. I guess she didn't have to tell them to sit still."

"No, I suppose not," Milford said with a laugh. "Fortunately, they were spared the sight of their headless bodies so they lack a certain look of horror in their expressions."

"What do you mean? If someone lost his head, how could he possibly know anything about the sight of his body?"

"Ah well, you see, it was once a practice for the executioner to grab the severed head immediately after the guillotine sliced it off, and turn it to face the body. Since there was still blood and oxygen in the brain, it was felt there was still awareness for up to thirty seconds."

"Is that true?"

Milford shrugged. "From the bulging eyes and moving mouths that have been described, you would think so. But maybe it was just the reaction of the nerves."

"Still, just the idea . . ." Indy's words trailed off.

"Yes, it's amazing what we do to each other," Milford said after a short silence. "We like to think of the past as the period of barbaric behavior, but look at our own century. Thousands upon thousands sacrificed themselves for country in the Great War. Quaint French villages stacked with bodies. Fields soaked in blood. If you ask me, it wasn't so great."

They wandered about the museum for nearly an hour. Indy didn't even bother asking Milford if he'd recalled what he was going to tell him. Today, apparently, wasn't one of his better days for testing the older man's short-term memory. Finally, he persuaded Milford to join him for afternoon tea at a small restaurant near the museum. After they were seated and their tea and biscuits had arrived, Indy talked about his plans to go to Scotland. He explained that he would be excavating St. Ninian's hermitage, a cave that had been used by early Christians as a place of meditation, and according to myth where Merlin spent his last years. He added that the cave might have been Merlin's *esplumoir.*

He watched Milford's expression at the mention of the *esplumoir,* but the old professor was slowly stroking his white mustache and frowning as he gazed through the window. Indy turned to see if he was looking at anything in particular, but it seemed he was just daydreaming.

Milford noticed that he'd stopped talking. He blinked, and looked down into his tea. "Damn it, Indy, there was something I was going to tell you. Now wait. Did I already tell you about it?"

Indy tried to be gentle, but he was irritated. "Dr. Milford, let's not get into this again. All you've told me is that there's something you wanted to tell me."

Milford scratched his ear. "Well, if I didn't already

tell you, then I'm sure it will come to me. Now what were you saying, something about Scotland?"

Indy repeated what he'd already said.

"Excavating for Merlin, eh?"

"Well, not exactly Merlin, but..."

Milford scratched his chin, and touched his mustache. "You know, it seems I was talking with someone recently on that very subject."

"Me."

"Huh?"

"You were talking to me about it the other day at the Tower of London. You had some strong doubts about being able to prove that he lived."

"Yes, of course."

Indy took a bite of his biscuit, and sipped his tea. "By the way, do you know anything about Merlin's *esplumoir*?"

Milford repeated the word. "Yes, yes. That's one of those words," he muttered.

"What do you mean?"

"One of those words that was probably a misinterpretation between the French and the English when they translated stories back and forth." He waved a hand, looking annoyed. "It's a mess. You could spend a career looking at those words, trying to straighten things out."

That was just the sort of career Indy was avoiding, by pursuing archaeology instead of linguistics. But he was interested in what Milford had to say, and asked him to explain.

"I don't know enough about this *esplumoir*, but I'll give you another example about your friend, Merlin. Do you know what a barrow is?"

Indy sipped his tea. "Sure, I've been an archaeologist a couple of months now. It's a mound of earth or stone built over a grave. Britain's literally covered with them."

"True enough, and if Merlin was an historical person, he was buried in one."

Indy was surprised by Milford's confident, self-assured tone. "Why do you say that?"

"I'm sure you know the story of *Le Cri de Merlin*, about how he cried out from his tomb."

Indy nodded.

"Well, it's a mistake." Milford slowly stirred his tea.

"What do you mean?"

"A mistake in the translation found in the French texts, then later repeated by the English. The original word was *cruc*, which is an early English word for barrow, but it was translated to *cri*. Then, Geoffrey of Monmouth took the French *cri* and translated it to cry."

Milford beamed at Indy. He was in full control of his faculties at the moment, and he wasn't finished. "For example, if I may return to the topic of losing one's head, when Eldol cut off Hengist's head, he 'raised a great cry over his head,' Geoffrey of Monmouth wrote. Of course it was supposed to be a barrow that was raised over his head. That was the custom in burying a Saxon chieftain."

Indy set down his cup. "Really?"

"Yes, of course. I've been arguing this point with your father for years."

"So you're saying that Merlin was buried in a barrow, not in a cave," Indy said.

"Exactly. The story about his being trapped in a cave didn't make sense, anyhow. Why would a savvy magician like Merlin allow a young girl to fool him? He was too wise for that."

Interesting, Indy thought. Milford's last point was more or less the same thing that Deirdre had said in her paper.

"So what about his last words? He said he was going to retire into his *esplumoir*."

"Like I said. I don't know this one well. But I do recall something about this *esplumoir* being his way of saying he was going to die, change his feathers so to speak. Or *so whylome wont*. I wouldn't be surprised if it meant something else altogether. Remember they wrote with quills, feathers, in those days. Look at the root of the word. The Welsh *plufawr*, 'feathers,' comes from the Latin *pluma*. It probably means he retired from the active life and went to some secluded place to take up the plume, to write."

It was a few minutes after four when Indy returned to the Russell Square flat after accompanying Milford back to his room at the club. He was tired and decided he'd lie down for a few minutes. Spending time with Milford exhausted him. Maybe it was because he was always on guard, uncertain of how Milford would act, whether he would slip into Middle English, mumble incoherently, or get angry at him. In spite of his forgetfulness, Milford seemed capable of getting around by himself, and never forgot—at least for long—what he was doing at any particular moment.

"Jack, you here?" he called as he closed the door.

No answer. Shannon must have left. Now he was committed to going out tonight, even though he was leaving early in the morning. He wished he hadn't made the promise, but maybe he'd feel more like going out again after he'd rested.

He glanced at his desk, looking to see if Shannon had left a note. He heard something. It sounded like a stifled cough. He turned his head. His bedroom door was closed. It hadn't been closed when he went out. He never closed it.

Not more trouble. He didn't need it, didn't want it. He considered heading for the door, and calling the police. But who knew what he'd find when he came back. He took a couple of cautious steps toward the door, and reached for the handle.

Suddenly, it burst open amid shouts and screams, and people spilled out around him. "Surprise!"

He looked around, baffled. For a brief moment he didn't know who they were. They looked familiar, but...

...Of course, his students.

"Professor Jones!" It was Deirdre. She moved forward from the throng that had surrounded him. "I hope you don't mind. Everyone wanted to say goodbye and wish you well on the dig."

He laughed. "No. I guess I don't mind. Hell, you're all here now." Red, blue, and green balloons bobbed near the ceiling, crepe paper streamers had materialized as if out of nowhere, and one of the students was holding out a cake. On the top of it the frosting spelled "Happy Digging," and below the words was a drawing of a man and woman, both carrying shovels and holding hands.

"What is this?" Deirdre peered at the drawing, her shoulder pressed against his arm. "I didn't have anything to do with that," she said emphatically. He liked the sound of her lilting Scottish voice, even when she raised it.

The crowd laughed and several students shouted lighthearted taunts. It was obvious that everyone thought something *was* going on between them, or that it should be, if it wasn't.

Indy's face reddened, and he avoided looking at Deirdre. Then he glanced beyond the crowd and saw Shannon across the room, leaning against the wall. His arms were crossed and there was a smirk on his face. "Jack, did you have something to do with this?"

"Me?" Shannon tapped his hands at his chest, brows lifting. "I just opened the door."

"Oh no, he was in on it," someone shouted.

"Right from the start," another voice piped in.

"I knew it," Indy said. "That's why you were so insistent on me getting back by four."

Glasses of soft drinks and wine were being passed out. "Cut the cake," someone said. The gangly young man who was supposed to write his term paper on views of Stonehenge in the seventeenth century stepped forward with a knife.

"I should get to cut it," he said. "I wrote my term paper on Stonehenge, comparing the ideas of the architect Inigo Jones with those of Professor Indy Jones."

"And he managed to pass," Indy added.

"Let's cut it on the table," the girl holding the cake said, and moved toward the kitchen, followed by a swirl of students.

Indy looked around and saw Deirdre standing back from the crowd. He moved to her side, touched her lightly in the small of the back. "Thanks. I appreciate this. I had no idea."

"No idea of what?" she asked.

He smiled. "No idea it was going to happen."

She looked up at him. "I wasn't sure myself." It seemed they were talking about more than just the party.

"I'm looking forward to Scotland."

"Me too. It'll be nice to go home."

"Are you from that region of Scotland?" he asked, realizing how little he knew about her.

"I'm from Whithorn. I grew up in the village."

"Oh." Indy was surprised. "I didn't realize that."

There was a rap at the door, and Indy turned to see Shannon opening it. Joanna Campbell stepped inside.

"Joanna! What are you doing here?" Deirdre exclaimed and moved across the room. One surprise after another, Indy thought as he trailed after her. He stopped short to give mother and daughter a chance to talk alone. They exchanged a few quick words, then Dr. Campbell turned and smiled at Indy.

He moved over to them, and she touched his forearm. "I hope you're not upset by this invasion of your privacy, but your students were insistent. You're probably the most well-liked professor I've had on my staff. I can't recall ever hearing such enthusiastic comments as I have about you."

Her compliment astonished him. "Why, thank you, Dr. Campbell. From the bored looks I see sometimes in class, I would've never known."

"You can call me Joanna. No need to be formal."

"Good. Let me get you a glass of wine, or would you like something else? And we've got cake." He was relieved that it was already sliced so he wouldn't have to explain the drawing.

"No, nothing for me. I'm not going to stay." She leaned forward, and spoke confidentially. "Actually, I wasn't officially invited, and I'm afraid I've embarrassed Deirdre." She glanced over at her daughter.

"Oh, that's not true," Deirdre protested.

Joanna flashed a smile, but her demeanor quickly turned serious. "There is a particular reason I've come here to see you. Deirdre, you should listen, too."

"I'm listening." Deirdre sounded sarcastic, yet puzzled at the same time.

"I'm afraid my plans have changed. I need to stay in London a few more days."

"But Joanna, you promised—"

Her mother raised a hand. "Let me finish, Deirdre. I don't think there's any need to disrupt our plans. I want you two to go on to Whithorn without me, and I'll join you as soon as I can."

"But what are we going to do?" Deirdre sounded exasperated.

"All the equipment is packed. You know the area well, and Professor Jones is a fully qualified archaeologist." She turned to Indy. "I've prepared written instructions for you as guidelines. You'll need to hire a couple villagers. Deirdre can help you with that. She knows everyone, including the ones I've worked with before. Anyhow, by the time the two of you get started, I'll probably be there. Is that all right with you?"

He felt light-headed. Everything was happening so

fast, but he couldn't think of a more interesting change in plans. "I guess we can make do until you arrive."

"I know you will," she said confidently.

Indy accompanied her to the door, and opened it. "One other thing I was wondering about. As I understand it, the intent of the dig is to look for the gold scroll mentioned in the monk's letter."

Joanna smiled. "Yes, of course."

"Well, it's just that . . . I don't see how you can assume from the letter that the scroll is buried in the cave."

"I'm glad you mentioned that. I've been so busy that we haven't had time to talk about all the background."

They moved out into the hall, and Indy closed the door, shutting out the noise.

"You see, after I read the letter," Joanna continued, "I contacted a friend of mine, who happens to have an excellent relationship with the Vatican. He found out that no such scroll or letter was ever received, and there was no request made to exorcise Ninian's Cave."

"I was wondering about that, since the letter was found in Whithorn."

"Exactly. It was never sent. Neither was the scroll. What I did find out was that Father Mathers remained in Whithorn until his death five years later. My theory is that since the scroll has never turned up, it was buried in the cave."

"Maybe the gold was melted down."

She shook her head. "That's not likely. There was an approved procedure which would've been followed. There would've been records, and there aren't any."

"It still seems a long shot."

A hint of a fey smile touched her lips. "This is something I feel strongly about, Jones. Very strongly. I can't explain it. It's just a sense I have that the dig will be productive."

"I hope you're right. By the way, I'm a little confused about Deirdre's paper now. I mean did you..."

"Did I write it? Of course not. But I did suggest the topic to Deirdre. I was hoping her paper would entice you into joining us."

"It didn't take much to pique my interest. I can't wait to get started."

Joanna met his gaze. "I appreciate your enthusiasm. But keep in mind that I'm also expecting you to behave in a professional manner while in the company of my daughter."

"Oh, of course."

10

WHITHORN WELCOME

The southwest coast of Scotland was wild and forested, a land where ranges of hills were interspersed with breathtaking lochs and glens. *A faerie land*, Indy thought as he rode horseback toward the village in the dying light of early evening. It was difficult for him to compare it to the rugged desert of the American Southwest where he'd grown up. There, a sense of immensity prevailed. Here, the scale was smaller, but more diverse. It was as if nature was aware that only so much space was available, so everything had to be compacted, scaled to size.

They'd arrived by train late the previous night, and this morning had begun preparations for the dig. They'd met with the village mayor, a longtime friend of Joanna's, and Indy had briefed him on their plans. Later, they found two carpenters who had worked with Joanna on her last dig at the cave, and made arrangements for them to begin work the next day.

It wasn't until midafternoon that they'd finally ridden out to the cave. Ninian's Cave was only a few feet wide at the mouth, but twenty feet or so beyond the entrance it opened into an expansive cavern. While Deirdre had returned to the village to assemble supplies they would need, he'd immediately begun work, taking measurements of the cavern, and laying out plans for the grid they would construct.

In the days after Joanna had invited him to the dig, he'd read everything he could about Candida Casa and Ninian's Cave. A report by the Royal Commission on Ancient Monuments of Scotland in 1914 described small slabs of hand-carved stone and fragments of two Christian crosses unearthed near the cave. Joanna Campbell was mentioned as the archaeologist in charge of the excavation. No mention of Merlin's *esplumoir* or the gold scroll was made in the report, and he suspected the work had taken place either before she knew about the letter or before she'd decided the scroll was buried in the cave.

He dismounted at the stable and walked to the quaint rooming house where they were staying. It was a three-story eighteenth-century stone building that had been remodeled to accommodate electricity and modern plumbing. He passed the large dining room, and climbed the staircase to the second floor where his room was located. His room was special, the landlady had said, because it was the only one with a bathtub in the room. He'd offered it to Deirdre, but she preferred the larger, corner room next door. He closed the door behind him, and turned on the light. Immediately, he heard a tapping on the wall from the adjoining room. He smiled, walked over to the wall, and repeated the same tapping pattern. Deirdre was no doubt getting ready for dinner, and it was time for him to do the same.

As he washed and changed his clothes, he wished that he and Deirdre were dining alone this evening. Things had been awkward between them, and he wanted to talk with her, to bridge the gulf that had opened. Although he'd been looking forward to spending time alone with her, he'd been haunted by Joanna's departing words, and had intentionally kept his distance. His job at the university was virtually assured now, but he knew Joanna could still retract her offer if he crossed some invisible boundary with her daughter. Now though, he wanted to make it clear to Deirdre that the way he'd acted on the train had nothing to do with his real feelings about her. He didn't know exactly *how* he was going to explain it to her, but he would.

Dinner that night would be a village affair. The event was being held in their honor at the local pub, and many of Deirdre's old friends were expected to attend. He straightened his tie in the mirror, left the room, and knocked on the adjoining door. He'd have to make good use of the time he had with her.

"Is that you, Indy?" she asked, then opened the door a couple of inches. She peered out at him, but didn't open it any farther. "I'll be right with you. I'm almost ready."

The door closed in his face. He didn't move for several seconds; a part of him expected her to reopen it and invite him in. When it didn't happen, he stepped back and leaned against the wall in the dimly lit hallway. Swell. Now she was the reserved one. Things were going just great. How the hell were they going to work together in a cave?

Finally, the door opened, and they headed down the hall. She was wearing a tartan skirt and a white, frilly blouse, and her hair was bunched primly on her head with a few strands falling to her shoulders.

"You look . . . very Scottish this evening," he said as they reached the top of the stairs.

"You look rather dandy yourself, Professor Jones."

"I do?" Indy owned two suit coats, a tweed one, which he wore to most of his lectures, and the navy blue wool coat he now wore with a white shirt and blue tie. He noticed her glance stray to his feet as they reached the stairway. He wore his boots, the only footwear he'd brought along. "I forgot my dress shoes back in the flat."

The shoes he'd found scorpions in, he thought.

"Don't worry about it. You're in Whithorn, not London. No one will notice, and if they do, they won't care." She laughed, a lovely trill, a sound that made him want all the more to break through the barrier separating them. "In fact, they'll probably approve," she added.

"That's good to know."

As they headed down the street, Indy did his best to turn the conversation to their relationship, or the lack of it. "You ever travel alone before?" he began.

"I didn't think I was alone."

"I meant on your own without your mother."

"Well, if you put it that way, I'm used to making journeys on my own and being away from Joanna for extended periods of time. She's a good mother, but she's also busy and gone a lot, attending conferences and meetings, going to digs." She shrugged. "The life of an archaeologist."

"I guess I've been sort of distant since we left London."

"Have you?" She looked away. "I haven't really noticed."

He cleared his throat. "Your mother told me to be careful around you."

Deirdre laughed. "She did? Why, am I dangerous?"

"No, I think she thought I might be."

"No *wonder* you were acting like I was going to bite you."

They moved on. "You can understand my situation, can't you?" he asked.

"Just relax. I think we'll get along a lot better."

Relax, sure. How was he going to relax around her?

Inside the pub, the smell of cooking food and cheery conversation greeted them. Back home, he thought, the town bar would be an unlikely spot for a dinner in someone's honor, especially a young woman. But pubs were more family-oriented here than their American counterparts. The place was crowded with villagers, and a quick glance around told him they represented at least three generations of Whithorn residents.

"There she is," said a man's voice. "There's the lass, Deirdre."

A woman from across the room chimed in: "And look there at her man."

Everyone fell silent, and stared. "They got you right," Indy muttered, "but I don't know about me."

Then the mayor, a pink-cheeked man with a receding hairline, stood up and motioned for them to join him at a long table in the center of the pub. He wore a kilt complete with a tasseled sporran dangling from his belt. Seated with the mayor was a matronly woman he introduced as his wife, Marlis, and Father Phillip Byrne, an elderly white-haired priest who wore a black cassock. Also at the table were several young women whom Deirdre introduced as old friends. They were all about her age and were dressed in similar outfits.

In spite of Deirdre's explanations about who Indy was, the looks and smiles of the others suggested they knew different, that the two were lovers. The priest's eyebrows twitched when he glanced at them, as if he was trying to decide if they were committing adultery. Indy imagined him taking Joanna aside when she arrived, and telling her that she must do something about the young archaeologist's libido.

A waiter arrived and poured Indy and Deirdre shots of a local brand of Scotch. Indy took too big of a swallow and felt it burning all the way down to his stomach. He coughed into his hand.

"A good batch, don't you think, Professor Jones?" the mayor said, holding up his glass.

"Great." He felt like fanning his mouth.

"Ah, it's too bad your mother couldn't be here," Father Byrne said to Deirdre.

"She'll be here in a few days, Father, and you can be sure she'll stop by to see you."

The priest's thick white eyebrows furrowed, and Indy thought he detected a look of concern on his face as if Joanna's absence, or maybe it was her impending arrival, somehow affected him. He wondered what the priest knew about the gold scroll, since the monk's letters had come from the archives of his church. He was about to ask when Byrne launched into a story about Deirdre's past.

At age twelve, she had organized a dance group of parish girls, and one time after they'd performed at a wedding reception, a dance choreographer from Edinburgh, who'd been in attendance, invited the group to perform in Edinburgh. "The girls were all excited about it, then they learned they would be performing for King George. Poor Deirdre, she was so excited as the day neared that she couldn't eat. I was worried that she would faint right there on the stage. But it all went very well, of course, and the king was heard to say that he was very impressed by the girls."

Deirdre, who had been chatting with one of the women, heard the end of the conversation. She waved a hand. "Oh, we were only one of several dance groups that performed for the king."

Byrne nodded toward the other women at the table. "They're all members of the original group, you know."

When dinner was finally served, Indy found himself eating haggis, a concoction of organ meats and oats served inside the lining of a sheep's stomach.

"What do you think of it?" Byrne asked, pointing to Indy's plate.

"Good, really good." He didn't like lying to a priest, but didn't think it was the right place to say that the idea of serving sheep guts inside a stomach didn't appeal much to him. He ate it, though. Hell, he'd eaten worse, and after a few bites he decided it really wasn't that bad.

"So what are the plans for the dig, Professor Jones?" Byrne inquired.

"Well, we're going to be working inside the cave. We're looking for a gold scroll, the one that was mentioned in the letter from the monk that was found—"

"Yes, I know. I found the letter in the archives."

"Oh, then maybe you can tell me more about it," Indy said.

Byrne shrugged. "Not much to tell. Why do you think the scroll is in the cave?"

"I don't know that it is. But Dr. Campbell seems convinced we'll find it there. I guess it's a logical hiding place. It's Merlin's Cave as well as Ninian's. Right?"

Byrne's expression changed, his features set in the stern look of a man who has spent a lifetime burdened by the weight of his position as guardian of his parishioners' religious life.

"It's St. Ninian's Cave," he said firmly. "Those who call it Merlin's Cave are people you would not care to meet."

"Oh, why not?"

Byrne seemed disturbed by the topic and quickly dismissed it. "Maybe we'll talk about it one day."

Indy took a bite of his haggis, and wondered about Byrne's reticence. "Do you know why Father Mathers never sent the letter to the Vatican?"

"As I said, one of these days we'll talk about these things."

Just then the mayor stood up and rescued them from the awkward silence. He gave a typical salutatory talk about Deirdre and her mother, their contributions to the community, and how they were missed.

Then he introduced Indy to everyone and presented him with a kilt. The mayor held it up and turned it slowly around, a broad grin on his face. Indy heard chuckles rippling back from the nearest tables, and saw heads tilting toward each other and mouths covered. He laughed with everyone else, uncertain what exactly was so funny.

"This kilt, Professor Jones, is a gift from the people of Whithorn; it also happens to be the tartan of the Campbell clan," the mayor explained.

Indy accepted the kilt. "Thank you. I'm not sure what exactly the pattern implies, but I've got an idea." Everyone laughed again, and he glanced at Deirdre. She was smiling, but her face was red with embarrassment. "It does look very nice, though," he added. "At first, I wasn't quite sure it was my style, but the more I look at it, the more I like it."

"That's what we like to hear," the mayor said. "Try it on for us, won't you?"

Indy grimaced. "You're kidding."

"Don't be shy about it," a burly, bearded man at the next table said. He stood up, and Indy saw his kilt. "Come on, lad. I'll show you to the back room, and you can change there."

Indy glanced at Deirdre, saw her nodding encouragement. He shrugged and followed the man. After he'd changed, he looked at himself in the mirror. He lifted the kilt up, uncovering his hairy thighs. He shook his head in disbelief. "Am I really doing this?"

As he walked back out into the pub, everyone looked up. To his surprise, Deirdre rose from her chair, walked over to him, and hooked her arm in his.

The crowd cheered as they headed back to the table. "Now we're dressed like twins," he muttered.

Deirdre leaned close, and whispered in his ear. "You look like a real man now, Professor Jones."

"That's good to know. You could've fooled me," he said as they sat down. "And just call me Indy, will you?"

"Indy," she said as if trying out the name.

Suddenly, the pub was filled with sound as a band of kilted bagpipe players marched through the door. Indy recognized two of the men as the brothers, Carl and Richard, whom they'd hired to work at the cave.

"Thanks for going along with everything," Deirdre said.

Their eyes met, and he sensed that the gulf between them had been bridged. Just then, several young girls in tartans joined the band and were performing a traditional Scottish dance. Indy touched the back of Deirdre's hand. He nodded toward the dancing girls. "So that's what you used to do?"

"What do you mean 'used to'?" She literally bounded out of her chair, and signaled her friends. They joined the younger girls. He watched as Deirdre, hands on hips, raised one knee high, and bouncing on the other foot kicked and twirled to the intoxicating sound of the bagpipes.

Indy couldn't take his eyes off her. He felt as infatuated as a kid with his first girlfriend. Maybe it was the Scotch he'd drunk, the wild sounds of the pipe music, Deirdre's beauty. All of it.

11

MERLIN'S CAVE

"Tea, Professor Jones?"

Indy looked up at Lily, the landlady, and nodded. He would prefer coffee with his breakfast, but he knew that wasn't an option. It was like the rest of the meal, bread toasted on one side, and fried eggs, watery on top and hard on the bottom. He either accepted them, or started a discussion about cooking, which at seven A.M. was a worse idea than eating the food the way it came.

He watched as the frumpy, middle-aged woman, who always wore a housecoat and curlers, poured him half a cup of tea, then filled the rest of it with milk, and pushed a bowl of brown sugar cubes in front of him.

"Thanks." He picked up a cube, but dropped it back in the bowl when she walked away. When he did drink tea it wasn't with milk or sugar, but one thing he'd learned from his travels was to adjust to local food and customs rather than try to change them for his particular needs. It made everything much easier, and today, the first day of the dig, he wanted everything to go smoothly.

A few minutes later, Deirdre descended the stairs. "Good morning, Indy."

She wore brown pants and a baggy checkered shirt. Her auburn hair was tied in a braid and covered with a scarf, and a pair of gloves protruded from the back of her pants. "Morning. Breakfast?"

She shook her head. "I was down earlier, and had my tea and scones."

Indy pushed his chair back from the table. "Well, you look like you're all ready to go out and strike gold," he said with a grin.

"Do you really think the gold scroll is in the cave? You know the monk found it in the ruins of the old monastery."

"I suppose he could have hidden it anywhere, but your mother seems confident we'll find it in the cave."

Deirdre's expression turned pensive. Her eyes were soft, violet pools that made him feel weak in the knees. "But Joanna is right. If the scroll is in Whithorn, the cave is the logical spot."

"It's worth taking a look. Meet you out front in ten minutes."

She nodded. "I'll be there."

Back in his room Indy pulled on his leather jacket, and put on his hat. He was about to leave when he remembered something. He opened his bag, and took out a coiled whip. He ran his hands over it. Maybe it was silly to bring it along, but he'd promised himself a couple of years ago in Greece that he'd always keep it with him on digs. He hitched it to his belt. What the hell. If nothing else, it was a good luck charm, a superstition he allowed himself.

Deirdre was waiting in the road in front of the house, holding the reins of two horses. She didn't see him and he watched her a moment from the doorway. She was stroking the muzzle of one of the horses and talking softly to it. He could overlook the fact that she still hadn't clearly explained the situation with her old boyfriend. It was understandable. Everything about her was right. She was attractive and bright, and they even had similar interests. Of the women he'd met in Paris over the last couple of years, all had lacked at least one of those attributes.

He stepped into the road, and his eyes were drawn toward the sky. It was a gray, windy morning and the clouds were so thick they literally pressed down on him. Maybe it was the contrast from yesterday's clear skies and bright sunshine that made him feel a sense of unease. Maybe it was his growing interest in Deirdre mixed with his concern about what would happen if his desires were fulfilled.

"Looks like rain today," he mused.

Deirdre looked up as if seeing the sodden sky for the first time. "Rain isn't an event here; it's part of everyday life."

"I grew up in a desert where it was a wonder," he responded.

As she mounted her horse, her mouth swung into that easy smile that seemed as much a part of her as her Scottish lilt. "I'm looking forward to uncovering a wonder, and soon I hope." With that, she prodded the sides of her horse, and galloped off. Indy quickly mounted his steed and chased after her, his eyes glued to her petite figure.

They rode past stands of immense beech hazel trees, drumlins and moraines, bracken and gorse, bog myrtle and thistle. And it was all a blur. The three-mile stretch of road from the village to the cave was historical in its own right. It was known as a pilgrim's way because Christians, including early Scottish kings, visited the cave after worshipping at St. Ninian's chapel in Whithorn. Indy had read in a French manuscript that the road was also known as a "royal route" traveled by King Arthur, who had visited the cave after Merlin's death. But the writers who had penned the tales of Arthur and Merlin were by no means in agreement that the cave was the site of Merlin's death, and no one called it the *esplumoir*.

They didn't slow until they reached Whithorn Isle, which was not an island, but a peninsula. They trotted along a trail until they came to the base of a bluff where they dismounted, and hitched their horses to a tree branch. "You ride well," he told her.

"Thanks. I'll show you my equestrian trophies sometime."

Another surprise, he thought, as they walked over to the two carpenters, Carl and Richard, who were busy unloading lumber. The men had arrived ahead of them with a wagon loaded with equipment and supplies. They were to build a work table and cabinets for storing gear. Since the cave was remote and rarely visited, Indy didn't think there was much likelihood of theft. However, Joanna had insisted they not only have locks installed on the cabinets, but hire someone to guard the ruins at night. So far, they hadn't had any luck finding someone for the latter job.

"Your gear is already in the cave, waiting for you," Richard said as he and his brother lifted several two-by-fours onto a cart. "And we've set up the torches."

"Great. Sounds like Dr. Campbell trained you well."

"We've worked on a half dozen or so digs with Dr. Campbell all over Scotland. We belong to the Scottish Amateur Archaeology League, you see."

"That's great," Indy said.

They climbed the winding trail leading to the cave, which was located high on a bluff. When they reached the mouth of the cave, Indy stopped and gazed out to sea. He watched a gull pinwheel across the sky, carried by the wind. Whitecaps dashed across the surface, the only contrast to the dark, moiling water and solemn sky. He clamped a hand over his hat as the wind nearly blew it off.

"I'm glad it's summer," he said. "I'd hate to see what it's like in winter."

"Actually, inside the cave it never changes much. The temperature remains about sixty degrees year-round."

"That's good to know." He stepped back from the lip of the cliff. "At least for the sake of the old monk who stayed here."

"And Merlin," Deirdre added.

"And Merlin," Indy agreed with a laugh. "But maybe the temperature didn't matter to him."

They moved into the cavern. "Did your mother do any work inside the cave on her earlier excavation here?"

"Very little." In the light of the flickering torches, her skin was an eerie orange. As she turned her head to the side and the glow vanished, shadowy skeins fell across her face. "She made a few sample bores, but that was before Father Byrne showed her the letter."

Indy knew that the areas outside of caves were favorite sites for archaeologists, especially at sites of ancient man. It was where the refuse of daily life—broken pottery, animal bones, discarded tools—was deposited. In this case, it was where the remains of stone crosses had been found. It wasn't, however, a likely place to find a gold scroll, or anything that was intentionally hidden.

"Why did Byrne show her the letter? Things related to Merlin don't seem like a favorite topic of his."

Deirdre laughed. "Joanna wondered about that herself. She thinks that he wanted to know if the letter should be taken seriously. He didn't know what to make of it. I don't think he expected her to start looking for the scroll, though."

"What's he say about it now?"

"Oh, he doesn't want to talk about it any longer. Joanna thinks he might even have destroyed the letter, which would be a shame."

"That's too bad if it's true. I had the feeling he wasn't too keen on our work here, from what he said at the dinner."

"He's an odd one in some ways. From what I gather, he's very concerned about druids. *Why,* I don't know."

So that was it, Indy thought. That was what Byrne had meant by his comment about those who call it Merlin's cave. The priest was worried about pagans.

"You know, lots of the local folks won't even go into it," Deirdre said. "They say odd things happen here, and that it'll bring them bad luck."

"What about Carl and Richard? They don't seem too concerned."

"They're not from Whithorn. They've only lived here a few years."

"Well, if we find the scroll maybe folks won't be so afraid of the place anymore. Let's get to work."

They spent the rest of the morning pounding markers and stretching cords across the markers to create a gridwork to use as the basis for defining the areas of excavation. At Joanna's recommendation, they were concentrating on the rear chamber, which had a fifteen-foot ceiling and spanned twenty-eight feet at its widest point, narrowing to six feet at its entrance.

It was early afternoon when they hooked cord around the last pegs, which were in the deepest corner of the cave. From here, the entrance was a barely visible aperture of light. Above his head a torch was propped in a holder on the wall, illuminating the floor of the cave. "That about does it." Indy stood up, looking over their work.

"Time for a break, don't you think?" Deirdre moved closer to him.

He thought he glimpsed something in her eye that had nothing to do with the cave or archaeology or Merlin. Indy's gloves dropped to the floor of the cave as Deirdre removed her scarf. She shook her head, and her hair fell loose. She looked dazzling in the torchlight. He reached out and pushed back an unruly strand which had fallen across her cheek.

The cave was like a cocoon. It shut out the rest of

the world, and all the considerations of propriety fell away. There was no need for words; their consent was mutual. His hands slipped around her slender waist. Deirdre lifted her head, her lips parted. He bent forward; his lips brushed against hers.

Then Deirdre pulled back. "What about Richard and Carl?"

He grinned. "They left for lunch fifteen minutes ago."

Her fingers traced Indy's brow, cheekbones, jaw. They felt his broad shoulders, his chest. "Indy, I've wanted this to happen. I wasn't sure you did, not until last night at the pub."

He ran his hands lightly along her sides, his thumbs grazing lightly over the swell of her small breasts. "Your heart's pounding," he whispered.

Deirdre's tongue darted into his mouth. She seemed to suck the breath from his lungs. His fingers threaded through her hair, and ran down her back. He pulled her to him, feeling her thighs pressed against his. They moved against each other, and suddenly, the world exploded; the earth shuddered.

It moved; it really did.

For an instant, the rumble and vibrating under their feet seemed natural, a part of them, self-created by the sudden fury and hunger of their passion. Then a concussion hurtled them to the ground and a sound like a thousand claps of thunder pounded their eardrums. Dust filled the cave. He heard Deirdre coughing from somewhere nearby.

"What happened?" she gasped, and she crawled into his view.

An earthquake, a cave-in, an explosion. "I don't know. You okay?"

"You bit my tongue."

"Sorry. Let's get out of here."

Indy helped her to her feet. They'd taken three or four steps when another shockwave rocked the cave. They dropped to the floor, and covered their heads as dirt rained over them.

Deirdre coughed. "I can hardly breathe. What's going on?"

Slowly, he lifted his head; he smelled the answer. "Gunpowder. Someone dynamited the entrance."

12

BAD AIR

Dust clogged Indy's throat as he dug through the rubble. He'd lost his gloves, and his fingertips were scraped raw after fifteen minutes. A dull, throbbing ache in his temples sapped his strength. Deirdre, her face smeared with dirt, worked beside him, clearing away stone after stone.

"This will take days at this rate," he said.

"The villagers will come for us. They won't leave us here." She uttered this with such certainty that he found himself believing it. But he kept digging, grabbing one rock after another and tossing them aside.

Deirdre was about to pick up another rock when she sat down and rubbed the side of her head. "I feel dizzy. My head hurts."

"Maybe we should put out the torch. I'm starting to worry about the air."

Deirdre frowned and looked around. "There's got to be air coming in somewhere."

Indy sniffed. "I smell something."

"What?" She sounded frantic.

"Fumes. That's why we've got headaches. There's gas coming in." He grabbed the nearest torch and buried its head in the dirt, killing the flame. He did the same with another.

"Leave one of them," Deirdre said, "or we won't be able to see anything."

"Smart thinking." He took Deirdre by the arm, and they moved toward the rear of the cave. "Stay down low. Take slow, shallow breaths." His forehead was gritty and wet with perspiration, but his headache eased somewhat as they moved to the recesses of the cavern. He stumbled over one of the picks, stopped, and turned it over in his hand. He planted the torch, then stabbed the ground with the pick.

"What are you doing?"

"Maybe the gas is lighter than the air. If we dig a couple of holes, we should be able to survive longer by breathing the air below the floor level."

Dirt spewed in all directions as he hammered the ground. Even if it *was* lighter than air, he knew they couldn't last very long before the effects of the gas would reach them. He wondered where Richard and Carl were. What if they *had* returned and run into trouble with whoever was out there? Nobody else would look for them for hours. Maybe days.

He dug a second hole for Deirdre, then dropped onto his stomach and put his face in his hole. Deirdre did the same.

"This is a hell of a way to die, Indy."

"I know. So let's not."

He rose up and scooped loose dirt out of the hole, enlarging it. He rubbed his fingers together, and held his hand close to the torch.

"What is it?" Deirdre asked.

"Ash. This was a hearth."

"Indy, this is no time for archaeology."

He looked up toward the ceiling of the cave, which he knew was about twelve feet over his head: "No, but it's time to find an escape route."

A hearth in the rear of a cave meant that there must be a chimney. He stood up and asked Deirdre to hold the torch. At first, all he could see was a rough surface with no opening. Then he realized there was an indention almost directly overhead. The chimney was covered, but how thick was it?

Deirdre followed his gaze. "A chimney?"

"That's right."

"But how can we get up there?"

Indy picked up a mallet, and a couple of the leftover metal stakes. "Climb."

He had to work fast. He pounded stakes in the wall every couple of feet and, holding the torch in one hand, quickly scaled the wall. Now he could see the chimney better. The indention at the base of it was about three feet across. It quickly narrowed and closed. Maybe he could wedge himself in the opening, and work from there. The problem though was that the indention began about five feet from the wall.

He climbed back down. "It won't work."

"I could've told you that." Deirdre sounded even more frantic now, and he didn't blame her. She looked toward the entrance of the cave. "Maybe we could uncover the wood the carpenters brought into the cave, and build a ladder."

He shook his head. "Too dangerous. The gas

would get us before we reached the first two-by-four. I've got a better idea."

He anchored the torch in one of the holders in the wall, then picked up the remaining stakes, and moved over to the wall across from where he'd inserted the other ones. He quickly pounded them into the wall at about the same levels. Then he grabbed a new spool of cord and started unraveling it. He wrapped one end around the bottom peg, then crossed to the opposite wall. There was plenty of cord so instead of cutting it, he moved up to the next stake, wrapped it and crossed back. He continued going back and forth, climbing the stakes as he went, until he'd created a webbing that reached the ceiling.

"Indy, we've got to hurry. I can smell the gas again. It's getting stronger."

Indy's head pounded again. "I know."

He grabbed a pick from the floor, and placed the handle in his mouth. Carefully, he stepped onto the bottom cord. His weight stretched it nearly to the floor, but it didn't snap. He lifted his foot, reaching for the second step, then the third. But his foot slipped off the cord and he caught it with his knee. The cord he was holding with his hand stretched. Suddenly, one of the stakes pulled out from the wall, and he toppled over onto Deirdre, knocking her to the ground.

He pulled the pick from his mouth. One prong had torn his shirt, scratching his chest. He felt a trickle of blood oozing over his stomach. He rolled over on his side. "Are you all right?" he asked.

"I'm okay. What about you?"

"Fine, just fine," he said and went right back to work. He found the loose stake and this time pounded it all the way into the wall. He did the same with the others on both walls, then moved beneath the chimney again. "Don't stand right below me this time."

Deirdre coughed. "Please, hurry."

Despite her plea, Indy took his time, cautiously scaling the web of cord until his head was finally even with the chimney.

"Damn it. I forgot the pick."

"I'll throw it up to you," Deirdre said.

Indy saw himself lunging for the pick, and the entire web collapsing. Either that or she'd stick it in his back, he thought. He had another plan. "No, just hang on to it for now."

He worked his way higher, turned, and managed to press his shoulder blades against one side of the chimney. He held his breath as he slowly lifted his right leg, and stretched it toward the opposite side. If the cord snapped now, he'd fall twelve feet and land on his back. His toes touched the wall, then his foot. With a quick move, he pulled up his other leg. He wriggled his shoulders until his back was flat against the wall.

Relieved, more confident now, he touched his whip, which was still coiled on his hip, and loosened it. "Tie the pick on the end," he said, letting the whip uncoil.

As he waited, he reached to the top of the chimney, and felt three rocks the size of basketballs covering the hole. Dirt, accumulated over years, filled the spaces between the rocks. This wasn't going to be easy.

He pulled up the pick, returned the whip to his belt, and started chipping at one of the rocks. His position allowed him only about six inches of movement with his hand. Clots of dirt dropped onto his chest and face; dust brought tears to his eyes.

After a couple of dozen blows, he stopped. The rocks were still firmly in place. Even if he did loosen one of the rocks, it could fall right on top of him and knock him off his perch. He was feeling desperate when a clump of dirt fell out of a crevice between two of the rocks and a ray of light filtered through a gap. The light gave him hope and he resolutely resumed his attack on the rocks. When he finally stopped to catch his breath, he was covered with dirt but had made little progress.

"Indy, I've got it," Deirdre called up to him.

"What?"

"Can you pound a couple more stakes in up there, inside the chimney?"

"I guess so. Why?"

"If you put them beside your hips, it'll give you a grip. Then you can work the rocks out with your feet."

He thought of several reasons it might not work. The stakes could pull out. His angle might be too sharp to allow him the leverage he needed. It would take too long. But he wasn't getting anywhere now. "It might work," he conceded.

He unfurled the whip again, and Deirdre tied two stakes and the mallet to the end of it. It was awkward hammering the stakes into the same wall his back was pressed against. He couldn't see what he was doing, and struck his fingers several times. But, finally, after far too many blows, they were both in place. He tested their strength by gripping the stakes and letting his legs drop down.

When he was confident they'd hold, he walked up the opposite wall until he was curled into a ball with his feet at the top. His knees pressed against his chest. Now he was ready. He attacked one of the rocks, pounding it repeatedly with the heels and soles of his boots. It held stubbornly in place. He struck the rock with a flurry of blows. Dirt rained down on him. His mouth was dry and gritty; his eyes watered.

And the rock didn't budge.

He stopped to catch his breath. "Deirdre?"

No answer.

He dropped his legs, looked down. He couldn't see her.

"Deirdre!" He yelled this time.

"Professor Jones? Where are you?"

Indy looked around, confused. It was a man's voice, not Deirdre's. It was muffled, and he couldn't tell where it was coming from. Then he heard it again.

He looked up. "I'm here."

"Where?"

He pulled the pick from his belt and banged the rocks.

"Carl, I found them. Over here."

God, the carpenters. "I'm right here," he yelled again.

Suddenly, more dirt was spilling down on him. One of the rocks was moving. He pushed at it with his legs, and felt it rolling out of the hole. Light poured in, blinding him. He dropped his legs back down into the cave, and looked down. He couldn't see anything now.

"Deirdre, can you hear me?"

He lowered himself so he was hanging from the two stakes, his arms fully extended. The smell of gas was stronger now. His head pounded; he felt dizzy. Then he saw her sprawled on the floor. Above him, fresh air seeped in through the hole. He pulled himself up, took a deep breath, held it, then extended his arms again. He dangled a moment about six feet above the ground, then let go. He couldn't see the webbing any longer, and his right foot caught on one of the lower cords. He crashed hard onto his side.

He winced, cursed, then crawled over to Deirdre. He turned her over, bent close to her mouth. Her breathing was shallow. She wouldn't last much longer and neither would he. Even though he was holding his breath, he smelled the gas. He pulled out a knife and quickly cut three of the cords, twined them together and tied one end under Deirdre's arms, and held the other end between his teeth. He considered moving her directly under the hole, but thought better of it.

He squinted up toward the chimney. His eyes were adjusting to the light, and he could see hands rolling back another rock. He unhitched his whip, snapped his wrist, and wrapped the tip of it several times around one of the stakes in the chimney. He slowly let out his breath as he pulled himself up. He tried to use what remained of the webbing, but his feet slipped off.

He was halfway between the floor of the cave and the chimney when he heard a creaking sound. He looked up just in time to see one of the rocks breaking loose. The men grabbed for it, clung to it for several seconds, then both rocks slipped, falling at the same time. One narrowly missed his left side, the other just grazed his right elbow.

But he had no time to think about his good fortune. The stake his whip was lashed onto was pulling out from the wall. He was about to tumble back-first onto the floor when one of the men grabbed the whip.

The faces of the two carpenters appeared above him and they pulled at the whip until one of them grabbed Indy's wrist. A moment later, he was lifted through the hole, and into the brisk fresh air. He jerked the twisted cords from his mouth. "Pull her up, fast. Gas."

He tried to sit up and help them, but he slumped back onto a bed of heather. Exhausted, he drank great gulps of the best air he'd ever tasted.

The next thing he knew Deirdre was lying a few feet away from him, and the two men were hovering above her. "We'd best get her straight away to the doc," one of them said.

"I don't know if she's going to make it, Richard. She's barely breathing."

13

VISITORS

Deirdre opened her eyes, not sure what had awakened her. She felt a mattress, sheets, a down pillow, a wool blanket. She didn't know how she had gotten here, or how long she had been here, or even where *here* was.

A knock.

"Who is it?"

"Me, Deirdre."

"Indy?"

"Who?"

That voice, that smooth syrupy voice. Not Indy. A cold terror crept through her as the door opened; she couldn't move. A wedge of chalky light filtered into the room and a figure appeared in the center of it. She couldn't see clearly, but she knew it was Adrian. She could smell him. That expensive French aftershave he used, his skin, his smile. Yes, even his smile had a particular odor.

"What are you doing here?" She tried to sound as though she were in control, but her voice betrayed her. It cracked. She knew he heard it.

"I heard what happened." He stood at the bedside now. His smile flashed, deepening the cleft in his chin. His wavy hair was as perfect as always. He looked exactly as he had in the pictures she'd seen recently in the newspapers. "I wanted to make sure you were okay."

"I know you did it." She drew the sheets up around her, willing him away, but he didn't leave. He brushed an invisible speck of dust from the lapel of his stylish suit.

"Not me, dear."

"You always get others to do your dirty work, don't you?"

He chuckled. "Ah, Deirdre. You should know that if I wanted to have you killed, you would be dead by now."

He moved closer. His presence chilled the room and she rubbed her hands over her arms. She could see the oil on his hair, holding the waves in place, and the flash of his smile again. He nauseated her.

"I told you I don't want anything to do with you. Just leave me alone."

"But that's not possible now. Arachne knows too much."

"What?"

He laughed then, a full, throaty laugh, and stepped back from the bed.

"Leave me alone!" she shouted.

He laughed again and then he just started to fade. She could see right through him—the outline of the doorjamb, the wall. His laughter seemed to linger in the air as she sat straight up, rubbing her eyes. She saw peach-colored walls, a portrait of a family who looked vaguely familiar, a painting of a castle, and another of a benevolent Jesus, his heart flaming red against his chest.

She fell back up on her elbows; she felt dizzy and weak. Her throat and lungs burned. She saw her suitcase next to the bed, but she still didn't know where she was. It wasn't the room where she'd been staying. Yet, it was familiar. She looked through the opening in the curtains, and saw a ridge of smoky blue hills in the distance. She knew immediately they were the Machars, and she recognized the view. She was in her old room. The walls had been painted, and the pictures were not hers, but it was her room in the house where she had grown up.

The door creaked open; Marlis, the matronly wife of the mayor, was in the hall. Of course. The mayor's family had bought the house after Deirdre and her parents had moved to London.

"Deirdre, are you all right?" Marlis's pale moon face poked through the door. "I heard you yell something."

Deirdre managed to smile. "I must have been dreaming." Adrian, she thought. Something about Adrian. "How long have I been here?"

"Almost two days now. Don't you remember? You've been awake a couple of times."

She vaguely recalled talking to someone: the doctor, or was it Adrian? She was all confused.

"We were worried about you. Everyone was so relieved when the doctor said you were going to be all right. Let me fetch him. He wanted to see you as soon as you woke up again."

"Wait," Deirdre said as Marlis started to close the door. "Joanna, my mother—"

"We sent a telegram to London. She should be here anytime now."

Deirdre thanked her, then settled back as the door closed. She dozed again, and was awakened when the doctor arrived. He was a quiet, middle-aged man who'd lived in the village since Deirdre was a child. He listened to her heart, and examined her eyes and throat. He took a few notes in a small black notebook, which he produced from his bag, and prescribed more rest. "The burning in your lungs will gradually disappear as the poison works its way out of your system."

"How long will it take?"

The doctor tapped his notebook with his pen. "Oh, a couple of days to a week. Depends. You've been very lucky, Deirdre. The amount of gas you swallowed wasn't strong enough to cause any serious problems. If you'd been any closer to the source or if you'd stayed longer, it might have been a different story."

"Why have I been sleeping so much?"

"You needed the rest. I gave you a sedative when I saw you were out of danger."

"I think I'm having a problem with my memory. I can't remember much of anything that's happened."

"That's not unexpected. It's a temporary condition. It'll disappear as the drug wears off."

As he was about to leave, he smiled and told her she had a visitor, that he would only stay a few minutes and she should try not to get excited.

"Who is it?" she asked suspiciously.

"Professor Jones."

"Thanks, Doc. Tell him to give me a couple of minutes." After the doctor left, she slowly swung her legs over the side of the bed, and reached into her suitcase for a brush. She felt as if she'd never used her body before. By the time she heard a tap on the door, she'd combed her hair and brushed her teeth. She was sitting up in bed when Indy knocked.

"Come in."

"Am I ever glad to see you with your eyes open," he said as he walked into her room. He looked concerned and happy at the same time.

"I'm glad to see you, too." His clothes were soiled, his face smudged. It looked as if he hadn't changed since the cave-in. "You went back, didn't you?"

"I've been helping Richard and Carl clear away the rocks from the entrance." He looked down at his clothes. "When Marlis told me you were awake, I wanted to see you right away. You've been asleep every time I've checked on you."

The streaks of dirt on his brow and cheek reminded her of a little boy. "You look fine to me, Indy. I'm just happy you're here."

"You don't know how worried I was." He sat down on the corner of the bed.

The intensity of his look made her recall their last moments together before the cave-in. It seemed like a dream now that had been interrupted by an alarm clock. She thought that he might be thinking about the same thing. Then she remembered Marlis and the doctor telling her how Indy had saved her. "Thanks for getting me out of there. They told me what you did."

"You better thank Carl and Richard, too," he said. "If they hadn't shown up, neither of us would've made it."

"Did they see who did it?" she asked.

He shook his head. "Hopefully, when we get all the rubble out, something might turn up to prove it was an explosion."

"Of course it was an explosion. What are you talking about?"

"There's no evidence yet. It just looks like the cave roof collapsed."

Deirdre sat forward. "But what about the gas?"

"No sign of it now."

"But Indy, I'm sure—"

He raised a hand to calm her. "Of course there was gas. We both know that."

She was about to say that she wanted to talk to whoever was investigating the incident, when there was a knock at the door. "Deirdre, someone else to see you."

Marlis opened the door before Deirdre could say anything. The mayor's wife stepped aside and Joanna swept into the room. She threw her arms around her daughter.

"I came straight away after I heard." She held Deirdre at arm's length, then sat on the bed. "Marlis said you're going to be okay. What a relief."

She turned to Indy. "Now what exactly happened? I want to hear it all."

Indy had stood when Joanna entered the room. He sat down on the chair next to the bed, and explained as best he could, leaving out only the part about what they were doing when the explosion knocked them off their feet.

"Maybe it was someone trying to frighten us away. I don't know." He ran a hand through his hair. "Who would be concerned about us digging in that cave?"

Joanna gazed out the window toward the hills. "There are those who might find what we're doing offensive," she said obscurely. Then, after a pause she added: "The old ways are not completely dead in Scotland."

"You mean those silly druids?" Deirdre frowned at her mother.

"Are there druids here?" Indy asked.

"There have always been rumors about a coven around here," Joanna said matter-of-factly. "I think they just visit here from time to time, though."

"But if they're so damn concerned about the cave, why would they blow it up?" Indy asked.

"Maybe they're more concerned about us. Getting us out of here," Joanna said. She rose from the bed. "I should have told you not to say anything about the scroll. I've been trying to keep it as quiet as possible in academic circles until we know more, but I didn't think it would matter around here."

"But why would anyone think we're a threat?" Deirdre asked. "I don't understand."

"Fanatics see threats where others don't," Joanna answered.

"What are we going to do?" Deirdre asked.

"I think you should go back to London. It'll be safer."

Typical, Deirdre thought. Joanna was always trying to protect her. "And you? What are you going to do?"

"Professor Jones and I will restart the dig as soon as the rubble is cleared. We'll hire armed guards to watch the cave. I'll send for a few of my students, and we'll give it our best for a couple of weeks."

"I'm staying, too, Joanna."

"Deirdre. Please. You're in no condition to work, and I want you to see a specialist in London."

"I'll do nothing of the sort. I grew up here. This is my real home. And why would I be any safer in London?"

Deirdre looked up at Indy for support, but he looked away as if to avoid putting himself between them.

"Don't bring Professor Jones into this, Deirdre. This is between you and me."

"If you don't mind, I'll go and wash up," Indy said. He walked to the door, then turned. "I know it's not my business, Joanna, but I think Deirdre would be safer staying with us than going back on her own."

"See, Joanna."

Joanna pursed her lips. Her shoulders slumped slightly as she let out her breath. "All right. You can stay, but please don't go wandering off anywhere by yourself. You don't know what we're up against."

"Do you?"

"I think I've got an idea."

A while later when Deirdre was alone again, Marlis brought her a tray and a large bowl of soup. As she ate at the side of the bed, she remembered bits of her

dream conversation with Adrian. He'd mentioned a
name, Arachne. She puzzled over it. It wasn't druids
who'd blown up the cave. It was Adrian. But why
hadn't she said something to Joanna?

She dropped her spoon in her bowl. No, Adrian
wasn't here. It was a dream. That was why she hadn't
said anything. It hadn't happened. Yet, it seemed so
real. It wasn't some dreamy landscape where nothing
made sense. It had been right here. Adrian had walked
through that door, and stood by the bed and talked to
her. But then she remembered he hadn't left; he'd just
disappeared. It had to be a dream.

She heard a knock, and froze. She stared at the
door, wishing that whoever was there would go away.
She didn't want to know who it was. Then the door
opened a few inches, and Marlis's head appeared.

"Deirdre, are you awake?"

She rubbed her temples. "Yes, and I'm done with
the soup. Thank you, Marlis."

"Father Byrne is here. Should I tell him you're too
tired to see him now?"

Deirdre thought a moment. "No, go ahead, show
him in." She lay back in the bed, and Marlis helped
her with the covers.

"I'll tell him he shouldn't stay long, that you're
tired," she said, and she took away the tray.

"Good evening," Byrne said as he walked into the
room. "I hope I'm not disturbing you."

"No, thank you for coming."

He sat in the chair next to the bed, and asked about
how she was feeling. Deirdre started to say that she
was feeling better when she suddenly burst into tears.
Like a child in a confessional, she told the priest

everything about Adrian, from the time she'd met him and ignored her mother's wishes to how she'd been followed. Finally, she told him about the dream.

While she talked, Byrne buried his face in his hands and bowed his head. She found it odd talking to him that way, but it probably was what he did when he listened to confessions. When she finished, she smoothed the bedsheets with her hands. "I'm sorry, Father. I just don't know what to do anymore."

He lifted his face from his hands, and blinked. His eyes were red at the rims, probably an attribute of his age, rather than an emotional reaction to her story, she thought.

His voice was soothing. "No, it's good that you told me. You needed to get it all out."

"But what am I going to do?"

Byrne leaned back in his chair, his arms crossed. "How do you feel about Professor Jones?"

"Well, I..."

"The reason I ask, lass, is because it seems that if you stayed away from him, this Adrian might leave you alone."

"No, I'm not going to allow him to do that to me. Indy is... I love him, Father."

Byrne held up a hand. "Okay, lass, that's what I wanted to hear. And how does Professor Jones feel about you?"

"I think he feels the same way."

"He would be crazy if he didn't," Byrne said, and he smiled. "I think the best thing for you to do is to leave Whithorn with Professor Jones and your mother as soon as possible."

"But Joanna is so set on the dig. She won't leave."

"It doesn't mean that you and Professor Jones must stay. I'm sure Joanna is concerned about your safety, and will do what is right."

"What about Indy? Do you think I should tell him about Adrian?"

"Well, you don't want to scare off the man you love."

"I know. But he deserves an explanation."

"Don't you worry. Things will work out. You'll see. Now just rest. You're safe here."

She watched the old priest hobble out of the room. She wished she had his faith.

14

ARACHNE

Indy picked his way through the rubble, turning over stones, scooping shovelfuls of dirt and rock into a wheelbarrow. The roof near the cave mouth had collapsed in the explosion, and rocks and dirt littered the cave, blocking the entrance to the rear chamber. He and Joanna had discussed working in the rear chamber, using the hole in the ceiling as their entrance, but they'd quickly decided against it. The chamber was strewn with rubble and too little fresh air entered from above.

Joanna had left an hour ago, after they had finally unblocked the entrance. She was anxious to restart the excavation tomorrow, and Deirdre was ready to join them. Richard and Carl were dedicated to Joanna, and were camping at the site, taking turns watching during the night. Right now the two carpenters were busy uncovering and stacking the remains of their lumber and locating buried tools. Indy, for his part, was focused on finding something else which still lay buried. No sign of explosives or the source of the gas had been uncovered.

He noticed a heap of rubble that he'd overlooked near one side of the cave. He pushed aside dirt and pebbles with his boot, and felt something solid. He dropped to his knees and scraped away more dirt with his gloved hands. Then he threw down a handful of dirt in disgust.

"Swell. Another rock."

Indy kicked the ground. It had to be here, something that would provide a clue to what had happened and hopefully something that would help identify the perpetrators. Joanna was still convinced that some pagan protectors of Merlin, druids who wanted to keep archaeologists from digging in the cave, were at fault. But in the back of his mind were memories of the spiders and the scorpions. And then there was the matter of Deirdre's old boyfriend. Maybe he was running amuck again. Indy didn't know what to think.

"Indy," Carl called out.

He turned and saw Carl's gloved hands clawing at the ground. He hurried over to where the carpenter was working near the inner edge of the area damaged by the explosion. A dull green cylinder lay partially buried. Indy bent down, sniffed, and wrinkled his nose. "This is it. You found it, Carl."

Indy dropped to his knees and carefully dug around the cylinder. Then both men lifted it, and removed it from the hole. They set it down on a pile of rocks.

Carl looked up as his brother approached. "You see this, Richard? A chlorine gas canister, or at least it was one."

Indy bent over and examined it. "How do you know, Carl?"

"It's like the kind they used in the war."

"You and Deirdre are lucky to be alive," Richard said. "They must have placed it here, opened it, then detonated the charge to block the entrance. What they didn't realize was that the blast was strong enough to bury the canister, too."

Carl rapped his knuckles against the canister. "We'll take it to the constable, Professor. I'm sure he'll be interested in seeing it. Maybe we'll get some action now."

"Where do you think it would come from?"

Carl looked at his brother, then to Indy. "My guess is the old army supply depot. It's a couple of miles from the village."

"Who has access to it?"

"Far as I know just the soldiers stationed there."

Indy rode back to the village, and when he reached the boarding house he headed for Deirdre's room. He was anxious to tell her about their discovery. But then he decided he would bathe first.

In his room, he turned on the bathwater and stripped off his clothes. As he slid into the tub, he heard noises coming from Deirdre's room. What was she doing, moving furniture? He leaned back in the tub and tapped twice on the wall. He thought it odd that she didn't tap back, but he didn't have much time to think about what, if anything, it meant because the door to his room suddenly flew open and two men burst in.

They wore black mesh hoods with holes cut for their eyes, noses, and mouths. Indy took one look at them and leaped up, but the man closest to him lunged, grabbed him by the shoulders, and shoved him down into the tub. Water splashed over the sides. Indy struggled to free himself, but the man was stronger. His thumbs pressed down against Indy's Adam's apple, pushing him deeper and deeper into the water. Indy wedged the heel of his hand under the man's jaw, shoved his head back, and glimpsed a scar on his throat—then the water covered his head. The image of the mesh-covered face hovered above him like a giant octopus whose arms were squeezing the life out of him.

Air bubbled from his lips. He fought, but to no avail. The man's thumbs kept pressing, pressing. He was beginning to fade. He saw himself as a child seated on his mother's lap, then he was standing next to his father at her funeral, wondering what death was. Now he was sure he would see her again. She was waiting for him.

He was about to lose consciousness when he heard a pounding. His heart, he thought dimly. His heart was in its death throes. The pressure on his throat lessened some and he took advantage of it. He kicked his feet in the air; they struck the man in the chin, knocking him back. His hands slipped away and Indy exploded out of the water, gasping for breath, and fell on his assailant. But he was so weak, he was no match for the thug. The man was forcing him back underwater.

He heard the pounding again. Someone at the door. His shout for help was nothing more than a futile choking sound. Desperate, he kicked again. His feet connected with the man's chest, and he shoved with all his remaining strength. The man fell back. Indy scrambled up, and had one leg over the side of the tub when the man hurled into him, ramming him against the wall.

Indy reached out, grabbed the still-life painting from the wall, and smashed it over the hooded man's head. Just then, the door swung open and a voice shouted, "Hey, what the hell's going on here?"

Indy saw it was Jack Shannon, but before he could warn him the other hooded man rushed up behind him, sank his fist into Shannon's gut, then kicked him in the side. "Let's get outta here!" he shouted to his companion, who was still wearing the frame Indy had smashed over his head.

The man slammed Indy against the wall once more, then let him go. He slid back down into the tub and caught his breath. Gripping the sides of the tub, he hoisted himself up. He crawled out and over to the closet, where Shannon was pushing himself up, groaning softly, a hand pressed to his side. "You okay, Jack?"

"Ask me next week."

Indy pulled his robe from a hanger, shrugged it on as he staggered to his feet, and barely made it to the sink before he retched. When he turned, Shannon was talking to Lily, who was peering in through the doorway.

"I'll get Dr. Campbell," she said and disappeared.

Shannon turned from the door. "You're keeping bad company, Indy."

"It looks that way." The room was a mess. Drawers were pulled from the dresser and dumped on the floor. The mattress was halfway off the bed. He suddenly remembered the noise that had come from Deirdre's room. He stumbled out of the room, still feeling queasy.

Shannon trailed after him. "Where're you going?"

He opened the door to Deirdre's room, and saw that it had been torn apart with the same savagery that had swept through his own. "What the hell were they looking for?" Shannon asked.

Indy lifted one end of an upside-down dresser drawer, uncovering a heap of clothing. "Gold, I'd guess."

"Gold?"

"Yeah." Indy turned around. "By the way, what the hell are you doing here?"

Before Shannon could answer, the sound of voices in the hallway interrupted him. "Indy?"

Deirdre stood in the doorway, and behind her were Joanna and Lily. Deirdre looked around, her eyes wide, her mouth open, as if the confusion of furniture and clothing disoriented her. She took a couple of faltering steps into the room and Indy moved swiftly over to her as she collapsed into his arms.

With the housekeeper's help, Shannon heaved the mattress back onto the bed frame, and Indy laid Deirdre carefully onto it. "I'm all right," she mumbled. "I'm all right. I just want to catch my breath a minute."

"Did you see who did this?" Joanna asked.

"He saw them all right. They almost killed him," Shannon said.

"Who are you?" Joanna asked suspiciously.

"He's an old friend, my roommate," Indy said. He looked over at Shannon. "Just came up for a visit, I guess."

"So what happened?"

Indy told her about the assault, and how Shannon's arrival saved his life. "They were big guys, wearing black mesh over their faces."

Joanna turned to Lily. "Did you see them?"

Lily shook her head. "I didn't see anyone come or go."

"Excuse me a minute," Joanna said, and she walked out.

Indy frowned, and turned back to Lily. "You sure you didn't see anyone?"

"Well, now, I was out for a bit and they might have snuck in, but I don't see how they would've gotten out. I was downstairs ever since your friend here arrived."

Indy thought a moment. "That can only mean one thing. They went to another room."

He walked out into the hall and down to Joanna's room. She was standing in the doorway as he arrived. He got one quick look inside before she closed the door.

"They got mine, too," she said. "They must have just left. The door was open, and it wasn't when we came up here."

"Anything missing?"

"I don't think any of us will have to worry about that. They're not common thieves. They're looking for the scroll."

"A scroll?" Shannon said. "I thought you said gold."

"Never mind. Let's look around downstairs." They hurried down the staircase and searched the first floor. Everything appeared in order, and no one else was around.

"I'll get the constable," Lily said.

Indy nodded. "We'll be upstairs."

"So what exactly *are* you doing here?" Indy asked as he and Shannon headed down to the pub after the constable had finished with them.

"I was going to send you a letter, but the more I thought about it I realized that you might not get it in time. Looks like I was right."

"What were you going to write me about?"

Shannon gingerly touched his side. "First I was going to tell you that spiders and scorpions are definitely related."

"Yeah. How so?"

Shannon smiled. "They're both arachnids. They've got eight legs."

"And their names both start with an S, too. But I don't think you came all the way to Whithorn to give me a biology lesson."

"Not exactly. Doesn't that name mean anything to you, Indy?"

"Arachnids?"

"You're the expert in Greek mythology. C'mon, Indy," Shannon prodded.

Indy didn't have to think long at all. "Arachne. She challenged Athena to a weaving contest, and was turned into a spider."

"Right."

"Let me guess, Jack. You think Joanna's the spider lady."

"So you know already."

"All I know is that I got a quick look in Joanna's room before the door was closed in my face. The place was a wreck, and scribbled on the mirror above her dresser was one word in big black spidery letters."

"Arachne?"

"You got it."

"This is getting more interesting all the time, and I just got here," Shannon said as they arrived at the pub.

The place was crowded and noisy, but they managed to find an empty table in the corner. They ordered ales and plates of fish and chips. "So what do you know that I don't, Jack?"

"Plenty. But first tell me what I've missed."

Indy quickly related what had happened since he'd arrived. He stopped once to get refills for their ales. They tipped glasses, then he continued, telling his friend about the explosion and the aftermath. Shannon listened quietly. If he was surprised, he didn't show it.

"Chlorine gas, eh? Someone high up with good contacts could probably get his hands on a canister of it fairly easy, I would think."

"I suppose," Indy said, wondering what Shannon was thinking about.

Their dinners arrived. "Okay. Your turn, Jack. Tell me a story."

Shannon sampled the fried fish. "Well, first of all it turns out that our eight-legged friends are coming from an exotic pet shop outside of London. You'd never guess who owns it."

"Go on," Indy said impatiently, as he bit into a fried potato soaked in vinegar.

"The owner is named Adrian Powell. He happens to be a member of Parliament."

"An MP?"

"You got it, a young Conservative Party politician on the rise. His big issue is opposing the plan for the Commonwealth of British nations, and he spouts off about it at every chance. He thinks it'll mean an end to the empire."

"I think I've heard of him. How does he have time to run a pet store, for chrissake?"

"He doesn't. Somebody else runs it."

"But why the hell would he be interested in making my life difficult?"

"Let me finish. You see, he bought the pet store from Joanna Campbell. Her husband used to own it before he died. Bit by a coral snake, by the way, in his own shop."

"Swell way to die."

"But just guess how much Powell paid for the shop."

Indy shook his head. "No idea."

"One lousy pound." Shannon took a deep swallow of his ale, then set the mug down.

"How do you figure that?"

"I don't know, but that's not all, either."

"I had the feeling there was more," Indy said grimly. "Go on."

"Powell developed a strong interest in your friend, Deirdre. They saw each other for a while until she cut him off. It seems that Joanna didn't want her to have anything to do with him."

"That still doesn't explain why he'd send me a candy box of spiders before I even got to London."

Shannon stroked his red goatee. "That's a tough one. There must be some connection we're not seeing yet. Unless it was just to annoy Joanna."

It didn't make much sense to him. "It annoyed me a hell of a lot more than it annoyed her. If she didn't like Powell, why'd she give him the pet shop?"

"Maybe she had a change of heart."

"What's this Powell look like?"

Shannon reached into his pocket, pulled out a folded piece of newspaper, and handed it to him. Indy straightened it out. The photograph was of a man about thirty, with wavy hair and a winning smile.

He shook his head. "That's not the guy in the library."

Shannon laughed as Indy handed the clipping back to him. "You think a member of Parliament would chase you around the British Museum Library? Not likely."

"I was chasing him," Indy shot back.

"You were chasing after someone he hired to watch you."

Indy set his ale down. "It's still hard to believe. I barely knew Deirdre, and I certainly don't give a damn one way or another about the Commonwealth."

"Maybe you should," Shannon said, and he laughed again. "You know, I bet Powell's got good military contacts with access to chemical weapons."

Indy scratched the back of his neck. "Yeah. No doubt."

"How are things with you and Deirdre? I couldn't help noticing the way she swooned into your arms."

"I don't know if that's exactly what she did, but you could say things have been heating up. At least they were until the roof fell in."

Shannon grinned. "She's a nice girl, I decided. I hate to see you disappoint her."

"What do you mean by that?"

"Here today, gone tomorrow, you know. You've always had a reputation as a heartbreaker."

"This time it's different. I think I love her. She's really something special."

"Sure."

"I don't know what it is, Jack. But she's on my mind all the time. I can't imagine finding anyone else who could be any better for me."

"My God, do I hear wedding bells?"

Indy was about to tell Shannon he wasn't *that* crazy about her, but he stopped short. "I've got to talk to her about Powell," he said vaguely.

"I can't believe you're ready to hang up your spurs already. Doesn't sound like you."

Indy stabbed a chip with his fork. "You've got a bad attitude, Jack. That's your problem."

"Yeah, well, that could be." Shannon looked around the pub. "Think I'm ready to hit the hay early tonight. I've had a long day."

"I'm going to see how Deirdre's doing."

"Funny, that doesn't surprise me. Just keep an eye out for Mother Campbell. It's hard to say *what* she's up to."

"I'll second that."

They stood up to leave. "By the way, before you retire tonight, you better check your bed real close," Shannon said.

"What for?"

"Mites. They're arachnids, too."

"Swell!" Just the thought made Indy's skin crawl.

15

After Dark

Lovesickness. That was her affliction.

Deirdre pushed her dinner tray away from the side of the bed after eating only a few bites. She was tired of being frail and sickly. It wasn't her nature. Besides, she didn't really feel sick. She'd just had a momentary relapse.

When Lily had rushed up and said that the professor was in a bad way, Deirdre had thought the worst. Her reaction was simply her relief at seeing that Indy was all right. She'd tried to explain that to Joanna without saying she was madly in love with Indy, but it was no use. Joanna was convinced Deirdre was ill.

She rested her head on the pillow, closed her eyes, and imagined Indy there, lying next to her. Just the thought of him thrilled her. She supposed it was the way everyone felt when they were in love, but she preferred to think of it as a personal, one-of-a-kind sensation. It certainly wasn't anything she'd ever felt toward Adrian or anyone else.

But it was no good imagining him with her when

he was so nearby. Restlessly, she climbed out of bed and for the third time in the last hour tapped lightly on the wall facing Indy's room. Again, no response. She wished she could just walk out and look for him, but she knew that was impossible. Joanna was worried that the hooded men would return, and had enlisted a villager to guard the door. Deirdre had overheard her mother telling the man not to allow her to leave the room alone.

She paced the floor. Why should she be stuck here? It wasn't fair.

She looked at her tray; she had an idea. She picked it up and carried it over to the door. She opened it and smiled at the guard. He was a husky man of about twenty-five, the son or cousin of the mayor. She couldn't remember which it was. She just remembered that he always won the log-tossing contests at the annual gathering of the clans. She held out her tray.

"Would you mind taking this down to Lily, please. I can't eat any more."

"Of course, ma'am."

As soon as he was out of sight, she grabbed her sweater from the chair and hurried down the back staircase and out the back door. She walked quickly down the alley through an evening fog. She wrapped her sweater tightly around her as she reached the corner, then headed over to the main street. The pub was just a block away.

The fog was denser now, denser than she could ever remember it in the evening. She couldn't see more than a couple of feet in front of her. Maybe this was a mistake. No, just one more block. She kept walking.

There was something odd about the night besides

the fog, she decided. It was so quiet she could hear herself breathing. And where was everyone? It was still early enough for villagers to be out for a stroll or shopping along the main street. But she hadn't seen anyone.

Then as she neared the pub, the fog started to dissipate and she felt better. She could see the buildings, and there were people, a group of them in front of the pub. But her sense of relief was short-lived. The men were garbed in black robes, and were huddled together, as if they were planning something. Even though none was looking at her she felt threatened, a cold, piercing menace that sent shivers across her back.

From somewhere came the sound of bagpipes playing an eerie melody that wasn't a melody at all. Notes that sounded familiar, but not familiar. What was it? It sounded vaguely like a march she had heard a thousand times, but it was all wrong. Then she realized what it was. The notes were being played backwards.

Her breathing came in quick gasps now. Despite the chill, sweat beaded on her forehead and the back of her neck. Backwards, she thought, like the men. Then suddenly they moved apart into two groups, their backs still turned to her, and a solitary figure seemed to glide between them toward her. He was dressed in a black robe like the others, moving closer, facing her.

Adrian.

She heard his laugh, recognized it, then she could see his features clearly, his wavy hair, his handsome face, the cleft in his chin.

"My dear, dreaming again?"

She took a step back. "Leave me alone."

"It's just a dream, Deirdre." He laughed, and this time the others joined him. Simultaneously, they turned around; their faces were shadows beneath their cowls. They were moving toward her. The laughter was horrible. Then she realized it wasn't laughter at all, but the sound of the bagpipes. The fog was rolling in; they were pressing in on her, reaching their hands toward her.

Adrian's face loomed in front of her. She screamed, and bolted upright in bed. She sucked in her breath, reaching a hand to her mouth. The door swung open. "Are you all right, ma'am?"

She stared at the guard. Her mouth was dry, but her hair clung to the back of her wet neck. "I'm . . . I'm . . ." She shook her head. "I don't know what happened."

He nodded uneasily. "The professor was here to see you. I told him you were sleeping. Would you like me to get him? He's downstairs in the dining room."

"Yes, please do."

She looked at the side of her bed as he started to close the door. "Wait."

"Yes, ma'am?"

"The tray with my dinner. What happened to it?"

"Miss Lily came and took it. She didn't think you would want any more, since you were asleep."

"She took it, you say. But . . . didn't I give it to you first?"

"No, ma'am."

She looked away. "Thank you."

She closed her eyes. What was happening to her? Was she losing her mind? She forced herself to get up and walk over to the sink. She splashed water on her face, dried herself, and picked up a brush.

"Deirdre?"

Indy's head peered through the doorway. Their eyes met, then he stepped into the room. "Are you all right? The guard said you screamed."

She dropped the brush into the sink, and the words spilled out of her. "I don't know what's going on, Indy. I was sneaking out to go look for you. I'm almost sure of it. I saw him, but it was a dream. I think it was. I don't even know."

Indy held up both hands. "Wait a minute. Who did you see? Sit down and start from the beginning. Take it nice and slow."

She nodded, and sat on the bed as Indy pulled up a chair next to her. She told him all about Adrian Powell, beginning with her first encounter with him. Her voice was laced with fear, anger, and frustration. "I should've told you about him, I wanted to tell you, but I was afraid you wouldn't want anything to do with me. He won't leave me alone."

He lifted her from the bed, took her in his arms, held her close to him. "It's okay."

"I wish it were okay." She looked away, wiped her eyes again.

"But why were you screaming? You haven't told me."

"It sounds so crazy," she said. Pacing the room, she told him about the dream she'd had in the mayor's house, and then described what had just happened to her.

"It was just a bad dream, Deirdre. You were thinking about the men who broke into the rooms when you were falling asleep and your imagination went wild. That's all."

She stopped in front of him. "But it wasn't like any dream I've ever had. Maybe it was a dream, but I was still awake."

He brushed the hair back from her face. "You couldn't have been awake. The guard said you never left the room, and no one went in." He stroked her cheek. "But I'm glad you dreamed about looking for me."

"I wish I'd found you," she said ruefully.

"You did. I'm here." He kissed her. There was no hesitation this time, no teasing. Her breath came faster; her pulse speeded; he felt so good against her. She never wanted the moment to end.

He whispered that he loved her, his mouth against her hair, and she pressed her head to his chest, wanting to purr.

"Indy?"

"Yeah?"

"The guard."

"I'll tell him to go home. You're in fine hands."

She stepped back, her hands braced on his hips. "I know. Let's go for a walk."

His face fell. "A walk?"

"Please?"

She knew he had other ideas, but she wasn't ready. Not quite yet.

"You sure you want to go out?"

"I think it'll help me get over this feeling that the dream was real, and that I'm not going crazy."

"Sure. Okay. But you can take it from me, you're not going crazy."

It was after eight when they left, and the village was neither dead nor lively. They passed several very normal-looking people as they moved along the cobbled street under the dim beams of street lamps. Even though it was August, the nights were cool in Whithorn, and she was glad she'd worn her sweater.

"See, no fog," Indy said, glancing up toward the gibbous moon. "It was just a dream. That's all."

She squeezed his hand. "I hope you're not a dream."

"Sorry, I'm real."

When they passed the pub, she stared at it and shook her head. "It was so strange, so different before."

A couple of blocks farther they reached the outskirts of the village. "It's a nice night," Deirdre said. "Let's keep going."

Indy glanced back toward the village. "Okay, but not too far."

The village quickly receded behind them, and stands of beeches bordered either side of the road. Their leaves were silver-tinged in the moonlight, an enchanted forest if there ever was one. She commented on the cool evening and the fresh smell of earth and forest. After a time, she said: "Did you talk to Joanna this evening?"

"No. Didn't get a chance."

"She's thinking about closing shop on the dig. She thinks it's too dangerous to stay here any longer."

"Maybe she's right."

Deirdre cast a sidelong glance. "I guess your friend, Jack, showed up at a bad time."

"He was right on time as far as I'm concerned. I doubt if I'd be talking to you if he'd hadn't shown up."

"Then I'm glad he did." She squeezed his hand again. "How did you meet him?"

"We were in the same dormitory at college. When we were juniors we got an apartment together. He was the only guy from the dorm who I felt I could stand living with."

"Why was that?"

"I don't know. Maybe it was because he approached life with a certain attitude. He was a business student, but he was also a jazz musician and that shaped his life."

"What is this attitude he has?"

"It's kind of like his music. The accents are on the offbeat. Where you're not expecting them." He glanced at her, wondering if she had any idea what he was talking about. "So the unexpected becomes the essential, rather than the exception. You understand?"

She nodded her head slowly. "Now I know where that American slang phrase comes from."

"What phrase is that?"

"When someone is called an offbeat person."

Indy laughed. "I guess so. I never thought about it that way."

"And you? Are you an offbeat person?"

He laughed. "Off the beaten path, maybe. Archaeology is like jazz in that way. You have a basic pattern you're working from, but you've got to innovate, to fuse what is known with what's still a possibility. At least that's the way I look at it."

They walked in silence for a few moments. "I want to know all about your past," she said. "I'm sure it's been much more exciting than mine."

"Oh, I don't know."

"Don't be modest. I remember what Joanna said that night at the restaurant about your experience in Greece. Tell me more about it."

She listened as he told her how he'd nearly lost his life in a deep chasm after his rope snapped, and how he had inadvertently discovered the Omphalos. He mentioned a woman named Dorian, and although he tried to skirt any mention of their relationship, she could tell from the way he talked about her that they had been lovers, and that she had disappointed him.

"It sounds fascinating."

"There's a lot more. This Omphalos, it's . . . Well, I'll tell you about it sometime. I think we better turn back now."

They walked in silence again. Pebbles crunched underfoot. In his story about Greece, Indy had mentioned that Jack Shannon had shown up unexpectedly at Delphi, and that made her wonder if his appearance here was more than just a friendly visit.

"Did you know Jack was coming?"

"No. But that's Jack."

"He just came to say hi?" she asked skeptically.

"He had some news for me."

"Oh? What kind of news?"

Indy paused as if he was considering how to answer. "You want to hear another story?"

"Sure."

He told her about an incident on a train with spiders in a candy box, and then another about scorpions in his room.

"Why didn't you tell me about this before?"

"I didn't tell you because I didn't know it had anything to do with you."

"Does it?"

"I'm afraid so." Indy told her that Shannon had discovered the source of the creatures, the pet shop her father had owned. Then he told her who owned it, and how much Powell had paid for it.

Deirdre stopped in the road. "I can't believe it. It must be some mistake. Why would Joanna give it away to him?"

"I don't know. Why would Powell try to kill me before I even met you?"

"He tried to kill both of us in the cave."

"We don't know that it was him."

"I've got to talk to Joanna," Deirdre said.

"So do I. Let's go."

Indy took her hand and started walking. "I'm sorry I got you involved in this mess. It's my fault."

"No it's not." Their faint moon-made shadows merged and stretched across the road. She hugged him as he stroked her hair. "Everything will work out. You'll see," he whispered.

"I hope you're not thinking that Joanna is responsible for any of what's happened here."

"My guess is that she knows more than she's told either of us, but I think she's been victimized, too."

Deirdre shook her head. "I don't understand any of it."

Then she heard something just ahead, a crunching sound. The trees were thick, and the pale moonlight cast shadows halfway across the road. She froze, and Indy's body went rigid. She sucked in her breath. "What is it?" she said under her breath.

Indy slowly turned and followed her gaze. She glimpsed a flicker of movement near the trees. Maybe it was just an animal scurrying along the side of the road. She heard the sound again, distinct this time. Footsteps. Someone was approaching, moving along in the deep shadows at the edge of the road. Whoever it was could see them in the moonlight.

"Indy, I'm afraid."

"Who's there?" His fists were clenched and he stepped in front of her. They should've never left the house. This was her fault. But it was too late now.

A dark form stepped from the shadows, a man dressed in black.

"Deirdre? Professor Jones?"

"Who is it?" Indy asked.

But as he spoke, she knew the answer. Moonlight cast on one side of the man's face and she recognized the old priest. "Father Byrne!"

"Sorry if I frightened you. I was out for a walk, and came upon you. You both seemed so wrapped up with each other that I thought it was a shame for me to interrupt."

"I hope we didn't startle you," Indy said.

The white-haired priest laughed, a deep, friendly laugh. "My God, why would the sight of a lad kissing his lass frighten me? I may be a priest, but I know what a kiss in the dark is like on a beautiful evening."

Then he corrected himself. "Or at least I know what it must be like."

"Actually, we're glad it's you," Deirdre said. "We thought you might be someone else."

"You mean Adrian Powell?" Byrne asked darkly.

16

REVELATIONS

Shannon jolted awake. The telegram!

He looked at the clock next to his bed. Nine-thirty. He'd been asleep nearly two hours. He ran his hands over his face. "Damn it," he muttered. "I'm getting as forgetful as Milford."

He climbed out of bed, and opened his cornet case. Beneath the velvet lining was a telegram from New York for Indy that had arrived after Shannon had already decided to go to Scotland. He dropped the telegram on the bed, and pulled on his clothes. He had to find Indy, and while he was delivering it, he might as well tell him that Milford had stopped by the flat the same day the telegram had arrived. It had taken him several minutes to convince the old prof that Indy was gone. Even reminding him that Indy had stopped off to say good-bye before he left hadn't helped. But finally Milford had accepted that Indy was gone. He'd babbled something that sounded like a curse in his Middle English and walked out the door.

Shannon had followed Milford into the hallway,

and told him that he was leaving for Scotland himself to see Indy, and did Milford have a message for him? Milford had turned, and considered what Shannon had said. "Yes, tell him..." Milford's pale blue eyes had gazed off over his shoulder. "Oh, never mind. I'll tell him myself." It was rather sad. Shannon guessed the reason Milford hadn't given him the message was that it had already slipped his mind.

He snatched the telegram and headed down to Indy's room. He knocked. Waited. No answer. He bent over and started to slide it under the door, but then decided to try Deirdre's room. As he waited, he heard voices coming up the stairway. When no one answered the door, he moved down the hall and peered over the railing.

Joanna was talking with a man in the alcove at the bottom of the stairs, but Shannon could only see his back. "If you were so interested in finding it, why did you blow up the cave?"

"That wasn't my doing. That was the work of the good Father Byrne and his young fanatics, who are trying to thwart my efforts as well as yours."

"I don't believe it."

"Believe what you like. I need that scroll and I'm going to get it one way or another. Sorry about your rooms, by the way, but I had to make sure you hadn't found it already."

"Just leave Deirdre alone."

The man laughed. "If you were so concerned about her life, you should never have tried to outwit me."

Joanna slapped him hard. His head jerked, and Shannon recognized Adrian Powell.

"You'll regret that." He walked across the dining room and out the door.

Joanna nearly ran up the stairs, and Shannon hurried back to his room, closing the door just as Joanna turned the corner. He leaned back against the door. "Damn it. Where the hell's Indy?"

He held up the telegram. It could be important, and with people breaking into rooms the way they were, he could lose it. He tore it open. INDY—BAD NEWS STOP OMPHALOS STOLEN STOP MARCUS

Indy wasn't going to like hearing that, but there was a more immediate concern now. He had to find Indy and tell him about Father Byrne. Just then he heard footsteps in the hallway. He cracked the door an inch and saw Joanna as she reached the stairway.

He jammed the telegram into his pocket, and crept out into the hall. Joanna was crossing the dining room and heading for the door. "Now where the hell is she going?" he muttered and descended the stairs after her.

Indy felt the pressure of Deirdre's hand on his forearm. It wasn't a squeeze signaling affection, but one of alarm. "You know Adrian, Father?" he asked.

Byrne motioned with his head toward the village. "Let's go to the rectory, and have a cup of tea and talk."

"Father, I don't understand," Deirdre said.

Byrne raised a hand. "Please wait until we get inside so we can talk in a civilized manner." He walked a couple of steps in front of them, as if leading the way. Deirdre looked over at Indy. He shrugged as if to say, what else could they do?

After a minute or so, Byrne slowed a step. "So what would you do with this gold scroll if you found it?"

The question surprised Indy. "I haven't really thought much about it. First of all, it would be Dr. Campbell's decision. But it's not really a major concern right now. I think Dr. Campbell is bringing the dig to a halt for the time being."

"It's probably for the better. But all that aside, what would it mean to you to find the scroll?"

"Well, it would be a startling archaeological discovery. I'd be happy to be part of it."

"It would change a legend to reality," Deirdre said.

Indy didn't think that was what Byrne wanted to hear. "To a point. It still wouldn't mean that the man Merlin accomplished all that was said about him."

Byrne fell silent, and no one said anything until they reached the outskirts of the village. When he spoke, it was as if there had been no break in the conversation. "What if the evidence you found in some way confirmed that Merlin did possess supernatural abilities?"

The archaeologist shrugged, and wondered why Byrne was so interested in Merlin and the dig. "Like I said, I can't really see that happening."

"Let's say it did. Wouldn't this change the entire way we look at the world?" the priest persisted. "Would it not give the magician's evil source of power a new life, a new grip on the world?"

Indy smiled, finally understanding what the old priest was getting at. He was concerned that they might find something which would place a positive light on paganism, the devil's work as he saw it, and therefore denigrate Christianity. "Father, I really wouldn't worry about it. If you want my opinion, that story about Merlin being the son of the devil and a virgin is pure fantasy."

Byrne laid his hand on the iron gate as they arrived at the rectory next to the church. "Someone has to worry, Professor. Ignoring evil will not make it go away."

For an instant, Indy saw a glint in the old priest's eyes, something he hadn't seen before, an obsession, a compulsion that said he would stop at nothing to carry out what he saw as his mission. Then the look was gone, and Byrne smiled, opened the gate, and let them pass in front of him.

They followed a walkway to a two-story brick house, and entered a sitting room where a fire burned low in a stone fireplace. The wooden floor was highly polished and a thick oval rug lay in front of the fireplace. Above the mantel, a crucifix was mounted on the wall.

"God above, the fire below," Indy commented.

Byrne stopped and looked at the fireplace as if he were seeing it for the first time. "Some people, through evil intent or just ignorance, might feed the flames of hell, Professor."

A housekeeper appeared, and Byrne signaled her to bring them cups of tea. Indy was curious about what the priest knew about Powell, and waited for him to begin. When it became apparent that Byrne was waiting for the tea, Deirdre told him what had happened at the rooming house. The priest listened closely, then questioned both of them about the incident until their tea arrived.

"Now, about Mr. Powell." Byrne stared into his

steaming tea and stirred it. His thick white eyebrows were furrowed, and he was slumped in his chair as if he carried a great weight on his shoulders. "I gather you both suspect by now that he is not the man most people think he is. I believe he is here in Whithorn and you can be sure that he is the source of your problems."

"I knew it," said Deirdre.

"How do you know him?" Indy asked bluntly.

Byrne mulled over the question. He took so long to respond that it almost seemed to Indy that he was making up an answer. "In the last ten years I've taken an interest in the various groups of druids in Britain," he began. "We hear lots of stories, and I wanted to find out for myself. Most of these druids are misguided individuals, poor souls who will suffer for their wayward lives. But they are relatively harmless."

He sipped his tea before he continued. "However, there's one group that I consider very different from the others, and extremely dangerous. They call themselves Hyperboreans."

"Hyperboreans?" Indy glanced at Deirdre. She looked as amazed as he was.

"Yes, and Adrian Powell is one of them," Byrne said. "Their leader."

"Father, what does he want? I was almost killed in the cave, and Indy was nearly drowned."

Byrne didn't hesitate to answer. "He's after the scroll. Just as you are."

"So he knows about it, too." Her voice was quiet.

Byrne cleared his throat, and stared down into his cup of tea. "Years ago, before I knew anything about the Hyperboreans, he came here inquiring about old records that might be related to the legend of Merlin. He was in college at the time and said it was research for a course he was taking. I tried to persuade him to pick another subject, but that only seemed to enhance his interest. Finally, I asked him to leave, but he came back the next day, and for some reason I showed him the letter. Even then I suspected his dabbling was more than just a passing interest, and yet I failed to stop him. The letter only gave him more impetus to pursue his devilry."

Indy thought it odd that the priest had relented to a college student's curiosity. He wondered if there was more to the story. "What does Powell want, anyhow?"

"Power. Power to rule, and control. You see, the Hyperboreans are men, and a few women, who are already either powerful or wealthy, or both. They're bankers, generals, lawmakers, and nobility, and they share the goal of stopping the formation of the British Commonwealth. They see it as the first step toward the decay of the British Empire. But stopping the Commonwealth is only the beginning. Powell's ultimate plans are to expand the empire and his own power, at whatever cost."

Indy shook his head, perplexed. "How could he possibly think a gold scroll will help him?"

Byrne threaded and unthreaded his fingers. "The devil's at his best when his works defy understanding." The old priest stood, and paced in front of them. "My investigation of the Hyperboreans has turned up something interesting. They believe that this scroll has something to do with an ancient, evil stone, and that great power will come to the one who brings the stone and the scroll to Stonehenge."

"How did you find that out?" Indy asked.

Byrne ignored him.

Deirdre shook her head in disbelief. "I wonder if Joanna knows any of this about him?"

Indy had the feeling Joanna knew a lot about Powell. As soon as they left here, he was going to confront her.

"Does he think he's going to become Merlin or something?" Deirdre asked.

"He doesn't want to be a Merlin," Byrne stormed. "He wants to be Adrian Powell, prime minister of England, an England firmly in control of world power, an empire ruled by the agent of evil."

"What's this stone you mentioned?" Indy asked.

Just then Joanna appeared in the kitchen doorway. She must have entered through the side door; she'd been listening. "You know very well what it is, Indy. It's the Omphalos. And Adrian already has it."

Indy's face drained of color, and his jaw slackened. "What are you talking about? It's in a museum in New York."

Joanna moved into the room. "To be truthful, Indy, the reason I hired you in the first place was directly related to the Omphalos. I was hoping that I could persuade you to work on Marcus Brody to move the stone to a more secure location. But now it's too late."

"Marcus?"

"Yes. I've been corresponding with him for the past year. I even went to New York and pleaded with him in person. I told him that as long as the Omphalos was on public display, it was in danger."

The more Indy found out, the more questions he had. "How did you know Powell was going to steal the Omphalos?"

"Because I know about the Hyperboreans. I used to be one of them until I saw what Adrian was doing."

"Joanna, you never told me any of this," Deirdre said.

"So you were one of them," Indy said. "Is that why you gave him your husband's pet store?"

Joanna looked at Deirdre, at Byrne, then finally back at Indy. "All right. I'll tell you."

"Joanna!" Byrne snapped. "Don't do anything foolish."

"No, Phillip, it's time to get everything out in the open. Deirdre, Adrian is your half brother. He was born illegitimately and put up for adoption five years before I met your father."

For long seconds, no one spoke or moved. Then Deirdre whispered: "My half brother? But who..." She stopped in midsentence, unable or unwilling to continue.

Joanna pointed at Byrne. "Phillip is Adrian's father."

"I don't believe it," Deirdre gasped, rising from her chair. "You never said anything to me."

Joanna took a couple of steps closer to her, but Deirdre backed away. She looked horrified. "You kept it from me even when you knew I was seeing him."

"I tried to keep you two away from each other. You don't know how much I wanted to tell you. But I was afraid of what he might do. I just hoped you would listen to me."

"He knows. Doesn't he?" Deirdre's eyes brimmed with tears.

"Yes, of course. Making friends with you was his way of getting at me. You see, he found me years ago. I told him the truth. I felt sorry for him, and when your father died, I gave him the pet shop, and I took him into the Hyperboreans."

"How could you—"

"Please listen to me." Joanna was pleading now. "If I had thought that there was any chance that you were serious about him . . ."

Like King Arthur and his half sister Morgan le Fay, Indy thought. Except in reverse. Powell was the black magician and the seducer; Deirdre, the innocent one.

"Why did you get involved with druids?" Indy asked, his curiosity piqued.

"For spite and revenge," Byrne bellowed. "She joined them when I refused to leave the priesthood for her."

"I can't believe what I'm hearing," Deirdre said, shaking her head. They were all on their feet, except Byrne, who remained seated with his tea as if attempting to save some decorum.

"The Hyperboreans never had any evil intentions," Joanna said. "The druid path is about nature, earth, and spirit. It involves legends, songs, and dance, all dealing with man's relationship to earth and spirit."

"What's it have to do with the Omphalos?" Indy asked.

"We believed that the Omphalos would be discovered and eventually returned to Stonehenge where it belongs, and that the world would be better for it. The druid quest is about bringing the earth into balance and harmony with the universe, and returning the sacred stone to Stonehenge was a symbolic step toward that goal. That was our only intention related to it."

"Why do you say it belongs at Stonehenge?" Indy asked.

"Ancient, secret knowledge. That's all I can tell you."

"You told Father Byrne about it, I guess," Indy said.

"We made a bargain," Byrne said. "She told me certain druid secrets and in return I showed her the letter from the monk."

"He also found out for me that the Vatican never received a gold scroll from Whithorn," Joanna said. "He didn't want to help me, but he was concerned about stopping Adrian as much as I was."

Deirdre grabbed Indy by the arm. "Please, let's leave."

"Let me finish," Joanna said. "Adrian is not the only one who is dangerous." She turned on Byrne. "I know about your soldiers, Phillip. You go out every week to the army depot, but it's not to take confessions, is it? You've recruited your own little army of fanatics to fight the Hyperboreans or anyone who gets in your way. They blew up the cave, and almost killed my daughter."

Byrne knocked over his cup of tea as he stood up. "We can't allow anyone to find the scroll, you or Adrian. Your ignorance of evil cannot be tolerated."

Just then there was a crashing noise from the kitchen. Everyone turned and the housekeeper appeared in the doorway. A pug-nosed man with black gloves covered her mouth with a hand, and held a knife to her throat. Indy saw the scar on his bullish neck and knew it was the one who had nearly drowned him. The man stepped into the room, and his partner, none other than Narrow Eyes, followed, revolver in hand.

Then Adrian Powell stepped between the two men. "You're right, Father, we can't tolerate ignorance, especially the kind you espouse."

17

THE CAVE OF DEATH

Adrian Powell moved into the center of the room. He wasn't particularly impressive, except for his eyes. Eyes that pulled you toward him, Indy thought. Striking eyes, those of a leader, a man of vision.

Powell stopped in front of Indy. "You asked about the Omphalos, Professor Jones? I assure you it's in good hands, and will be put to the best use possible."

"I'd watch out with that stone if I were you, Powell. It can do strange things to you."

Powell laughed. "Strange and wonderful. I have no doubt about that. Only fools would leave such a powerful relic in a museum case. You see, Professor, I've learned the art of necromancy, and I've learned it well. Look where it's gotten me. It's given me everything I've achieved. But it will be nothing compared to what's ahead."

He smiled at Deirdre. "I'm happy you survived the mad priest's poison, my dear sister. A terrible way to die, I would think."

He turned to Byrne and Joanna. "Mother and

Father. You know, I've never seen you two together. It warms my heart."

"What do you want, Adrian?" Joanna asked.

"You should know, Mother. You were the one who introduced me to the knowledge. You brought me into the druids. What you didn't realize was that I would not only find their way a legitimate and powerful vision, but that I would usurp your own position."

"The devil speaks within you," Byrne growled. "You can't escape the laws of the Lord."

"Father, Father. Fornicater. Failed murderer. And still speaking for God." He moved closer to the priest. "It's been many years since I've seen the letter from the monk. I want to see it again."

"Never," Byrne snarled.

Powell turned to the man who held the housekeeper. He nodded, and the man pushed the woman forward, still holding the knife to her neck. "You want to see her throat slit or are you going to cooperate?"

The woman's eyes bulged as the priest assessed his choices. "I don't have it any longer. I burned it."

"You lie. Kill her," Powell commanded.

"No. Stop. I'll get it," the priest snapped.

Powell signaled Narrow Eyes to follow Byrne and they left the room. He turned back to the others. "Now where were we?"

"You turned to the black arts, and that has nothing to do with the intent of the Hyperboreans," Joanna said. "The Omphalos is to be used for the good of mankind, not as a personal tool for power."

Powell laughed. "The good of mankind. What does

that mean, Joanna? What's good for some people is bad for others. It's always been that way."

He turned to Indy. "Don't you agree, Jones? You're a down-to-earth, rational man."

"And you're a very disturbed one," Indy answered.

Powell stepped closer to him. Indy could smell the scent of his aftershave. His hypnotic eyes seemed to tug at him. "I knew the Omphalos would be found and that the one who found it would be my enemy to the death. I knew that you would come to England, and try to block the inevitable return of the Omphalos to its true home, Stonehenge."

Indy looked away, and Powell laughed again.

Narrow Eyes returned, and he was carrying more than the letter. "He was hiding it in a box under his bed. But look what I found in the closet." He held up a canister like the one uncovered in the cave. "Chlorine gas. He's got another one, too. Maybe more."

Powell examined the canister, then looked at the priest. "Shoddy, my father. Very shoddy." He took out a pair of reading glasses and sat down with the letter. The two thugs, meanwhile, pushed everyone together and kept a close eye on them.

Finally, Powell lowered the letter. "Father, tell us, why was this letter never sent to the pope?"

The priest stared at his son, and remained silent.

Powell turned to Joanna. "Any ideas to contribute, Dr. Campbell?" When she didn't answer, Powell added: "Your contributions will be taken into account when we decide what to do with you."

"You'd kill your own mother without a second thought, wouldn't you, Adrian?"

"And the good father would kill to get what he wants. It's a cruel world, Mother. Sentiment only goes so far."

Powell was the most detestable person Indy had ever met. How pleasant it would be to sink his fist into the member of Parliament's pretty face.

Suddenly, Byrne spoke up. "They didn't have good transportation in the fifteenth century. The letter probably waited for months for a mail pickup. It must have been misplaced, or maybe the monk decided not to send it. It wound up in the records and diaries of the era."

Consorting with the enemy, Indy thought. Where was the good father's self-righteous ardor now? He wasn't any better than his treacherous son.

"Thank you, my father. I appreciate your help. Do you think the scroll is buried in the cave?"

Byrne hesitated. "I don't know."

"Well, friends, family members, my hunch is that the dig will be productive. What dig, you ask? Ours. We're all going to spend the night at the cave. No one will leave until we've found our answers." He turned to Deirdre, and smiled. "A night in Merlin's *esplumoir*. I spent a couple of days at your house after you left and had a chance to read your paper."

"What were you doing in the house?" Deirdre demanded.

"Talking with Joanna, trying to persuade her to join my quest. It's too bad she wouldn't listen."

"Why do you want the scroll, Powell?" Indy asked. "You've got the Omphalos."

"The scroll contains the key for unleashing the power of the Omphalos. Now you know a bit of ancient Celtic knowledge, Professor, that only initiates of the orders are told."

"I'll be damned," Shannon said as the parade of captives was led away from the priest's house, and into a waiting wagon. "Now what?"

He'd followed Joanna here, and watched her peer into a window, then stealthily sneak up to the side door. She'd moved about the property with a sense of knowing that was confirmed when she pulled out a key and opened the door. He'd moved to a front window and had just spotted her entering the room with the others when he heard a truck approaching. He'd ducked down and waited as Powell and two cohorts moved along the side of the house and quietly entered the same door Joanna had used.

It hadn't taken long for Shannon to see that his buddy was in deep trouble, and it was up to him to help. But he hadn't thought of a thing he could do. Now he watched as the wagon pulled away. He moved away from the house and saw the direction it took. He was almost certain they were headed to the cave.

"Oh, hell." Shannon started walking after the truck. When he'd arrived in Whithorn, he'd stopped at the pub and found out where the archaeologists were staying, and then when Lily had told him that Indy was at the cave, she'd given him directions. She'd assured him it was a pleasant walk. Good for the blood. But it had been late in the afternoon and he'd decided a lager or two at the pub would be even more pleasant.

It took about ten minutes before the last traces of

the village were gone and he was walking in the countryside. Shannon kept glancing into the dark woods on either side of the road. The place gave him the creeps. He walked about big cities in the middle of the night all the time never thinking twice about it. But out here it was different. Uncivilized. It had a feel to it that anything could happen.

Just then he heard the sound of breaking branches off the road somewhere, and he stopped. *What the hell was that?* He waited. He couldn't see a damn thing. He considered turning around, but he realized he was probably halfway there already. Anyway, he couldn't abandon Indy. They had their differences, but he'd never met anyone who would risk his neck for other people the way Indy did. Back in Chicago, Indy had saved him from trouble in South Side bars on more than one occasion. Besides, Indy was the only other guy he knew who was willing to go to some of the places where jazz was being played those days.

Shannon moved on. Whatever it was out there had better stay out there in the dark where it belonged. Playing hero wasn't Shannon's idea of a good time, and the farther he walked the more he wondered what he was doing out here. He thought about the telegram again. That stone, the Omphalos, had something to do with the trouble Indy was in right now. He'd bet on it.

Finally, Shannon arrived at the bottom of the cliff and found the empty truck. He knew the cave must be around here, but he had no idea where. He listened for voices, and heard none. He walked as far as he could along the base of the cliff, but saw nothing that looked like a cave entrance. Then he pushed aside a branch, craned his neck, and saw flickering light emanating from high above on the cliff wall.

"Figures, the hardest place to get to." He made his way back to the truck, and after some effort found the trail leading up the cliff. He climbed a step at a time, pausing frequently, making an effort not to curse aloud when branches snapped at him.

He stopped when he came within sight of the cave entrance, and huddled behind a rock outcropping. He was still too far away to hear anything or see into the cave. Heaps of rubble left over from the explosion were piled on the far side of the cave entrance, and he knew if he could get there without being seen he'd find a sheltered spot with at least a partial view.

Every few minutes someone pushed a cart filled with dirt and rubble to the edge of the cliff and dumped it over the side. Shannon waited until just after the cart pusher disappeared into the cave, then took a deep breath and darted forward. He was in full view, the moonlight casting his shadow across the rocky wall.

He reached the other side of the cave entrance, and hid amid the rubble. His heart pounded. He almost expected a guard to appear out of nowhere and stick a gun to his head. When nothing happened, he peered into the cave. He could see torchlights on the walls, and about a dozen people digging in the dim orange light. Powell stood apart from the others. He'd removed his coat and loosened his tie and was smoking a cigarette.

A gaping hole in the roof of the cave, the result of the explosion, started about ten feet back from the entrance. The sight of it gave Shannon an idea. If he could climb up to the relatively flat surface atop the cave he could watch from there without worry.

He moved away from his hiding place, running on his toes, bending low in a furtive manner. He kicked a rock, stumbled, caught his balance, then slipped behind a rock outcropping. Shannon waited, expecting any moment to be set upon by Powell's men. But again, they'd neither seen nor heard him. Then he spotted what looked like a route leading up to the top of the cliff.

He hurried over to the path, which was actually a series of footholds and ledges. It was the sort of trail which, under normal circumstances, he'd never even consider climbing during the day, much less at night. But the circumstances were far from normal, and here he was. He crawled, climbed, sidled his way up the cliff.

He'd give anything to be on stage right now in a dimly lit, smoky club blowing his cornet, drifting, relaxing, escaping. But here he was caught up in the world he despised, the place of schemes, deceit, hatred. And it was all taking place in the great outdoors, in the moonlight.

There was nothing archaeological going on in the cave, Indy thought. Nothing at all. It was like digging a well, a ditch, a grave. Yeah, a grave. That was a distinct possibility.

At least three hours had passed. No one had found anything in the rear chamber where they were digging but rocks and dirt, and more rocks and dirt. When they'd arrived, they'd found Carl and Richard, bound and gagged. Four others, all Powell's men, were busy digging holes. Powell had immediately taken over, and ordered the bound men to be released and given shovels. He'd ordered two of his men to haul dirt out of the cave in a cart while everyone else dug pits to a depth of four feet.

Deirdre was digging near one wall a few feet from him. Joanna was working along the opposite wall, and Byrne and the others were scattered between them. No one was talking; everyone's mood was sullen, including Powell's.

How long could Powell possibly expect them to go on? Byrne's housekeeper was already curled up in a corner where one of the thugs had shoved her when she'd repeatedly dropped her shovel and begged for mercy. It could take a couple of days to lower the entire floor level by four feet, and their progress would be considerably slowed near the entrance where piles of rocks and dirt were strewn from the explosion.

But maybe the longer it took to find the scroll, the longer they would live, and there was the growing possibility they would never find it. Maybe it was never buried here, or someone had dug it up long ago and melted down the gold. The thought had no sooner come to mind when he heard Deirdre call out to him.

"Indy." Her voice was raspy.

He moved closer to her. "What is it?"

"I think I've found something."

She'd stopped digging, and was on her knees. He glanced over his shoulder, and saw that no one else had heard her. He moved over beside her. In the hole, about three feet below the surface, was a partially exposed ceramic vase with a narrow neck. The top was sealed with a cork and wax, and the neck alone was at least eight inches long.

"You think it could be inside?" she whispered.

Indy started another hole, hoping to avoid attracting attention. "I don't know. Keep digging. Look busy."

Deirdre chipped dirt from the side, widening the hole. Indy tossed another scoop of dirt aside, then with a quick move jabbed the neck of the vase with his shovel. It snapped and crumbled against the hard earth beneath it. He knelt down, and carefully reached inside.

"Someone's coming," Deirdre warned.

He tossed a shovel of dirt over the vase, then returned to his hole as one of Powell's men wheeled the cart past them.

"Did you feel anything?"

Indy shook his head.

Deirdre stooped down, brushed the dirt off the vase, and turned it upside down. "Indy, there is something."

"What is it?" he whispered.

"I think it's a parchment."

He moved over next to her, bent down as she pulled it out. "Keep it out of sight," he hissed as he saw someone moving toward them.

"Well, what do we have here, little sister?"

Powell stood behind them, brandishing a gun.

"Nothing," Deirdre said.

"What did you just bury?"

"I said nothing."

Powell pressed the gun to the back of her head. "You'd better not be lying, little sister."

"Give it to him," Indy said.

"Ah, so you are hiding something." Powell called a couple of his men over. He snapped his fingers and pointed to the hole, and they quickly uncovered the broken ceramic and the parchment.

"So, what could this be?" Powell sounded curious and at the same time disappointed that it wasn't a gold scroll. "Watch them, closely." He moved over to where one of the torches was mounted on the wall.

"I hope it crumbles in his hand," Indy muttered.

"Don't say that," Deirdre said. "It may be something important."

Her face was streaked with dirt, her auburn hair hung loosely over her cheeks. "That's just what I'm afraid of." He craned his neck to watch as best he could.

With the help of one of his men, Powell slowly unraveled the scroll. But he was inexperienced with parchment and it broke into three pieces. His glasses were on again, and he was poring over the words. Indy decided that if he was asked to decipher anything, he'd intentionally mislead Powell.

It didn't take long for Powell to make up his mind on what to do next. He moved over to where a couple of his men stood. "Okay, tie them up. Their wrists to their ankles. Everyone but the good father."

"What are you going to do with me?" Byrne demanded as the thugs went to work.

"You are going to be my translator, dear Dad. I know your Latin is excellent. You are also going to be my scapegoat. You will get the blame for their deaths, because the constable is going to find the other canister of gas in your house."

"He won't believe it," Byrne snarled.

Powell shrugged. "Maybe not. But if they conduct a thorough investigation, the truth about you and your recruits will come out. I'm sure with a little pressure, one of those vulnerable young soldiers will talk."

"You won't get away with this," Byrne thundered. "God's rule will prevail."

Powell laughed. "I'll take that into consideration."

Narrow Eyes grinned at Indy as he looped the rope around his ankles. That was all the archaeologist needed. He jerked back his legs, bucked, slammed his feet into the man's chest. Narrow Eyes was caught off guard; he tumbled over onto his side. Indy lunged for his holstered gun, and pulled it free, but Narrow Eyes locked his hands around Indy's wrists. They struggled, but Indy had better leverage. He jerked his hands free, and backed away swinging the gun from side to side.

"Hold it, Jones!" Powell held his revolver to Deirdre's head, "Drop it. Now. Or she's dead."

Indy dropped the gun.

"On your face!" Powell yelled.

Narrow Eyes grabbed the gun and slammed the butt against Indy's back, knocking him to the ground. He rubbed Indy's face in the dirt, and with the help of one of the others he lashed his wrists behind his back, then tied them to his ankles.

Indy spat dirt. Powell smiled wanly. "The survival instinct is strong. So strong." He nodded toward Narrow Eyes. "Get it ready. It's time for us to leave."

Narrow Eyes disappeared from sight. When Indy saw him again, he realized what Powell had in mind for them. The thug laid the chlorine canister down on a flat rock less than ten feet from where he and Deirdre were tied. Nearby were Joanna and the housekeeper, and a few feet past them lay Carl and Richard. Their only hope was that the canister was already spent or faulty.

Powell bent down and picked up the crumpled pieces of parchment which he'd dropped when Indy had attempted to escape. He held it out to Byrne, as Narrow Eyes finished his preparations with the poisonous gas.

"Read, Father. Now."

"I won't."

Powell sighed. "Suit yourself. You're not the only one who knows Latin. But now you will die with the others."

"All right. Give it to me."

Shannon lay flat on the ground, staring down into the cave. He could see Indy and Deirdre lying on the floor, and the lower half of Joanna. He couldn't see Powell, but knew he was nearby from the sound of his voice.

After he'd reached the top of the cliff, he'd stretched out alongside the jagged-edged hole in the roof and waited. He could see the light of the torches, but nothing else. They were working too far back from the entrance. All he heard was the occasional sound of a shovel hitting a rock or the creaking of the cart wheels.

Shannon imagined himself entering the front of the cave. While everyone listened to Byrne, he would slink along the wall unnoticed, passing directly under a couple of the torches. Maybe he would drop into one of the holes, and grab Powell by the ankle as he walked by. He'd disarm him, and everyone else would drop their guns when they saw their boss was caught. That was the sort of thing he'd like to do, but he knew he'd never make it out alive. Those sorts of things happened in the serials. This was real; too real for him.

He considered rushing back to the village for help, but then remembered what Indy had said about how he had escaped from the gas and explosion. There must be another hole. He backed away from the edge of the cavity, and crawled on his hands and knees through the darkness, searching for the opening. Finally, Shannon stopped to rest near a rock, and there was the hole on the other side of it.

He just hoped that Powell and his buddies would leave with whatever it was they'd found. When he was sure they were gone, he'd climb back down and untie everyone. But what was going on? He leaned forward as far as he could, and listened.

He could see Byrne's legs now, and saw he held something in his hand. One of Powell's goons must be standing nearby with a torch because light flickered behind him.

Byrne cleared his throat. " 'Time of five months hath passed since I wrote of the gold scroll. The messenger from the Vatican arrived this day, but I fear some spell is cast upon me for I could not send the letter or scroll. Forgive me for what I do, but I am compelled to follow this path be it right or wrong. The Lord will judge my guilt or innocence.

" 'The words Merlin hath writ truly astonish, and

mankind in time shalt know of them. I am compelled to send the gold scroll to the place closest to where it truly does belong. It shalt go not to the pontiff, but to my sister at the convent in Amesbury with directions to conceal it in the most secret of places within the convent. Therefore, he who seeks the gold scroll of Merlin must seek it there.' "

"Amesbury, a walk down the road from Stonehenge," Powell said. "It makes perfect—"

Suddenly, there was chaos, shouts, movement. Shannon pulled his head back, and looked around. Had he leaned too far, had someone spotted him? He scrambled to his feet, poised to run, but then stopped short as he heard a scream.

Indy lifted his head as Byrne charged away with the parchment, racing for the entrance of the cave. One of Powell's men, fast in pursuit, tripped in a hole. Another one tumbled on top of him, cursing loudly. They crawled out of the hole and rushed toward the entrance.

But before the men had taken more than a half dozen steps, Indy heard a cry of terror, a hollow, horrible sound that faded and died. For a moment, he didn't know what had happened. Then he realized the priest must have tumbled off the edge of the cliff.

Whether intentional or by accident, Father Byrne was gone, and the parchment went with him. He no longer had to worry about Powell, or the police. His mission to save the world from the words of Merlin was over.

"One fitting ending deserves another, and another, and so on," Powell said as his two thugs returned.

"Adrian, come to your senses," Joanna said.

"I'm sorry it had to end this way, Mother. Good-bye. Have a pleasant journey."

He smiled sadly at Deirdre. "Little sister, it's too bad things didn't work differently. If you hadn't spurned me, we could've become great friends and al-lies. You know, not all love requires physical union. I was going to tell you. I really was."

"Adrian, don't do this," Deirdre pleaded.

But Powell ignored her, and turned to Narrow Eyes. "Let's go."

"Deirdre, honey, when the gas comes, breath deep and it'll be over fast," Joanna said.

"Don't listen to her," Indy said. "Hold your breath. Pray for a miracle."

Mother and daughter said their good-byes; Indy re-fused to say good-bye. He heard a noise as the gas hissed out of the canister, and sucked in his breath one last time before the chlorine contaminated the air. From his ground-level view, he saw Powell and his men retreating. He squinted his eyes against the chlo-rine. He couldn't help inhaling some of it; he felt it burning the inside of his nose.

Somebody save us. At that moment, a figure dropped from the sky, from the roof, from some-where. A creature, a god, with cheeks like balloons. Then he saw who it was; he could hardly believe it.

Shannon, his lungs and cheeks filled with air, knew exactly what he had to do. He grabbed the first shovel he found. He scooped up the canister, tossed it in the half-filled cart of dirt, and smothered it as best he could. Then, without hesitating another second, he wheeled it around the holes and between the piles of rubble until he was out of the cave. With one last shove, he pushed the cart over the side of the cliff.

It vanished into the night, and he collapsed onto his hands and knees. He sucked in great lungfuls of fresh, clean air. Finally, he thought of the others. He had to help them. He stumbled to his feet, and hurried back into the cave.

"Indy!"

No answer.

God, were they all dead?

He coughed and choked as he was engulfed by the nebulous remains of chlorine gas. He knelt next to Indy, and laid a hand on his shoulder.

"Shannon," a voice croaked. "Get us out of here. Fast."

He pulled out his pocket knife and sawed at the rope binding Indy's feet and hands. He heard the two guards coughing, and Deirdre moaning and weeping, and saying something over and over. At first he thought it was the effects of the gas; she was in pain. Then as the rope snapped, he understood what she was saying.

"Mother Joanna. Mother Joanna." Over and over.

Indy worked the rope over his wrists, then rolled over to help Deirdre. Shannon turned to Joanna. He saw right away it was no use.

Joanna was dead.

18

THE DOWNS

Tears gathered in Deirdre's eyes as the casket containing her mother's body was lowered into the ground of Whithorn Cemetery. The graveside ceremony was over, and villagers were streaming away. Another one of their own had been laid to rest.

Indy knew that many of the same people had been here the day before for the funeral of Father Byrne, and that few, if any, knew the real circumstances of his death or Joanna's. The rumor was something about a gas explosion relating to the work at the cave. Joanna Campbell had died; Father Byrne had fallen off the cliff trying to escape. If anyone wondered what the priest was doing at the cave, they hadn't asked Indy about it.

"I wonder if she saw Jack coming to help us before she died," Deirdre whispered.

Indy didn't know how to answer. "Don't think about it."

"I can't help it. She could've lived, Indy."

Maybe she didn't want to live, he thought. "We better go."

"Give me one more minute."

Indy stepped back. Three days had passed since the incident in the cave, and neither Indy nor Deirdre was in great shape. There were times when their lungs still burned, and their heads ached. But they had decided that as soon as the funeral was over, they would leave for Amesbury and join Shannon, who had gone ahead of them.

The reason was simple; Powell had to be stopped. It wasn't because they feared what would happen if he found the gold scroll and joined it with the Omphalos in some druid ceremony at Stonehenge. That was irrelevant. The man was deranged, and dangerous. Just the thought that he held a position of influence in the British government and was aiming even higher made Indy shudder. He wasn't sure what they would do, but they had to do something, and Amesbury was the place to do it.

Deirdre turned away from the grave. "I'm ready."

Indy took her hand as they walked away, but she pulled it back, crossed her arms, and stared ahead. As they neared the gate of the cemetery, Indy saw Carl waiting for them.

"How's Richard doing?" Deirdre asked.

"Still in bed. I'm afraid he got the worst of it. Besides Dr. Campbell, I mean."

"Wish him well for us," she said.

He nodded, then looked at Indy. "Have you heard? The investigation is over."

"No, what did they decide?"

"The constable found two canisters of chlorine gas in Father Byrne's house, and he's saying that the priest was responsible for Dr. Campbell's death."

Indy nodded. "Nothing about Powell?"

Carl shook his head. "It's all politics, if you ask me. Not a word in the constable's report about him."

"Thanks, Carl. I expected as much." They started to walk away. "All the more reason to get to Amesbury as fast as we can," he muttered.

"Indy," Carl called and hurried after them. "Please take this with you."

He handed Indy something wrapped in paper and tied with a string. It was heavy, and felt like a gun.

"What is it?"

"A .455 Webley. You may need it."

It was a case of down being up, Indy thought, gazing out the window as the train rattled across the Western Downs. In spite of its name, the Downs was not a lowland, but a plateau rising several hundred feet above sea level. They'd crossed into Salisbury Plain, which was indistinguishable from the rest of the Downs, except that it was bordered by two rivers and a rim of hills. To Indy, it all was one vast, barren landscape.

Deirdre leaned forward. The closer their journey took them to Amesbury, the more anxious she became. "Can you see the village yet?"

He shook his head. "Stop fretting. We're almost there."

"I can't help it. I'm worried, and scared."

Indy slipped an arm around her shoulders, and brushed a strand of auburn hair from her face. He felt her stiffen, pull back from him. He knew she was still grieving about her mother's death, but there was something more to it.

He suspected it had something to do with her relationship with Powell. He wanted to tell her that it didn't
matter what had happened between them. But it was
difficult to find the right words. He knew she might mis-
interpret what he said, or worse, assume he was saying
one thing while thinking another. So he had said nothing and the barrier remained.

"Deirdre, what's wrong?"

"I just told you."

"No, I mean between us."

Silence filled their compartment. She avoided his
gaze. "I didn't know there was anything between us,
right or wrong."

Denial. "I think there is, and you know it, too. We
may not have known each other for long, but there's
something special that's developed."

"What?"

"I'm in love with you, that's what."

She bit her lower lip, and looked up at him. Her
eyes glistened. She blinked, fighting back tears.
"Damn it, Indy. How can you say that? How can you
love me? I feel so dirty. He was my half brother."

"It's all right." But he wondered what exactly she
meant.

"No, it's not."

"Deirdre, did you and Adrian . . ."

"No, of course not. But he kissed me, and . . ."

Indy laughed. "So what? Brothers and sisters do
kiss each other."

She shook her head. "Not like that they don't.
God, he knew, Indy. He knew, and he wanted to make
love with me. He's horrible. I hate him."

"But you didn't. You just said you didn't."

"It doesn't matter. I still feel sick just at the thought. No wonder Joanna made such a dither about him. But she didn't tell me, either, and I still can't forgive her for that."

"Deirdre, it's over. Forget about it." Indy knew that wasn't exactly true. He was almost certain they hadn't seen the last of Powell.

She slipped her arms around his neck and pressed her face against his shoulder. When she spoke, her voice was muffled. "I just wish it *were* really over."

"You'll see. It's going to be over soon."

"I love you, Indy."

He kissed her neck, her jaw, her mouth. Their tongues dueled. He hungered for her, and he knew she felt the same yearning, the same passion, but that part of her was elsewhere, distracted by events that surrounded them.

She pulled back a little. "Maybe we can find Jack, and just go back to London and forget about Adrian. Forget about all of this."

He would like nothing better than to forget. But he wanted to know what Shannon had found out. He said as much as his fingers slipped through her hair, as the scent of her perfume washed over him, intoxicating him.

"Indy?"

"Mmm?"

"I don't have a good feeling about what's going to happen."

"Don't worry," he said with more conviction than he felt.

"I always worry."

"Tell you what." He touched her jaw, lifting her

face toward his. "When we get back to London, I'd like to get married."

He couldn't believe he'd just said the words, and she seemed equally amazed. "To who?"

"To, uh, you."

She laughed softly, very softly. "Is that a proposal?"

"Yeah." His smile grew. "Yeah, I think it is."

"Yes." That was all she said, just *yes,* the sweetest word he had ever heard.

"Amesbury," the conductor called out, moving down the aisle between compartments.

Just then the train slowed, and Indy glimpsed the village. It was situated in a hollow in the plain where the Avon River made a crook in its route across southern England. It was built on the site of ancient stone ruins, but was best known as the village nearest Stonehenge.

"Well, here we are."

"I sure hope Jack's okay."

"He may not be the greatest physical specimen, but I guarantee you Jack can handle himself."

"You think we'll have trouble finding him?"

"We made a plan. He was going to leave a message at the first inn he came to when he left the station."

As they disembarked, a kid with an unruly thatch of blond hair and protruding ears came up to them, and asked if they wanted a carriage ride to the ruins. He looked to be eleven or twelve, but was big for his age.

"Not right now," Indy said and kept walking.

"You won't find a room," the kid yelled after them.

"Smart aleck," Indy muttered.

They headed down the main street of the village. Most of the white-walled houses were trimmed in pale blue, red, or black and provided the only contrast under the slate gray sky and dull brown plain. They found the first inn two blocks from the station.

An old man was seated at a desk behind a wooden counter in a cramped lobby. Thick muttonchops rimmed his jaws like silver fur. He was drinking tea, and didn't look up until Indy cleared his throat. "You're lucky, young man. We've got one room available for the weekend. Someone canceled."

"Only one room?" Deirdre asked.

"Good," Indy said. "Do you have a message for Henry Jones?"

"Henry Jones." Muttonchops scowled, and walked over to a wall of cubical cubbyholes. "Let me see here," he said, reaching into a corner one.

Deirdre looked over at Indy. "Henry?" she mouthed.

"My undercover name," he whispered.

Muttonchops moved back to the counter, carrying his tea. "No, not a thing here today."

"How about yesterday or the day before?" Indy asked, unperturbed.

"Well, I did have a message for a Mr. H. Jones, but that couldn't be you."

"Why not?"

"Because Jones already picked it up."

"He did? What did this Jones look like? I think I might know him."

Muttonchops studied Indy a moment, then shrugged. "Can't remember."

Indy reached into his pocket, and placed a few

coins next to the bell on the counter. "You sure about that?"

Muttonchops eyed the money. "Come to think of it, I do remember something about him now. A nice-looking fellow, real friendly. A good dresser. He had a little dimple in his chin."

Powell. No doubt about it. "Thanks. Is Mr. Shannon in his room?"

Muttonchops rubbed his jaw, and looked over at the cubbyholes as if Shannon were hiding in one of them, then back at the coins on the counter. "Shannon, Shannon. The name does ring a bell."

Indy added a few more pence to trigger his memory. "He's the one who left the message."

"Oh, of course. He canceled. Stayed one night, paid for three. That's why I've got a room."

"Did he give a reason?" Deirdre asked.

"Didn't say. It was Jones who canceled for him actually. Picked up his belongings and took them with him."

"Is Jones staying here?" Indy asked, and added the last of his coins to the pile.

Muttonchops set down his tea. "You know this Jones fellow?"

"Sure. He's my brother."

"Why didn't you say so? He's at the old convent. There's a whole crew of 'em over there."

"What are they doing there?"

Muttonchops scowled at him. "Didn't he tell you?"

"Not all the specifics," Indy answered. "I got the feeling he's going to put me to work, and I just want to find out what I'm getting into."

"Smart thinking. They're inspecting the whole

structure, foundation, everything. Been closed for years. Now seems some money may be coming along for restoration, but they've got to know what shape the old place is in."

"That's nice," Deirdre said. "I mean that someone wants to fix the place up."

"Whole thing came up real fast." He leaned forward, tapped the coins, then made a face. "Crafty politics, if you ask me."

"If my brother's involved, I can understand that." Indy turned to Deirdre. "Why don't we go over and take a look?"

The old innkeeper peered curiously over his wire-framed glasses at them. "Might you not be needin' that room first? All the inns are booked full. Know that to be a fact."

"Why's that?" Indy asked. The village didn't seem particularly flooded with visitors. In fact, Indy had seen few people that he could identify as outsiders.

"The festival."

"A festival?" Deirdre asked.

"Once every nineteen years, the druids hold a great festival and people come from all over Britain and the continent." He leaned over the counter, and held a hand to his mouth. "Superstitious folk, you know, that sort. They take over Stonehenge for two nights."

"When is it?" Indy asked, wondering if the festival had something to do with Powell's plan for the gold scroll and the Omphalos.

"Started last night. Went on till dawn."

"How many people were there?" Indy asked as he signed the registry.

"Hundreds, I hear. This one, they say, is special

because it comes along at the same time as an eclipse of the sun. You see, they think those old stones were placed there to watch the stars. Heard that all my life. It may be true. They come here for the solstice, too. They're out there every June twenty-first before dawn, watching the sun rise right over the big rock on the outside, the one they call the heel stone." He leaned forward, winked. "Hell stone, that's what I call it."

Indy was familiar with the summer solstice ritual, but that didn't interest him at the moment. "Where are all these druids now? I didn't notice many people on the street."

"They're all back out there again. Slept a few hours, then went right back. They're serving a meal before the eclipse, I heard."

"When's the eclipse?" Indy asked.

Muttonchops looked over at the grandfather clock behind him. "Three-twenty-two. About two hours away."

Indy glanced at Deirdre. "Why don't we have a look before we visit my brother at the convent?"

"Good idea."

"You wouldn't get me out there, least not at night with those folks," Muttonchops said.

"Why not?" Deirdre asked.

"The last time they had one of these festivals, nineteen years ago, two boys from the village about your age snuck out there. They came back, but they were never the same again. One killed himself a year later. Smashed his head against one of the stones out there. The other one has been in some asylum in London for years."

Indy picked up their bags. "Thanks for the tip."

The old man handed Deirdre the key, and scooped up the coins. "Room's at the top of the stairs on the left."

"What about Jack?" Deirdre asked as they climbed the stairs.

"If I know Jack, he probably got wind that Powell was onto him and disappeared before they got him. Maybe we'll find him at the eclipse."

Indy unlocked the door and they stepped inside the room. He looked with disappointment at the two single beds, then set the bags on the floor.

"What about the message he left?"

He sat down on one of the beds, testing the springs. "Powell probably picked it up when he found out Shannon was gone." At least, that was what he hoped had happened.

"But then Adrian must have known we were on our way. Why didn't they have someone waiting to nab us?" she asked.

"The eclipse, that's why. We must have arrived at the right time."

"Maybe we should go to the convent instead, if everyone's at the ruins."

Indy thought about it. "We could, but what if Powell's already found the scroll and has it with him? It may be our only chance to stop him."

"But how?"

He stood up. "Let's just see what happens. If we can somehow get the Omphalos away from him, everything else might just come together on its own."

He was about to open the door when Deirdre touched his forearm. "Indy, will you answer me truthfully about something?"

He turned, leaned against the door, and slipped his hands around her waist. "I'll try."

"Do you really believe me when I say I never slept with Adrian?"

He laughed, squeezed her shoulders. "Of course I do."

She hugged him. "I was so worried before that you were thinking . . . I don't know. That I was unclean or something."

"Deirdre, forget about it." He pushed back her hair, then stroked her cheek. Her head tilted back, and he kissed her.

Her lips parted; she pulled him closer. Indy opened one eye and looked at the bed just steps away. "No sense getting out there too early," he whispered in her ear.

She smiled. "It could even be dangerous if we got there much before the eclipse."

He nodded, walking her back toward the bed. "I agree, wholeheartedly."

19

ECLIPSE AT STONEHENGE

Stonehenge was two miles west of the village, but Indy had no idea if they were heading toward the ruins or away from it. He just wanted to find a ride, but Amesbury wasn't London, and of the few cars parked along the road, none looked like taxis.

"If we have to walk there, we're probably going to miss the eclipse," Deirdre said.

Indy gazed skyward. The solid gray cloud cover was unchanged. "It's not going to be much of an eclipse. I'm sure it's just a partial one, and with the clouds we might not even notice it."

At the moment, he didn't care whether they made it to the ruins or not. He was still soaring from his love-making with Deirdre. If Shannon turned up right now, he might even consider forgetting about Powell and the druids and going back to London on the next train. They could report what happened to Joanna to Scotland Yard and tell them that the local investigation had been a sham. That, he supposed, was the civilized way to handle it, but he also knew that Powell would probably get away untouched.

Just then they heard the clopping of hoofs, and turned to see a horse and buggy approaching at a slow gait. Indy stopped and was about to wave down the driver when he saw it was the blond-haired kid.

"Stonehenge now? You can still get there before the eclipse."

"You're just who we're looking for," Indy said as the kid bounded down from his perch and opened the carriage door.

"You're not druids, are you? Didn't think so," the boy quickly added, answering his own question.

"How can you tell?"

"You're not carrying any robes, and they're all out there by now."

"Lots of business today, I bet," Deirdre said as she climbed into the carriage.

"No. The druids walk." He shook his head as if druids were synonymous with nuisance. It was the same sense that Indy had gotten from the old innkeeper. They were tolerated, but not particularly liked by the villagers.

"Is it okay for us to go out there?" she asked.

The kid laughed, shutting the door after Indy. "You won't be the only tourists there. You just have to stay together on one side."

Like hell, Indy thought.

"Drive carefully, please," Deirdre called up to the kid as he mounted the buggy, and picked up the reins.

"I've been driving carriages half my life," he said in a weary voice that no doubt was supposed to sound grown-up.

Indy smirked. "He'll be ready to retire before he's twenty-one."

The kid looked back at them. "Three more years and I can get a car. They say that one of these days the cars are going to push the horses right off the roads here just like they've done in the cities."

"That's progress, kid," Indy said. "Let's go."

"My name is Randolph, but you can call me Randy. Everyone does, except my father."

"I'm Deirdre. This is Indy."

Indy gave her a sour look. "Nice going. Tell everyone we're here," he said under his breath.

As the carriage rolled forward and left the village behind, Indy strained to see the ancient embankment and megalithic remains that bordered three sides of the village. But most of the massive, crude stones had been broken up and carted away long ago, and the site was hardly as impressive in appearance as their destination.

A few minutes later, Indy spotted Stonehenge. The stones rose across Salisbury Plain like an assemblage of towers reminding him vaguely of a castle. Yet, the circle of stones looked small and isolated, not the center of the world, but a misplaced relic, lost in time, out of place, like a shipwreck in the desert.

As they neared the ruins, he saw a line of lilliputian figures garbed in billowy white robes moving beneath the looming stone pillars. As they drew closer, he realized the hooded figures were full-grown men and women who were dwarfed by the massive stones. The buggy circled to the right, veering toward the tail end of the line. He could see that some of the druids carried oak branches, others held long trumpets, and a few held incense burners surrounded by clouds of smoke. None of them seemed to pay the carriage any heed.

He estimated there were between two and three hundred druids present, and he was almost certain they represented several different orders. He recalled that when the owner of the property turned it over to the national government in 1918, at least five orders of druids had requested permission to hold ceremonies here. He also knew the orders coexisted in a shaky alliance and that misunderstandings were threatening to tear it apart.

They stopped near the heel stone, a huge rock that looked like a gigantic potato standing on end. Several other buggies were parked close by, and gathered around the stone were a cluster of spectators, outsiders looking inward toward the circle of stone. Two robed druids, both massive men with full beards that hung over their chests in the traditional druidic style, kept an eye on the spectators.

As he climbed out of the carriage, Indy surveyed the crowd. Shannon wasn't among them, and somehow that didn't surprise him. He paid Randy, and left his fedora on the seat. The kid said he'd be back in an hour. With that, he turned the buggy around and left. "Guess he doesn't care to stick around for the eclipse."

"He did seem sort of anxious to leave. So now what?" Deirdre asked as they walked over to the crowd at the heel stone.

"Let's play it by ear."

"You just made it here in time," said a woman wearing a large, floppy hat and a purple, ankle-length dress. "Eclipse starts in less than fifteen minutes."

Indy ignored her. He walked over to the pair of

druids. "We overslept, and we were in such a hurry we forgot our robes. Any extras?"

Neither looked anxious to help. One of them frowned at Deirdre, then looked at Indy. "Who are you with?"

"Order of the Bards...and Ovates." He remembered reading the name and thinking that they probably accepted women in their membership since *ovate* was related to egg.

"There are no extra robes," the man growled.

Indy stepped forward, his hand inches from the whip attached to his belt, and the Webley pressed against his lower back. He stared the man in the eye. "We are here to honor Adrian Powell, chief of the Order of Hyperboreans, and if we are not allowed to enter you will be responsible for a schism that could damage all druids." He tapped his index finger against the man's chest, and added: "*Vae victis!*"

The last two words, Latin for "Woe to the vanquished," made the men uneasy. They looked at each other, then with a shrug one pulled off his robe. The other man did the same.

"This is better than the eclipse," the woman in the floppy hat said. "Just fascinating how these people relate to each other."

Indy handed one of the robes to Deirdre. "Here, one size fits all." They quickly slipped into the robes, and pulled the hoods over their heads. "Ready?"

"Do I have a choice?" Deirdre was lost in her voluminous robe. She picked up the sides with her hands and they hurried away. The end of the processional was passing through the main axis of the sarsen circle by the time they caught up. The druids were murmuring a low, repetitious chant that sounded like a swarm of angry bees.

Indy glanced at Deirdre. Her eyes were wide; he could tell she was frightened. "You've got a way of getting involved in some of the strangest things," she whispered.

He smiled, hoping to reassure her, then turned his attention to the stone pillars ahead of them. The procession was curving around the inside of the circle and he gazed in awe at the nearest trilithon. He knew that the upright stones weighed up to forty tons, and the sandstone lintels resting atop them each weighed ten to twelve tons. He was enthralled just at the thought that the structure dated back at least thirty-five centuries.

"Look, Indy!"

He saw that the front of the procession had circled the stones, and the white-robed marchers were gathering around one of the stones that was lying flat. The slaughter stone. Just as druids did not build Stonehenge, the slaughter stone was most likely not a site of ancient sacrifices. It was simply one of the stones in the sarsen circle that had fallen over. But the history of druid rituals and the imaginations of early researchers had left their imprint, and Indy wouldn't have been surprised if the druids actually considered the stone a place of ritual sacrifice.

"Let's take a closer look. Maybe we'll find Powell."

They broke off from the tail of the procession and moved around the inner horseshoe of trilithons until they were amid the growing crowd of chanting druids. Indy tried to make out the words. He kept hearing the phrase *axis mundi* over and over, but there was more he didn't understand. Then he listened closely to a bearded druid standing near him. *Axis mundi est chorea gigantum.* So that was it. *The center of the world is the Dance of the Giants.*

"You see Powell anywhere?" Deirdre whispered.

He shook his head.

The light was already noticeably dimmer, but clouds obscured the sky and the vanishing sun. Now the last of the procession arrived and the crowd spilled out from the slaughter stone, filling the space around the inner horseshoe. The place possessed an eerie feel to it, Indy thought, as though the very texture of the air itself had changed.

Suddenly, as if orchestrated for the benefit of the crowd, the clouds parted and pellucid rays the color of a tarnished gold artifact flooded the ruins. Cowled heads turned upward. The chanting stopped. Crows cawed from their nests in the stone pillars. Three quarters of the sun had blackened; dusk fell on the ruins.

The crows lifted abruptly from their perches, lifted in a thick flock, their wings beating the dusky air, their cries a strange paean to unknown gods. Goose bumps crawled up Indy's arms. Deirdre reached for his hand and he held hers tightly, not entirely certain who was drawing comfort from whom.

Several robed figures, their faces shrouded by cowls, mounted the slaughter stone. "Who're they?" Deirdre whispered.

"Probably leaders of the different orders."

The men conferred for a few seconds, then one of them stepped forward. Indy wasn't surprised that it was Powell. He turned toward Deirdre to make sure that her face was still buried deep within her cowl, then tugged at the sides of his own.

Powell raised his hands over his head to draw everyone's attention. He began by welcoming the various orders to Stonehenge, which he called the druids' most sacred place. "You know the story of how Merlin built this great circular temple. It originally had seventy windows, and was Merlin's observatory of the cosmos. It was the entry point for the gods to our world. This festival not only celebrates the return of our sun-god Apollo for his nineteen-year trip to his homeland, but will see this great monument restored to its place as the sacred navel of our world. Once again Stonehenge will be the Dance of the Giants, the entry point of the gods."

Indy looked over the assembled druids, and wondered how they could swallow this mishmash of myths. Powell made it seem that Merlin and Apollo lived at the same time, or even that Merlin, as builder of Stonehenge, preceded Apollo. It didn't make any sense.

"Most of you, I'm sure, are knowledgeable about the deeds of our ancestors. In the year 280 B.C. an expedition of Celtic warriors and druid priests landed in Greece and marched to Delphi. Their goal was to capture the Omphalos, the sacred stone which belonged to Stonehenge and marked the center of the world.

"But fate turned against our brave ancestors. The oracle itself prophesied that it would be saved by the white virgins. The warriors laughed at this prediction, and said they couldn't wait until the white virgins appeared. But the priests, knowing the wisdom of the oracle, were not so amused. They worried and puzzled over the strange prophecy, but decided to continue their march on Delphi. That day, a ferocious snowstorm appeared out of nowhere and buried our warriors, killing many and forcing the survivors to retreat. Humbly, they recognized that the white virgins, taking the form of the snowstorm, had been victorious, and the oracle had been right."

Indy listened, both fascinated and angered. He knew what was coming next, and he realized that Powell was a genius to invoke this story of a failure, and now follow it with his victory tale.

"With the waning of the oracle at Delphi, the Omphalos was lost to mankind for many centuries," Powell continued. Then he recounted its recovery two years ago.

"During those two years it has been displayed in a museum, and not surprisingly many people have said recently that New York, the very site of the museum I speak of, will soon replace London as the center of the civilized world. But the Omphalos does not belong in a museum. It belongs here at the Dance of the Giants. Magnetic forces radiate out across the earth from here. It is a great center, a cosmic center, balanced above by the polestar. Now I am very pleased to tell you that today the Omphalos has finally returned to Stonehenge."

He bent over, reached into a leather bag, and lifted the cone-shaped relic above his head. He held it for several seconds, then lowered it, cupped in his arms. "By dawn tomorrow, before this festival is over, the great prophecy will be fulfilled. Merlin will indeed speak from the past directly to us, and with those words the power of the Omphalos will take effect."

The sight of Powell holding the stolen relic and speaking so blithely sparked a sudden, unreasonable rage in Indy. He fingered the whip on his belt as his rage mounted. His hands itched to crack the whip, to snag Powell around the ankles with it. His legs shrieked to rush forward. Adrenaline raced through him. He took a step, and Deirdre's fingers closed around his arm.

"No. Don't."

He blinked. The rage receded some. As he looked around at the sea of robes, he realized that any attempt to attack Powell here would fail. No one would listen even if he *did* get a chance to shout a few words before Powell's thugs pounced on him.

Deirdre pulled him back and he melted into the crowd. Powell was still speaking, but Indy heard only a word here, a phrase there. It was as if Powell were speaking a foreign language.

As he calmed down, he mulled over what he was seeing. He was perplexed that Powell held the Omphalos as if it were any ordinary stone. He seemed unaffected by it. The sight caused Indy to question what had happened to him when he'd held it at Delphi. Did the uncanny experiences, the visions, really happen as he remembered them? How could a stone cause such a thing? The Omphalos was a valuable artifact, a symbol of power, a focal point. But maybe all the rest of it had simply been his imagination.

Then he remembered what Powell had said at Byrne's house. According to the order's secret knowledge, the Omphalos would not possess its power until the message of the gold scroll was read. That hadn't been necessary before. Why now?

But Powell didn't have the gold scroll. If he did, Indy was sure Powell would've brought it here for the eclipse. It was still missing, and somehow he knew it held the key to unraveling both Powell and the enigma of the Omphalos.

The blackness was receding from the sun just as his rage had receded from him, as though the two events were connected. The field of white robes began to ripple and Indy realized that Powell had stopped talking and everyone was moving away. Deirdre squeezed his hand.

"Let's get out of here."

Outside the ring of giant stones, Indy felt a sense of relief. It was as if some power had gripped him when they were on the inside, and hadn't let go until they'd left. Ahead of them a disorganized file of druids, many of them in the process of removing their robes, streamed away from the ruins.

"There's Randy," Deirdre said.

The horse and carriage with the kid perched atop the driver's seat waited for them near the heel stone. Indy expected to hear a surprised remark from the kid about their garb. Instead, Randy told them something that made Indy forget all about the druids.

"Indy, Deirdre." He grinned. "I'm glad you found me. Do you know a man named Freddie Keppard?"

"No," Deirdre said, just as Indy said, "Yes."

"You do?" Deirdre looked confused.

Indy spoke under his breath. "That's the name of one of Jack's heroes. A cornet player back in Chicago." He turned to the kid.

"He's looking for you," Randy said.

"Where do we find Kep?" Indy asked, knowing that it was Shannon himself.

"The old convent. C'mon with me. I'll take you there."

20

THE CONVENT

Randy parked the carriage in a grove of trees a short distance from the convent. He jumped down, and signaled them to follow. "C'mon. Your friend wanted me to take you in the back way."

Indy looked around warily. There was no one in sight, but he still felt exposed and vulnerable. If Shannon hadn't used Keppard's name, he wouldn't be here. He knew that much.

"I don't know about this, Indy," Deirdre said as he held open the door. "This is the last place I'd expect to find him."

"Me too, but maybe that's exactly what Jack was thinking. It would be just like him. Besides, the message must be from him. No one else would use Keppard's name."

They cut through the grove, then stopped as the convent came into view. "This place is legendary, you know. Queen Guinevere sought refuge here after abandoning King Arthur's court, and remained until her death."

"And Arthur found her here, and bade her farewell before his last battle with the Saxons," Deirdre added.

Indy looked over at her, and smiled. He'd never met a woman before who could respond so quickly and knowledgeably to one of his mythical allusions. They moved ahead toward the convent and passed under an archway, then Randy opened the door at the rear of the building and motioned for them to enter.

Indy peered down a long, dank corridor with a high, arched ceiling. "Swell place to hide, Jack," he said to himself as they stepped inside.

The sound of Indy's boots on the flagstone floor echoed in the corridor. At the end of the hallway, Randy motioned to the right, and they headed down a shorter hallway until they reached a large oak door with a rounded top.

Randy rapped on it, and assured them they would see Shannon soon. The kid's solicitous tone tipped him off; Indy sensed something was wrong. Then the door opened, and he saw a middle-aged man with strawlike hair, a craggy face, and protruding ears not unlike Randy's. The man stared at them, then gestured for them to enter. Indy took a step forward. The man crossed the room, and opened another door. "Wait here," he said, then closed the door behind him.

Indy walked over to the door the man had exited, and tried the handle. "He locked it."

The door they'd entered slammed shut behind Deirdre. The bolt slid into place. "He locked us in," she exclaimed, pulling on the door. "I *knew* something was wrong about this."

"He suckered us."

"I can't believe he did this to us."

"I can't believe we let him." Indy looked around. The room was long and narrow, about ten feet wide and twice that in length. There were two small openings high on the wall through which gray daylight filtered. Candles were stuck in several holders on the walls. An aged table with two chairs were the only furniture. It looked like a waiting room, or maybe it had once been used for storage.

Suddenly, the inside door opened and Shannon walked into the room. He looked haggard, but Indy didn't have time to even greet him. Right behind Shannon were two men, Narrow Eyes and Ears.

"Well, give the mouse a little cheese and he walks right into the trap," Narrow Eyes laughed.

Indy reached for the Webley, but Narrow Eyes was ready for him. He lifted a hand, and aimed a gun at Indy's head. "Drop the gun and the whip on the floor, and I'll take that knife on your belt, too."

Indy did as he was told.

"What's going on?" Deirdre demanded.

Narrow Eyes uttered a short choking sound, part laugh, part scoff. "I'm not the man with the answers, lady, but I can tell you that before long you'll wish that you died like your mother in that cave."

Ears scooped up the whip and knife, and the two men left.

"Sorry," Shannon said after the door slammed shut. "They were onto me right away."

"Us too, I guess," Indy answered.

"Did a blond kid bring you here?" Shannon asked.

"He sure did."

"That no-good little bastard. I gave him a message for you just before they got me. He was supposed to tell you to go to Salisbury. That's where I was headed. It would've been safer to stay there."

"And you used Keppard as your alias."

"You got it."

"I guess the kid doesn't know the good guys from the bad ones," Indy muttered, and he paced the room, which now seemed smaller. "Speaking of bad guys, who was the one with the ears?"

"Williams," Shannon answered. "He's the caretaker of the convent, but he's working for Powell now. Does whatever he says."

"Swell. Is there anyone else here?" Indy asked.

"Just Powell's men. He convinced the mayor that he's here to see if Parliament should provide money to fix it up. He's got the run of the place."

Deirdre slumped into one of the chairs, and crossed her arms. "He can do just about anything he wants."

Shannon paced back and forth as Indy leaned against the wall next to Deirdre. "They've been tearing the place apart looking for that scroll. But I think Powell's getting worried. He wanted to find it by today."

"For the eclipse," Indy said, and he told Shannon about their excursion to the ruins, and Powell's talk. "If he doesn't get the scroll by tonight, he's going to let down a lot of druids. They'll see him as a failed leader, a false prophet, and there won't be another festival for nineteen years."

"Why do they have to wait nineteen years?" Shannon asked.

"That's when they say Apollo returns," Deirdre said.

"It's also the time it takes for the solar year and the lunar year to realign on the calendar," Indy added. "In other words, it takes nineteen years before the moon is full on the same date again. It's called a metonic cycle after Meton, an ancient Greek astronomer."

"But if he finds the scroll now, everyone will know he is the chosen leader," Deirdre said. "Am I right, Indy?"

"That sums it up pretty well," he answered.

Shannon continued pacing. "Whether he finds it or not isn't going to matter much to us. Either way our futures are not exactly going to shine. Not if Powell has his way."

Deirdre found a box of stick matches by one of the candle holders. "Maybe if we get ourselves a little more light, things won't look so bad." She lit one of the candles. "Who knows, he may just let us go when the festival is over."

Shannon leaned against the wall and kicked it with his heel as if to make one final protest of their situation. "Not much chance of that. We know too much."

Deirdre lit the candles in the holders. A yellow glow filled the room. "You're right. He's been cleared of murdering my mother, but I know he did it and I won't let him get away with it."

Shannon didn't answer. He'd dropped down to one knee and was examining the wall.

"What is it?" Indy asked.

"This stone's loose. Too bad it's an inside wall." He stood up, kicked it again, and turned away.

But Indy didn't take his eye off the stone. He knelt down, ran his fingers over it, and scraped away the crumbling cement around the edges. "I wish I still had my knife. I'd like to see what's behind this wall. It could lead us to another way out."

Shannon reached inside his boot, and pulled out a knife with a four-inch blade. "Try mine. They didn't search me very well."

"Great," Indy said. "Deirdre, hold the candle down here."

"What if they come back?" she asked.

"We'll say it's mice."

Carefully, Indy inserted the blade between the stones. He twisted it back and forth, then pulled it out. "The cement isn't very thick. It shouldn't take long to see what's on the other side."

He stabbed at the cement, chipped at it. When most of the cement was cleared away, he pulled on the block of stone, but couldn't get a good grip. Instead, he pushed, and it moved. Shannon placed a hand on the stone and they both shoved, and with a heavy thud it dropped onto a stone floor on the other side of the wall. Indy glanced toward the door, but no one opened it. He guessed that no one was standing guard.

Deirdre, meanwhile, squatted down and peered through the dark hole, holding the candle in front of her. "It's another room, but I can't see much."

She moved back, and Indy tested the stones above and below the one they'd removed. He decided the top one would break free more easily. "If I can get one more loose, I should be able to squeeze through."

"And if you can't, I will," Deirdre informed him.

He stripped off his leather jacket, then stabbed at the crumbling cement. After a few minutes, he stretched out on his back and kicked the stone again and again. Finally Shannon moved in and grabbed hold of it. With one quick thrust, he shouldered it into the next room.

Without even raising himself up from the floor Indy worked his legs through the opening, and crept forward until his waist was through the hole. "Now, if I can just get my chest and shoulders through, I'm in."

He extended his hands over his head, and sucked in his breath as Shannon pushed him by the shoulders. He'd almost made it when he scraped his armpit. "Ouch!"

He jerked his head and it bounced against the underside of the wall. Cement crumbled onto his face and hair. "Hold it, Shannon," he hissed. "Stop pushing."

He closed his eyes, and wriggled the rest of the way through the hole until he was sitting up in the other room. He gingerly touched the sore spots on his head and under his arm. The room smelled dank, and he couldn't see any better than he had with his eyes closed. Then Deirdre passed the candle through the opening, followed by his jacket and fedora.

The room was larger than the one he'd come from, and devoid of furniture. The walls were bare. The only ornament was a stone fireplace on the opposite wall. Nothing else. "Not much here. Not even a door."

"A room with no doors," Deirdre said. "Let me see. I'm coming through."

She crawled headfirst through the opening. Indy helped her up, slipped an arm around her, and kissed her. In spite of their predicament, he was glad he was here with her. But if he was going to have a life with her, it meant getting out of the convent alive.

"You okay?"

"Fine. Didn't even bump my head." She lit a candle from the one in Indy's hand and moved along the walls. "You're right. No doors."

Shannon grunted as he crawled through the hole, but he was skinnier than Indy and made it with ease.

"I'd guess that the entire wall we entered through was added to close off the room," Indy said. "That's why the other room is such an odd size."

He bent down in front of the fireplace, and closely examined the floor and walls of the hearth. He held the candle above his head and craned his neck. Without saying another word, he ducked inside the hearth and stood up inside the chimney.

"I wonder why they'd close it off?" Deirdre said. "Indy . . . where are you?"

"Right here."

"Where?"

Indy squatted down and stepped away from the fireplace.

"What's up there?" Shannon asked.

Indy held out a hand. "Take a look at this."

"What is it?" Deirdre asked.

"Dust."

"I'm impressed," Shannon said. "He found some dust."

"Right, dust, but no soot. The fireplace is a fake. There's an iron ladder inside the chimney. My guess is that it leads to a trap door on the roof. It was an escape route."

"Why would they need that in a convent?" Deirdre asked.

"Keep in mind how old this place is. The Saxons weren't the kindest warriors. They didn't draw the line at killing nuns."

"Who cares why it's here," Shannon said. "Let's get out of here."

"Not so loud, Jack," Indy said. "You two go ahead. I'm going to put the stones back in place to slow them down."

"Can we help?" Deirdre asked.

"No. I'll get it."

"Be careful," she said, and gave him a hug. "And please hurry." She ducked into the fireplace.

"Don't do anything stupid," Shannon added, and followed her.

Indy crossed the room, and started to lift one of the stones. But then he put it back down. He knew Powell could walk in at any time, but he also realized blocking the hole wouldn't do any good unless he hid their tracks, and created a diversion.

He crawled back through the hole, and crushed the crumbs of concrete with his boot heel, then spread them across the floor as best he could. Next, he snuffed out the remaining candles, dimming the light in the room. He moved over to the door through which Shannon had entered, and pulled the knife out of his jacket pocket. He gouged at the wood around the lock, chipping away one chunk after another.

Hopefully, Powell would see the splintered wood around the lock and think they had somehow gotten out, and were hiding inside the convent. He and his cohorts would search the interior, while they escaped through the chimney. Indy was counting on Powell to react quickly and not pause to think out what he was seeing. Eventually, when Powell couldn't find them, he would reassess the situation and realize that, if they had broken out of the room, they would have chosen the other door, the one leading outside. Then he would probably check the wall and find the loose stones, but by that time they'd have found their way to the ground, and escaped.

Suddenly, Indy froze as he heard a key turning in the lock just inches from his hand. He was caught off guard. There was no time to flee. He backed against the wall, and held up the knife, ready to defend himself. The knob turned, and the door creaked open several inches. He drew in his breath, squeezing the knife.

Then he heard Powell's voice. "I didn't say to open it yet. Wait until their food trays get here."

The door slammed shut, and Indy literally dived through the hole. Quickly, he hefted the stone from the lower part of the wall, and worked it into place. Then he picked up the other one, and pushed it end-first into the opening. Finally, he turned it and shoved until it fit firmly into place.

The darkness closed tightly around him. He patted

his pockets, then snapped his fingers. He had a candle, but no matches. He crossed the dark room, guessing at the location of the fireplace. But the distance was shorter than he'd estimated and he bumped his nose against the wall. He cursed under his breath, then moved to his left feeling the wall as he went. After three steps, his hand touched the edge of the fireplace.

He crawled into the hearth, and stood up inside the chimney. A soft flickering light emanated from the wall several feet over his head. They must have left him a candle. Convenient, he thought. His hand found one of the iron rungs, his foot another, and he started climbing. As he neared the light, he saw that it was set back from the wall, and realized there must be a hole. Then he heard murmurs.

The hole in the chimney wall opened into another room. It was narrow and confining, and a few feet inside it Deirdre and Shannon were huddled together, examining something on the floor.

Indy stared in astonishment. "What the hell are you doing?"

"Look," Deirdre said, her voice bubbling with excitement. "This is it, the gold scroll."

"What?" He climbed through the opening, and Shannon moved aside. In the candlelight, resting on a purple velvet cloth, was the scroll. Deirdre had partially unrolled it, and engraved on the dull yellow metal was row after row of handwritten script.

"It was lying right here, wrapped in this cloth," Deirdre said.

Indy crawled closer and touched the scroll as if he

didn't actually believe what he was seeing. "It looks in really good condition."

"I know," Deirdre said. "I think we can unroll it the whole way without it breaking or cracking. Can you read it?"

"It's Old English, from the fifth or sixth century, I'd say." And he *could* read it. It was one of the skills his father had taught him, and his ability to decipher the language was one of the reasons his father had encouraged him to pursue linguistics as a career.

"I say we get out of here, and look at it later," Shannon said.

"No, let's find out what it says first," Deirdre countered.

Indy wasn't sure what to do. He wanted to know what it said as much as Deirdre, but he knew that Shannon was right, too.

"Jack, why don't you go up and see if you can find the trapdoor, and find a way to get down off the roof. We'll be up in a few minutes."

"So I'm the scout. Is that it? Remind me never to go up a chimney with a couple of scholars again." Shannon crawled out the hole and onto the ladder. He peered back at them. "Don't take all day with that thing."

Even before Shannon was out of sight they were unrolling the scroll. After several more inches were revealed, Indy started reading as Deirdre gazed over his shoulder. "It's about Merlin," he muttered. "It's in first person."

"My God, he wrote it," Deirdre said in a hushed voice.

"Wait a minute. This doesn't make sense." He tapped the scroll. "Look at the year he gives as his birthdate. That's not possible."

"I can't read it. What's it say?"

"That he was born more than four thousand years ago." Indy laughed. "Very early Old English, and the date's based on the Julian calendar, which didn't come into use until 46 B.C." He smiled and shook his head. "Well, they said Merlin was a trickster. C'mon. Let's go."

Deirdre shook her head. "Wait. I don't understand."

"It was probably written more like four hundred years ago, not four thousand." His tone of voice reflected his disappointment. "In other words, just another Merlin legend with a fancy gold touch. Probably the monk, Mathers, wrote it himself. He no doubt knew enough Old English to fake it."

"But why?"

"He was probably bored being stuck in Whithorn, and thought it was a good joke to put the mighty pagan enchanter's words to rest in a monastery."

"Read it, anyway. Please?"

"All right." Indy touched its clinquant surface. He spoke slowly, translating the script to modern English. " 'As a young man I was a student of necromancy, an initiate in the wyrding ways. One day while traveling in distant mountains across the waters a fiery black stone fell in my path. That day my life was changed for all time. When the stone cooled and I picked it up, I could hear the gods speaking to me.

" 'They said that I was to build a great circular temple using rocks from the very mountain range upon which the fiery stone had fallen, and they told me where I was to build the temple. But I said that it was impossible to do such a thing since the place was so far away. They answered that with the stone all things were possible. The gods needed the temple as a doorway allowing them to enter our world. I built the temple and when I saw how the gods cavorted about when they arrived, I called it Dance of the Giants. Finally, at the gods' request I buried the sacred stone in the center of the temple.

" 'Only then did I discover the powers that I had gained from the sacred stone, powers beyond belief. I was a god, immortal, and the stone allowed me to pass through time as if I were walking through a gate. I lived a life in Greece, and at my bidding, a messenger was sent to Britain, and he returned with the sacred stone. I placed it at Delphi and it was called the Omphalos.' "

Indy stopped reading to unravel more of the scroll. " 'I moved again through the gate of time to the distant future in which I now exist as Merlin. I came here for a particular reason. This being an era when the powers of the old gods are waning. Fallen rocks are all that remain of Delphi and the Dance of the Giants long ago lost its strength. Yet, I trusted that my powers were great enough so as to revive the old ways. But soon I saw that was not to be, for the Omphalos was now lost.

" 'I spent my life as best I could. I guided three kings, and although my powers remain ample, they are much weakened with the loss of the sacred stone, and no longer am I immortal. Damned am I, to die in this time as the old gods take their last breaths. I am old and tired, and do not have long to remain. I now surrender myself to the place where no one will seek me, on the very hearth of the new religion. I will take my last breath soon on the day when the light dims at midday.' "

"There's still more," Deirdre said, and she unrolled the scroll to its last lines.

" 'My final words are ones of hope, for my vision of future times remains unhindered. The Omphalos will return to the Dance of the Giants when once again the light dims at midday as the stars align for Apollo's festival. He who reads these words, remember what you know of the Omphalos, for it will remain true to its nature. That is all you need to know.' "

Indy looked up, speechless.

"What does that ending mean?" Deirdre asked.

"It's sort of cryptic, isn't it?"

"You still think the monk wrote it?"

Indy gathered his wits. "Well, it would explain why it was never sent to the Vatican." Even as Indy said it, he knew that the explanation didn't ring true, and Deirdre was quick to say it was too easy to just reduce the whole thing to a joke.

"You're overlooking what it says. It's about the Omphalos, Indy."

"Well, it is fascinating that it links Stonehenge and Delphi."

"And who would've guessed that Merlin and Apollo are the same?"

Indy laughed. "You can't believe everything you read, Deirdre, especially if it's about Merlin. But

Merlin's not the Apollo stand-in we need to concern ourselves about right now."

"Are you saying that Powell thinks he's Apollo?"

Indy carefully rolled up the scroll. "Well, their names are close. I'm sure he'd be happy to accept the role of a god."

21

WICKER WALLS

"Did you hear that?" Deirdre said.

Indy wrapped the purple cloth around the scroll as he finished rolling it up. "What was it?"

"Voices. They must have found the loose stones."

"Let's get out of here. Fast."

Deirdre crawled toward the opening in the chimney. "Where's Jack?"

"Waiting for us on the roof. I hope." He tucked the scroll into his jacket pocket, and watched as Deirdre stepped out onto an iron rung and started climbing. She reached the top and Indy was right behind her.

"I can't see anything," she whispered. Then she moved aside as he climbed around her, sharing the same rungs.

"Let's see here," he said. His arm was wrapped around her waist, and he could hear her breathing. Her hair fell against his cheek, and memories of their recent lovemaking came to mind again. He nuzzled her neck.

"Indy, this is not the time or place. Can't you see? It just ends."

"And I thought it was just beginning." He pecked at her cheek.

"Look at it, will you?"

He pressed his hands to the roof, felt the beams. "There's gotta be a way out. Shannon didn't just disappear."

"Maybe if I light the candle..." But she didn't finish. The voices from below were louder, and a soft glow of light suddenly filtered into the fireplace. Powell's men had moved into the room and Indy realized the seriousness of their predicament. They needed to find a way out.

"Hey, are you two through playing around?" Shannon hissed from somewhere to Indy's left.

Indy patted the wall of the chimney and felt an opening just below the ceiling. Then suddenly light exploded in his face as Shannon lit a match in front of his nose. Indy blinked his eyes rapidly, adjusting to the light, and saw Shannon in a crawl space a few feet away.

"Go ahead," he whispered to Deirdre. "Quick."

Just as she climbed into the crawl space, a lantern was shoved into the hearth. Indy quickly wriggled through the opening after her. "Don't say a word," he whispered.

They crawled through into the darkness, but after ten yards or so the tunnel broke into two channels and Shannon took the one which seemed to lead toward the interior of the building.

"Jack, did you find a way out?" Indy called after him.

Shannon stopped. There was just room enough to

sit up. "I tried the other way. It divided into two arms and both of them were dead ends."

"There's got to be a way out, somewhere," Deirdre said.

Unless it's been blocked, Indy thought. "Let's see where this goes."

"You can go first," Shannon said. "I've done my time as scout."

Indy heard voices, and knew Powell's men were climbing the chimney. He edged past Shannon and clambered forward into the darkness. The crawl space was stuffy and smelled of rotted wood. He stopped as he saw another passage opening to the right, and a faint light leaking from somewhere in the distance.

He waited for the others to catch up. "Looks good this way. I see light."

"Damn it, something just bit me," Shannon complained.

"Quiet, Jack. I can hear them back there," Deirdre said.

Indy felt something crawling on his neck and brushed it off. He moved ahead, but stopped and ran his hands over his arms. Ants. Swell. They were scampering over his fingers, hands, wrists, and arms, and probably heading up his pant legs as well. They had to get out of here and Powell was no longer the only reason.

He heard guttural sounds, slaps, a screech cut short as he crawled forward, and knew that they were all under attack. The light gradually grew brighter. Then, he stopped as he saw that it was coming from below, not above. It was a knothole in the wood, and beyond it was another dead end.

"Indy, there're ants everywhere," Deirdre said in a harsh whisper. "They're all over me. They're biting."

He looked back and in the light saw Deirdre frantically running her hands over her arms and legs. Now he could see hordes of fire ants crawling everywhere. Shannon twitched and rubbed and cursed. "Don't stop now, damn it. We're sitting in a goddamn ants' nest."

"I can't go any farther. We've gotta go back."

"We can't go back now," Deirdre said.

The ants were feasting on his legs; he slapped at his pants legs.

Desperately, Indy squatted and pushed his hands against the roof, hoping that a trapdoor was right above him. He drove his legs downward, thrust his hands and shoulders into the roof. It didn't budge. Then something else did. The rotted plank under his feet sagged, then ripped through the plaster on the ceiling of the room below.

"What the hell!" Shannon yelled.

Light flooded over Indy; he tottered, balancing by his toes and fingertips. But gravity prevailed. His feet slid off the plank and he plunged downward. His chest slapped against the rotted board; he slid over the end of it. At the last moment, his hands grasped the sides of the board. It bent under his weight and he dangled.

Above him, he saw Shannon's feet and Deirdre's legs. Below him, the late afternoon sun shone brightly through a window. He saw a room with two single beds, and standing in the doorway was Adrian Powell. He heard something strike the floor and knew it was the gold scroll. The room swirled; ants bit his fingers and arms, legs and ankles. He heard a creaking as the board bent farther.

"Indy, we're going to fall," Deirdre cried out. Then, suddenly it snapped, and the floor jumped up at him.

"Damn train. One stop after another. No one told me I'd arrive in the middle of the night. Slowest mode of transportation since walking. *So whylome wont.*"

Leeland Milford scratched his bald pate, and his thick, white mustache twitched as he surveyed the Amesbury station. He wore his long dark overcoat and carried a black leather case with a lock on it. He was on a mission of sorts, and this time he wasn't going to forget about it. He'd even written himself a note just in case.

"A ride, sir?"

Milford stopped and looked around, confused by the voice, then turned and saw it was a boy barely five feet tall. "You talking to me, young man?"

"Yes, sir. I'm wondering if you would like a ride in my carriage."

"A ride? Do ye tyke me a fool, young master? It is known well by yours truly that no place in this tiny village cannot be found in five minutes or less on foot. *So whylome wont.* Do ye hear me right?"

"I think so. Could I carry your bag for you."

"Not on your life. Now move on." Milford walked off at a determined pace, but after he'd passed through the station he noticed that the youngster was following him. "I'll show the little urchin," he muttered. He spun on his heels, pointed a finger, and bellowed, " 'I knowe whome thou sekest, for thou sekest Merlyn; therefore seke no ferther, for I am he.' "

The boy backed away. "You must be here for the festival."

"Not likely. Not likely." Milford headed down the sidewalk. He hoped he didn't have to check too many lodgings before he found Indy. Of course, there certainly couldn't be many here to check.

"You missed the eclipse."

The rascal was still with him. Milford stopped, turned, and considered the towhead a moment. "Maybe I spoke too soon. Merlin, after all, was known from time to time to disguise himself 'lyke a chylde of fourtene yere of ayge in a beggars aray.' "

"My name's Randy."

"Well, Master Randy, I don't take trains to eclipses or festivals. You can be sure of that. But you might tell me if you've seen a man who . . . Oh, never mind."

"Are you looking for a man who carries a whip?"

"Good God, no. I've never heard such a thing. The man does wear a leather jacket, though, and a fedora."

"He does? That's Indy. I know where you can find him."

"You do?"

"Yes, and we can go there in my carriage."

"Why didn't you say so in the first place? Let's go."

When Deirdre awakened, she moaned, grimacing in pain. Her body ached. She sat up, rubbed her head, and felt a lump behind her right ear. She was staring at a sturdy wicker pole in front of her and wondered what it was. Then she remembered what had happened, and saw she was surrounded by wicker poles. She was in a cage, a wicker cage.

"How are you feeling, Deirdre?"

Adrian's voice sounded strange, distant. She couldn't tell where it was coming from, and she couldn't see him. She looked around; she was in a large empty hall with a high ceiling. There were tall, stained glass windows on the walls, but no light shone through them.

Then she saw him to her right. He'd been there all the time, staring at her from across the room. He wore a robe and was flanked by two men in similar garb. Their cowls were pulled over their heads. Adrian started toward her, and the other men followed.

No, this wasn't right, she told herself. Hadn't this already happened? Yes, in front of the pub, but that had been a dream, and this must be another one.

"Thank you for finding the scroll for me. I doubt that I would've found it in time without your help. My guess is that the room you found when you and your friends removed the stones was a very special one, the very one where Guinevere stayed. The monk's sister probably hid the scroll in the chimney just before the wall was built closing off the room for all time."

Deirdre hugged her arms around her, waiting for him to vanish so she could wake up. But he kept moving closer, and she could see the details of Adrian's face, his smile, the cleft in his chin, and those dark eyes that looked right through her.

"You can't fool me. You're not real. I'm dreaming this."

"Oh, dreaming, are you? Can't you remember falling through the ceiling? You were lucky. You landed on one of the beds, but unfortunately you fell off and hit your head."

"Where're Indy and Jack?"

Adrian stopped outside the cage, and ran his fingers along one of the bars. "What does it matter? This is a dream, isn't it?"

He laughed. The hair rose on her arms. She closed her eyes, wished him away. She ordered herself to wake up. She and Indy must have fallen asleep after they made love, and she'd dreamed it all. None of this had happened. They hadn't gone to Stonehenge, or to the convent. They certainly hadn't broken through a wall and climbed up a chimney. She'd just dreamed they'd found the gold scroll and that they'd crawled through passages under the roof and then fallen through the ceiling of a bedroom.

She'd had dreams of wandering around large, old houses before. But then she felt the bites on her arms and legs, and she recalled something else. When she last saw Adrian in her dream, he was wearing a black robe, not a white one like he wore now.

"Don't go back to sleep, Deirdre. I'd hate you to miss all the fun."

The voice sounded so real. She opened her eyes, and he was still there. She touched the sore spot on her head, and rubbed her arms. Not a dream. It was real and it was horrible.

"Let me out of here. You can't get away with this, Adrian."

He walked around the cage as if he were inspecting an animal.

"Where's Indy?" she demanded.

"I'm afraid you've seen your Professor Jones for the last time, Deirdre." He signaled the men, and they each took one corner of the cage. They lifted it, and carried her toward a set of double doors.

"Put me down!" she shouted, but no one paid her any heed. She clung to the bars as she was rocked and bounced through the convent's musty air. "Adrian, please stop this. It isn't funny."

He stopped at the double doors and turned to her. "You are truly fortunate, Deirdre. Truly fortunate. You are the chosen, the select. You will be remembered."

She didn't know what he was talking about, didn't want to know. Powell pushed open the doors, and the night swallowed her.

22

MILFORD REMEMBERS

Indy was seated on a cold stone floor. His hands were tied to either leg of a bed that was behind him. Shannon was next to him, tied in the same way to another bed. They were captives in the room they'd fallen into. Indy had landed on his feet after the fall, but Shannon had dropped on top of him and they'd both crashed to the floor. When Indy had untangled himself, he was staring into the barrel of a gun that Powell was holding.

Indy had tried to help Deirdre when he saw her slumped on the side of the bed, but Powell had kept him away from her. When his thugs finally showed up, they took her away, and he hadn't seen her since. He hadn't seen Powell either.

Now Williams stood guard at the door with Indy's Webley in his hand, Indy's knife on one side of his belt, and Indy's whip on the other. Indy had asked him how Deirdre was, and where they'd taken her, but the caretaker hadn't responded. He hadn't said a word, except to tell them not to talk.

They'd been quiet a long time now so Indy decided to try again with a different tack. "You have any experience with whips?"

Williams ignored him.

"Indy could give you a quick lesson if you untie the rope for a while," Shannon said.

"Jack, let me—"

"I told you, no talking." Williams smacked the butt of Indy's revolver against his palm.

"Sorry," Shannon mumbled.

Now he'd have to wait, Indy thought, and try again.

The bolt in the door was pulled back and Powell entered the room in a white robe. "I hope you're comfortable, gentlemen. I'm leaving now, but we will be back for you later. Thank you, by the way, for finding the gold scroll. The timing could hardly have been better. It makes me realize that everything is working as it is intended."

"What did you do with Deirdre?" Indy demanded.

"Don't worry. She's in good hands. She has her role to play." He opened the door to leave.

"You hurt her, Powell, and I'll shove that Omphalos down your throat."

A cruel smile twisted on Powell's lips. "No, I don't think so. The Omphalos will be buried in the center of Merlin's Precinct, and no one will dig it up for a thousand years."

"Or until the next archaeologist picks up a shovel," Indy said.

"That won't happen," Powell said confidently. "Just last week Parliament passed a proclamation allowing for the planting of a tree at the center point of

Stonehenge, and marking the site as off-limits to all digging. In fact, I am here as Parliament's representative. Of course, my colleagues don't know about the Omphalos or that Deirdre's blood will consecrate the ground above the sacred stone when the tree is planted at dawn. But it's all part of the prophecy, our legacy."

"Like hell it is!" Indy shouted, struggling against his bond.

"You'll spend the rest of your life in prison," Shannon said. "Someone will talk."

"Not likely. Not likely. You know so little about me. But enough talk. The others await my arrival."

The door slammed shut after him, and Williams stepped in front of it.

"Sounds like he's got a big night planned," Shannon muttered.

"We've got to do something," Indy said under his breath as he eyed Williams. If he could get the guard to move within reach of his feet, he could trip him, and knock him out with a kick to the head. They could lift the beds and work the ropes under the bottoms of the legs. But he was tied to the bed farthest from Williams and that made the plan tougher to pull off.

"Indy, you must know something about druids," Shannon said. "Do they really sacrifice people like Powell was saying?"

"The old druids. The real ones." As Indy spoke, he watched Williams out of the corner of his eye. "They were involved in animal and human sacrifice."

"Then I guess Powell is picking up their bad habits," Shannon said.

"Stop talking like that," Williams said. "Both of you."

Williams looked uneasy. What they were saying obviously bothered him more than the fact that they were talking. "It might do you good to hear what kind of things your friends are up to," Indy said. "Druids killed by burning, hanging, or drowning. It represented the three elements: fire, air, and water."

"There's no water or trees at Stonehenge, and no fires are allowed," Williams said.

"They also stabbed victims," Indy said. "They used their entrails for divination."

Williams silently mulled over what he'd said.

"I guess you don't know much about Powell," Shannon said.

The man grunted, looked away.

Indy decided to push him further. "You're not a druid, are you? You're not wearing a robe, and you're not going to their ceremony."

"Maybe he's in training," Shannon said.

Williams took several steps forward, and cracked the butt of the gun against Shannon's ribs. "I'm not a druid. I'm a carpenter, and the caretaker here."

"You're an ass," Indy shouted.

Williams raised the Webley by the barrel, and moved toward Indy. Good. Now was his chance. He tensed his legs, prepared to bring Williams down with one quick swipe. *A little farther; one more step. Come on.*

But the caretaker abruptly stopped and turned as the door creaked open. Indy cursed under his breath as Williams moved out of his range. Indy saw it was the kid, Randy. *Thanks, you little bastard.*

"What are you doing here, Randolph? I told you to stay away," Williams snapped.

"Dad, listen to me. We have to let them go."

"What are you talking about? It's none of our business. We can do nothing about it, or the others will kill us."

Randy looked past his father to Indy and Shannon. "They're forcing us to do these things. My father is not a bad man. They paid him too much money to make a cage, and made him take the money."

"A cage?" Indy asked. "What kind of cage?"

"Made from wicker. Dad is a very good carpenter. But they said he owed them services, because of the money he accepted. He couldn't say no. The first day it was just a few chores, then they made him guard your friend, and they made me watch the train station. And even now I still have to watch the station for unusual people every time the train arrives."

Randy turned toward the door, and at that moment the last person Indy expected to see stepped into the room. "Dr. Milford, what are you doing here?"

"Never mind that now." Milford set his black leather case down on the floor, and looked around. "What the devil is going on here?" He scowled, and turned to Randy's father. "I order you to release these men. They're not criminals. At least, not that I know of."

Williams looked as baffled as Indy. "I can't. Powell will kill me."

"Then I'll do it," Milford said, and he slickly pulled the knife from the man's belt before he could react. He moved over to Indy, and sliced at the rope.

"Stop that," Williams ordered. He raised the butt of the gun above his head.

"No, Dad. Don't." Randy grabbed for the gun, and father and son struggled for it.

Indy pulled his arm as hard as he could as Milford sawed away at the rope. Suddenly, it snapped, and Indy rolled over, lifted the foot of the bed, and freed his other arm. He leaped to his feet and jerked the revolver out of Williams's hand.

The man backed against the wall. "What are you going to do to me?"

"Hand over my whip."

Williams hesitated, then did as Indy ordered. "Don't hit me. I wasn't going to hurt you."

"No, you were just guarding us so someone else could kill us later."

Randy lifted the other bed and Shannon freed himself. "Now I remember where I know you from," Milford said to Shannon. "You're the one who played the horn after dinner at Indy's."

"That's right." Shannon sounded amazed.

"Yes, it was so loud my ears hurt for days."

"Sorry about that," Shannon said as he moved over to Indy. He grabbed Williams by the shirt collar. "I didn't appreciate the way you smacked me with that gun."

"You can hurt me, but don't hurt my son," Williams said.

"We're not going to hurt either one of you," Indy said. "We just want some cooperation, and if things work out our way, you won't have any trouble with Powell."

"We'll help you," Randy said. "You can count on it."

His father looked away, then nodded grimly.

"Where's Deirdre?" Indy demanded.

"They took her to Stonehenge in the cage I built."

"Swell. Keep an eye on him, Jack," Indy said, then he turned to Milford. "Now what in the world are you doing here, Dr. Milford?"

"I'm on an important mission."

Indy stared at the old professor. "You are?"

"Yes, I am." He bent down to his black case and fiddled with the catch. "Locked. Now what did I do with my key?" He stood up and started searching his pockets.

"How did you know I was here?"

"Well, you weren't home, and..." He pulled out a key from his pocket, examined it, then knelt down and tried it. He shook his head. "No, that's not it. Don't know what it's for, either." He stood up, and continued his search through his pockets.

"I wasn't home, so you just figured I was here?" Indy asked in a skeptical tone.

"No, Marcus figured that out."

"Brody?"

"That's right. Marcus got worried and sent me a cable, asking if I'd carried out his instructions."

"What instructions?" Indy asked.

"That's exactly what I wanted to know. So I cabled back and asked what he was talking about." He pulled out a handkerchief, was about to wipe his forehead when a key fell to the floor. "That's where I put it. Wrapped it up so I wouldn't forget it."

"What about these instructions from Marcus?"

"Well, he sent back another cable reminding me that I was carrying something I was to give to you. I'd had it in the bottom of my bag all the time, but it was in a box under some papers, and—"

Indy was exasperated. "Dr. Milford, what are you talking about? What is it?"

"The Omphalos, of course."

"The Omphalos." Indy shook his head. "It was stolen by Adrian Powell, the man who tied us up here."

Milford waved a hand. "No, that one's a fake. Marcus got the idea of making a duplicate after a Dr. Campbell kept asking about the Omphalos and warning that it was going to be stolen. So when the duplicate was ready, he put it in the display."

"How ingenious of ol' Marcus." Indy paused, looking perplexed. "And then he gave you the real one so you could give it to me."

Milford beamed. "That's right. I was already going to London, and he didn't think anyone would suspect what I carried." Milford scratched the fringe of white hair on the side of his head. "Of course, things got fouled up when I forgot about it. Then to top it off, when I found it, I couldn't find you, but Marcus said something about an eclipse at Stonehenge and that you'd probably be there, one way or another."

"He got that right."

Milford opened the case, and lifted a plain, square box. "Here you are, Indy. By the way, Marcus told me it's best not to handle the stone for some reason."

"Yeah, I've heard."

23

REVELRY

"I need to borrow your carriage for a while," Indy told Randy. "I've got to help Deirdre."

Shannon opened the door. "I'm going with you."

"Not me," Williams said. "I won't go out there."

"Dad! You said you'd help."

"We don't need any more trouble, Randolph."

"Okay, you stay here with your son and Dr. Milford," Indy said. "Go to the constable, and tell him the druids are planning on murdering a woman at the ruins."

"Can't do that," Williams said.

Indy gave the man a sullen look. "Why not?"

"Because the constable's out there wearing one of those robes. He's a druid."

"Great. That's just swell. Let's go, Jack. Dr. Milford, thanks for your help. I'll see that the Omphalos gets back safely to Marcus."

"Do you want to leave it with me?"

Indy didn't especially care to take it with him, but he didn't like Milford's suggestion any better. "I'll take it with me."

"Suit yourself. If you don't mind, I'm going to lie down in one of these beds. It's well past my bedtime."

Indy opened the top of the box and looked down at the black, cone-shaped artifact with its petrified, net-like lacing embedded on the surface. It amazed him how much trouble such an unattractive, nondescript relic could cause. He didn't believe much of what the gold scroll said about Merlin's life, but one thing about the Omphalos was true. It had fallen from the sky. It was a meteorite that in the ancient past had been worked into its present shape, probably by having been rubbed with an abrasive while under running water.

He held open his jacket pocket, and tipped the box upside down. The Omphalos fell nose-first into the pocket. It protruded slightly, but Indy zipped the pocket closed. He patted his bulging jacket, feeling the added weight.

"Okay, let's go."

Indy and Shannon left the room and moved through a maze of hallways and finally into a chapel. They headed directly to the main door, moving at a determined pace. They hit the double doors at the same time, but were stopped in their tracks.

"Locked," Indy exclaimed.

Shannon backed away. "Now what?"

"I know the way out," Randy yelled from the other side of the chapel. "Follow me."

Indy shrugged. "Let's go."

They crossed the chapel, and headed through another door and into a hallway, which led to an exit at the side of the building. The horse and carriage were waiting nearby. "I'll drive," Randy said. "You're going to need my help."

"Is it okay with your father?"

"Yes, it is," Williams said, approaching the carriage. "I'm going, too," he said, grudgingly. "We're already in trouble. Can't get much worse."

Indy climbed atop the carriage with Randy, while Shannon and Williams sat inside. They pulled away from the convent and headed for Stonehenge. He didn't know what to expect, but he knew it wasn't going to be a quiet night at the ruins.

Deirdre lay in her wicker cage near the slaughter stone. She was aware that Powell was talking to the crowd and some of the druids were standing just a few feet away. But she had no will to call out for help. Nothing seemed to matter. She felt heavy, sleepy, and unconcerned. It was a magic sleep. That's what Adrian had called it. Maybe he'd put something in the water she'd drunk, or maybe it was just Adrian's voice. He had ridden with her in the back of a truck, and all the way he had talked and talked about druid things, about the sun-god and Merlin, the underworld and the other world, and she had wondered what had happened to the man of Parliament.

Now though, as she listened to him relate a Celtic myth, she saw the connection. It was a story of a boy hunting in a time when many in the land were lacking will and were faint of heart. The boy came upon the castle of the King of Suffering and in an interior court spied a gold bowl. He discovered the bowl had the ability to restore the dead to life and to heal, and when he took it from the castle and showed it to the people, the despair vanished and the people were strong again. Deirdre realized it was a parable for Powell's quest to stop the Commonwealth, which he saw as weakening the strength of the land, and those who supported it were lacking will and faint of heart.

Somewhere far off, she thought she heard a steady pounding and the distant sound of horns. But Powell continued talking. "The gold bowl is not unlike the gold scroll, which, as I promised, I have brought to you. It brings us great hope and returns the power of the Omphalos to the Dance of the Giants. Listen now to Merlin's amazing story."

Then she heard Powell reading the scroll. She grasped the wicker bars in both hands and pulled herself to her feet. She could see Powell atop the slaughter stone, and noticed that he wasn't reading from the scroll, but from a sheet of paper. One of his more knowledgeable cronies must have translated it for him. When he finished, Powell spoke in a ritualistic voice. "What was written here in ancient times confirms what we knew, but many have doubted. Merlin, a druid, was indeed the architect of Stonehenge. He is the envoy of the Omphalos, and foresaw this day when the gates of power would reopen at the Dance of the Giants.

"Now, we will bury the Omphalos and at dawn, after the consecration is completed, the great powers of the Omphalos will spring forth as Apollo and Merlin merge as one, and I, your servant, take their place in the flesh. Believe what I say, colleagues of the great orders. If what I say is not true, may the sky fall upon my face, and the wrathful flames of the gods destroy me."

I hope they do. The thought seemed to pop into Deirdre's mind from outside of her, and it made her start to think about her predicament, and about what was going on. *What am I doing here? I've got to get out of here.*

The beat of drums grew closer; the horns sounded like a wild, howling wind. Deirdre looked over the field of white robes and saw Adrian moving to the center of the inner horseshoe. He lowered something into the ground. As he stood, he stared directly at her, holding her gaze.

No matter how hard she tried, she couldn't look away. Finally, he smiled, and she shifted her eyes to the crowd. She couldn't believe what she saw. She sucked in her breath, and gaped. She squeezed her eyes shut. She refused to look. *It can't be. I don't believe it.* Then she made herself look. With an odd sense of relief, she welcomed the sight of the robed druids. What was wrong with her? For an instant, she was sure that she had been looking at a herd of deer.

"This is not a night for speeches; this is our night of revelries, of high adventure," Powell shouted. "Listen now to the drums, and the horns as they approach." His voice was hypnotic. "Release, fly, soar with the night. Release, fly, soar with the night."

Randy stopped the carriage near a truck outside the ruins. "That's how they brought the cage out here." Randy pointed at the truck.

They walked over to it, but as soon as Indy saw that it was abandoned, he turned his attention toward the stone monument. He could hear music, and see shadowy figures moving about in jerking, swirling motions. "Let's get a closer look."

"You better stay here, son," Randy's father told the boy.

"I've come this far. I want to go, too."

"I said stay here."

"Your father's right, Randy," Indy said. "It's better if you wait out here."

"Oh, all right." He gave them a hurt look, then stomped off to the carriage.

"Watch out," Shannon hissed. "Someone's coming."

The three men ducked behind the truck, and watched as two robed figures approached the carriage. "What are you doing here?" one of them demanded when he saw Randy.

Williams started to stand up, but Indy jerked him down.

"I've come to see if anyone wants a ride back," the boy said innocently.

"We're not through, and besides we like to walk," one of the druids said. "You go on now."

"Let him stay for a while," the other man said. "Maybe someone will need a ride back."

"Just stay here. Don't come any closer," the first man warned. "You understand?"

"Yes, sir."

"Good going, Randy," Indy whispered in a voice that only Shannon and Williams could hear.

When the guards had disappeared from sight, Indy

motioned forward and they darted for the outer ring of stones. They stopped beneath one of the trilithons, blending into its giant shadow. Indy gripped his gun tightly, looked around, but no one had seen them.

The drumming was loud. It pounded in Indy's ears. The horns blared, and the air was riddled with sounds. Several bottles of wine were being passed around the crowd. He saw someone costumed like a bull, someone else wearing a bird headdress. For an instant, he glimpsed a man wearing only a loincloth, dancing and playing a harp.

Some of the druids, both men and women, were writhing about on the ground, moving their arms as if they were birds soaring through the night sky. He knew the practices of the old Celtic druids were derived from ancient shamanism, and these new druids were obviously following the same pattern in their ritualistic practices. He still remembered how one of his professors at the Sorbonne had described the process in a lecture on shamans of the Upper Paleolithic: "Sensual stimulation, emotional stress, and disorientation induce disassociation, trance, vision, ecstasy."

But now wasn't the time to ponder druid behavior. They had to take advantage of the situation. He had to find Deirdre before she became a victim of the revelries. He signaled Shannon and Williams to wait, and edged away from their hiding place.

Just a few feet away one of the druids was twirling and staggering in his direction. Indy grabbed the man by the cowl and cracked the butt of the gun over his head. He slumped to the ground, and Indy immediately pulled off his robe and put it on himself, dropping the revolver into a pocket. Shannon and Williams looked from the fallen man to Indy, surprised by the swiftness of his actions.

"Watch him while I find a couple more robes." Indy pulled up his cowl, and slipped away from the shadows of the trilithon. Several robed men were building a bonfire on top of the slaughter stone and Indy knew he had to hurry. He felt a hand on his shoulder, and froze. He turned and recognized the same bearded, overstuffed druid who had been standing guard at the heel stone before the eclipse. The man held out a bottle of wine. Indy took it, and gulped the last of the wine. "Thank you, brother."

The druid was frowning now. "Say, you took my robe and didn't return it to me."

"I see you found another one, though. Mind if I borrow this one, too?"

"What?"

Indy cracked the bottle over the man's head, and the man toppled over. He grabbed him under the arms and quickly dragged him back to the trilithon. "This guy needs to lose some weight," he huffed as Shannon and Williams helped him.

They stripped off the big man's robe, and Shannon put it on. It fell over his feet. "You could've found someone a little smaller."

"No time to be picky. They're already stoking the fire."

"Watch out! Someone's coming," Williams said.

Indy looked up just in time to see another druid. This one, however, was approaching warily.

"What's going on here?" he demanded, looking

down at the prone robeless figures. Indy grabbed Williams by the collar.

"We caught them spying on us."

"Williams, what are you doing here?"

"You know him?" Indy asked.

"I'm the constable. I'm in charge of security." He bent over to look at the two men on the ground and Shannon grabbed him by the neck and rammed him against the upright block of stone. But the constable was only stunned. He staggered a couple of feet, then pulled a gun from his robe. Indy shoved Williams out of his way, and at the same time reached into his own robe for the Webley. The constable leveled his weapon at Shannon. A gun fired. Shannon jerked back in surprise. But the constable fell.

"God, I shot him." Indy stared at the motionless body, and suddenly felt sick.

"Thanks," Shannon said. "That's why I'm alive." He pulled the robe off the constable and handed it to Williams.

"I don't want to wear it," Williams said, pointing at the hole in the chest and the patch of blood.

"It looks like spilled wine," Shannon said. "Either wear it or go back. Make up your mind."

Reluctantly, Williams put on the robe, and the three of them, with cowls pulled forward, moved away from the trilithon. Shannon immediately tripped over his robe, but caught himself. He pulled the robe up and held the hem in one hand as Deirdre had done. His awkward movements didn't attract any attention since nearly everyone was moving in spastic turns, gyrating to the music, and more and more of the revelers were falling into trances, quivering, shaking, undulating.

All to their advantage, Indy thought as he tried to shake off the sickening feeling in his gut. They moved toward the slaughter stone and he saw the bonfire blazing. He thought of Deirdre and toughened his resolve. A dozen or so druids cavorted around the stone. Among them were robed figures beating drums or blowing horns, and one pranced about wearing feathered wings and a scaly, snakelike headdress. "Back there, behind the slaughter stone," Indy said to Shannon when he spotted the wicker cage. He turned to Williams. "Start dancing, and follow me."

Indy kicked his feet, swung his arms in a swimming motion and snaked his way around the massive stone. He looked back once and saw Williams imitating his moves, and Shannon improvising his own. His hands were at his mouth as if he were playing his cornet, and he was gyrating to his own beat.

Then Indy saw Deirdre lying on the bottom of the wicker cage. She wasn't moving. *Bastards probably drugged her,* he thought. They were so confident she wasn't going anywhere that no one was guarding her.

He hurried to the gate of the cage, and Shannon positioned himself behind him and continued dancing. "Deirdre," Indy whispered. "Wake up."

She turned her head, blinking her eyes. Her jaw dropped. "Indy!"

"Shh!"

He jerked the lock on the latch, felt the wicker bars. Williams crouched down next to him. "Give me my knife. I can open it fast without the key."

Indy looked over at Williams, wondering once again if he could trust him. "Okay. Here."

The carpenter took the knife, held it up, smiled, then turned and went to work. Ten seconds later, the latch snapped and the door popped open. Deirdre started crawling out; but then the trouble began.

24

AXIS MUNDI

"Indy!" Shannon shouted.

He turned, and saw white.

A horde of druids descended on them. Shannon raised the constable's gun, but didn't fire it. Williams dropped his knife, and Indy simply stared at the surging robed mass of men and women. At the last instant, he snapped out of his lethargy, and dropped to the ground. He pulled Deirdre after him. He crawled under legs, zigzagged, twisted, rolled. He was stomped on and kicked. Hands grabbed him, pulled his hair, tugged his arms and legs. He bit, clawed, and punched. But all to no avail.

He heard someone yelling. "Lambs, lambs. Get the lambs. Don't let the lambs escape."

More and more hands grabbed him; they pulled, poked, shoved. Finally, he was pushed through an opening, and he felt a jumble of arms and legs around him. Someone pushed his feet, and a door snapped shut. He rolled over, and bumped into someone.

"Indy, you okay?" It was Shannon.

He managed to sit up and get his bearings. He was in the cage, and crowded with him in the cramped quarters were Deirdre, Shannon, and Williams. "I guess we didn't make it."

The cage door was bound by a rope and the druids were turning away to continue their merrymaking as if nothing had happened. "This is my fault," Deirdre said. "You should have just gotten away while you had the chance."

"That wasn't even an option," Indy said.

"But now look at us."

Indy reached for Deirdre's hand. "Don't worry. Powell can't kill us in front of all these people. He may think he's a druid, but he's living in the twentieth century like the rest of us."

"What's that you say, Jones?"

Indy looked up, and could hardly believe his eyes. Powell wore only a loincloth and a wreath woven from laurel leaves and twigs. He held a harp under one arm and his face was so caked with makeup that it looked like a mask.

"I said you can't kill us in front of all these people. They're not all corrupt like you. You'll never get away with it."

Powell laughed, and strummed his harp. "Jones, you have no idea of my powers. They see what I want them to see. You will be sacrificial lambs, and that is all. Even now, they are laughing and talking about how the little lambs almost escaped when their cage door broke open." Powell playfully strummed the harp again. "Now, my little lambs, I've got to wassail awhile, but we'll be back for you very soon."

Powell skipped off, like a carefree child.

"He's crazy," Shannon snorted.

Deirdre squeezed Indy's hand. "I think it's true what he said. He must have some ability to make people see what he wants them to see."

Indy stared through the wicker bars at the revelers. "Mass hypnosis. I've read that the ancient druids had mastered it." Powell was even more dangerous than he'd thought.

"That explains why I couldn't fire the gun," Shannon said. "I just let them knock it out of my hand."

"It's witchcraft," Williams wheezed. "That's what they are, witches. Something made me drop my knife before they even touched me."

"Any way you look at it, we can't do anything against him," Deirdre said, rubbing her hands over her face. "We're like ants about to be squashed under his thumb."

"Let's not talk about ants," Shannon groused. "My legs are still on fire from where the little bastards were chewing on me."

Indy tried to find a more comfortable position. From where he sat he could see the glow of the bonfire from beyond the slaughter stone. "Okay, let's think about this a minute. First of all, Powell isn't invincible. He may have created some sort of temporary effect on us, but he doesn't control us. Otherwise, he wouldn't have to keep us in this cage."

"So? We're still not going anywhere," Shannon said.

"So we've just got to figure a way to outmaneuver him."

"But how?" Deirdre asked.

"First of all, we've got to take advantage of his arrogance. He *thinks* he's more powerful than he is. He's put us in a cage, but we're not tied up, or gagged." He patted his side. "They took my gun, but not my whip."

Or the Omphalos, he thought.

"He doesn't need to tie us up or watch us," Williams scoffed. "We can do nothing against him."

"Maybe you should've stuck with the bad guys," Shannon said dryly.

"I was never with Powell. There was nothing I could do."

"Sounds like a regular problem of yours," Shannon commented.

Indy waved a hand to cut him off. "Jack, that's enough. You're wasting time."

"Psst. Psst." They all turned and saw Randy crouched behind the cage.

"Get out of here," Williams growled.

"Be glad that he's here," Shannon said.

"I've got a knife. I can cut your way out."

Indy reached his hand through the wicker bars. "Give it to me. Now get back to the carriage, and wait for us, or you'll end up in here."

Randy nodded, then crawled to the outer ring of stones and scampered into the darkness as Indy went to work carving at the rope holding the gate closed. "Take off your robes. You'll be able to run faster," he said.

"But they'll see us," Shannon protested.

"It doesn't matter. They see us as lambs, not druids." He kept slicing at the rope and was almost

through the rope when Shannon touched his forearm.
"Hide the knife."

He tucked it away as several men approached.
They surrounded the cage and grasped hold of the
wicker bars. One of them counted to three, and they
lifted the cage in unison. They moved it several feet,
then lowered it to the ground and regrouped.
"They're heavy," one of them said.

"Yeah, we're not lambs, boys. Open your eyes,"
Shannon said.

One of the men looked up, and Indy recognized
Narrow Eyes. "Not all of us need the veil. But your
yells and screams won't work with the others. Adrian
is powerful. All they'll hear is the bleating of lambs
before their sacrificial deaths."

They lifted the cage onto their shoulders this time
and started walking. The crowd moved back, making
way for them. Indy saw orange tongues of flame lick-
ing the night sky as they neared the bonfire. He had to
act, and fast.

He pulled out the knife and started hacking at the
hands gripping the cage. The men yelped and howled.
Blood spurted from the wounds. The cage rocked,
plunged downward, smashed against the ground, and
broke apart. But the knife slipped from Indy's hand as
he fell.

Indy pried away the broken wicker with his hands
and feet and rolled out the hole. He reached to his
belt, and unhitched his whip as the others crawled out
after him. The crowd stared, perhaps uncertain what
they were seeing. He grabbed Deirdre by the arm.

"Dash for it," he yelled.

"Get the animals before they get away," someone

shouted, and the crowd surged. Robes flapped; arms lunged. The escapees dodged between the ghostly figures, but finally they were corralled, surrounded on all sides.

"Get down!" Indy shouted to the others and unfurled his whip. He swung it over his head hard and fast, and the knotted tip slashed across cheeks and chins, noses and foreheads. One after another the druids nearest them crumpled to the ground, holding their faces.

"They've got claws," someone yelled.

"Go, go," Indy yelled as gaps in the circle opened. While the others scrambled away on all fours toward the nearest trilithon, Indy covered them, snagging the neck of one of the druids who attempted to stop Deirdre. He spun the man around and pulled him to the ground, and several other druids tripped over him.

Indy jerked back the whip, and hurtled ahead like a leather helmeted fullback. He bowled into a couple of druids, then raced past the trilithon, and away from the ruins.

Two druids were in close pursuit, but he saw the carriage and ran as hard as he could. The others were already aboard it and Randy was perched on top, ready to set the horses in motion.

Thirty more feet. Twenty. Fifteen. Almost there.

Then one of the men dived, caught his ankle. Indy stumbled, skidded, and rolled. He tried to get up, but the other man pounced on him. He grabbed the assailant by the neck, and punched him in the jaw. The man's head jerked back, and Indy rolled away from him. He leaped to his feet, but the other man grabbed him by the shoulder. Indy spun around, pulling back his fist. The man ducked and raised his hands, and Indy just pushed him away, turned, and charged after the carriage, which was rolling ahead now.

Shannon grabbed Indy's wrist and pulled him onto the running board. "You made it," Deirdre yelled as the carriage picked up speed.

Indy tried to catch his breath as he clung to the carriage door. "We all did."

"You gave them something to think about with that whip, lad," Williams shouted gleefully.

"They must think those were the meanest lambs they'd ever seen," Shannon laughed.

Indy looked up. Something was wrong. Then he saw the outline of the massive trilithons coming into view. The carriage was making a wide turn. It was heading back.

"What are you doing?" Indy yelled.

"I can't help it," Randy shrieked. "I can't control them."

The horses charged across the plain, rushing toward Stonehenge, galloping so fast that Indy almost lost his hold on the carriage door. He pulled himself up the side of the carriage, crawled over the roof, and grasped the back of Randy's wooden seat. The kid was bent low, reaching for the reins, which had fallen from his hands.

Indy climbed over the seat, and gripped Randy by the shoulder. "Move back. I'll get it."

The kid scrambled out of the way and Indy leaned over as far as he could. But he still couldn't reach the reins; they dangled over the back of one of the horses. There was only one thing to do. He jumped headfirst, landing on one horse's back. He grabbed the reins and pulled. But the horses seemed to go even faster.

He needed a better position. Holding the reins for balance, he stood up, placing a foot on the rear of each horse. Then he leaned back, and yanked hard on the reins. The horses suddenly reared up, catapulting Indy from his perch. He hit the dirt and rolled.

Indy must have lost consciousness for a few seconds because when he opened his eyes he saw the carriage lying on its side, and he heard calls for help. He raised himself up on his hands and knees. Just then his fedora, which he'd left behind in the carriage when they'd arrived, dropped in front of him. Next to it were feet. Legs.

"Don't forget your hat, Jones."

He looked up to see Powell, now garbed in a robe. He pointed a gun, and behind him the stone monument loomed in the night, silhouetted by the orange glow of the bonfire.

"Did you enjoy your ride, Professor? The horses heard my call, and came at my command. I have a very special affinity with animals, as you can see." He laughed. "Maybe it comes from owning a pet store."

Powell motioned the gun toward the upended carriage. "Now gather up the rest of the little lambs. There's more fun ahead."

Suddenly, Randy limped out of the darkness, and behind him was Narrow Eyes. "Caught this little runt trying to crawl away."

As Indy walked over to the carriage, he felt a pain in his side, and touched his hand to his bulging jacket pocket. He'd landed on the Omphalos and bruised a rib. But he was relieved it was still there. The relic was his last hope.

The horns and drums had stopped, and the druids were swaying and chanting again. *Axis mundi est chorea gigantum.* Over and over like the rumble of a car being started.

Powell led Deirdre into the horseshoe formation of trilithons at the center of Stonehenge, while Indy and the others were held at gunpoint to one side of the horseshoe, a short distance from the bonfire.

Powell held up a hand, and the chanting faded and died. "Now, finally the most sacred of our ceremonies will begin," Powell told the crowd. A druid moved forward with a small oak and planted it in a hole next to Powell. Indy guessed it was the spot where the fake Omphalos had been buried.

Another druid approached and handed Powell a long knife with an ornately carved handle. "Don't let him do this," Deirdre yelled.

"Listen to the lamb bleating before its sacrificial death," Powell said.

"It's a woman; open your eyes," Indy yelled.

Narrow Eyes jabbed his gun into Indy's back. "No one can hear you. They don't believe lambs talk so they don't hear anything."

Somebody out there had to see them, and hear them, Indy thought, frantic now. No one could control that many minds. But there was no time to wonder what the crowd was seeing. As the ground around the oak tree was patted flat with a shovel and the druid moved away, Powell raised the knife to Deirdre's throat.

Indy unzipped his jacket pocket. "Powell, you don't have the Omphalos. It's right here. Yours is a fake."

He pulled it from his pocket and raised it above his head. "Stop, Jones," Narrow Eyes ordered. "I'll shoot." But Indy stepped toward Powell, ignoring the threat. He heard murmurs from the crowd. "Who is this man? Where did he come from? Is he one of us?"

Now they saw him. He was sure of it, and Narrow Eyes didn't pull the trigger.

Powell was caught off guard. He lowered the knife as Indy stopped several feet from him. Indy didn't know what to do next, but suddenly, as he pressed the Omphalos to his chest, it didn't matter any longer.

He saw an eagle. His eagle. He knew this eagle. It was part of his past. It was his protector. He'd last seen it when he'd held the Omphalos at Delphi. Now it was here, soaring above the ruins, etching a circle above the trilithons.

"What am I going to do?" Indy asked, not knowing whether the words were spoken or thought.

The eagle completed its first circle, and suddenly Indy saw the stones illuminated in an ethereal light that seemed to emanate from within them. They were different now. The sarsen circle and the rest of the temple was completed. Where the slaughter stone had been a moment ago was another trilithon.

Indy was so fascinated with what he saw that he didn't realize at first that a tall man in a gray cloak stood to his left. The man was gazing off and an owl was perched on his right shoulder. Indy could see part of a long white beard, but nothing else.

The man spoke: "Ask."

"Ask what?"

"Try again."

"Where am I?"

"You know."

"But it doesn't look the same."

"Seventy windows look out to the universe and the universal mind."

"Where is everyone?"

"They are here."

Indy peered at the man, trying to get a better view. "Who are you?"

"You've already read my tale, false as you believe it to be. I have many names, and in not too many years will be reborn again in lore as Gandalf. I like that name." The man turned slightly, and Indy saw a pale, wrinkled face, a long nose, and a hint of crinkled smile. "But don't waste time. Ask what you don't already know."

Indy didn't know what to ask. "Why is it called Dance of the Giants?"

"The dancing gods once charged the stones, which are great batteries of power and healing."

"Can the power be used for evil?"

"The energy is neither good nor evil. It is."

"Will Adrian Powell become prime minister?"

"I say one from the orders will become prime minister. But you can stop Powell."

"How?"

"By giving to him what he wants."

He felt a tug and looked down to see a pair of

hands pulling on the Omphalos. Suddenly, he found himself in a tug-of-war with Powell for control of the relic, and everything was back as it was. The cloaked stranger was gone, and so was the eagle. But the words of the old enchanter were still in his mind. Indy let go and Powell clutched the Omphalos to his own chest. He seemed startled that Indy had given it up so easily. Then his expression changed. He looked stunned. His mouth opened; he took an unsteady step, then dropped to one knee.

Narrow Eyes moved forward to Powell and asked him if he was all right. Powell rose to his feet. His eyes bulged but he stared at Narrow Eyes as if he didn't recognize him or understand what he was saying.

"Now, the ceremony must be completed," he said in a monotone. He let go of the Omphalos with one hand and pulled the ceremonial knife from his robe. With a quick thrust, he stabbed Narrow Eyes in the stomach, then pulled out the knife and slashed upward to his collarbone. Narrow Eyes staggered back, blood spurting from his stomach and chest. He collapsed.

Indy snatched the Omphalos from Powell's grasp, and clutched it. He was about to reach for Deirdre, but was stopped in his tracks. Again, he saw the eagle soaring above the ruins. It swept down and lit on Indy's shoulder, and he knew he was protected. The gray-cloaked figure stood next to him in the ruins, which were no longer ruins. The conjurer raised a hand as if motioning him to speak.

This time Indy didn't hesitate. "What's going on?"

The tall man laughed. "More than what you see."

"What did Powell see when he held the Omphalos?"

"The landscape of his own mind. A mind of great strength, but equally great greed, with little concern for others. Everything is collapsing around him, including the very sky above him. He has lost his vision."

"If not Powell, who is the druid who will be prime minister?"

"That's none of your concern. Don't worry about it. He will be a strong leader, but not much of a druid." He stroked the head of the owl on his shoulder. "Isn't that right, Churchill?"

Then he turned to Indy one last time. "Now look what's going on."

Suddenly, Indy felt a jolt, and saw that Powell had jerked the Omphalos from his hands again. He backed away from Indy, holding the Omphalos above his head. "I am invincible. My strength is beyond all measure. I control."

Then Indy saw Narrow Eyes behind Powell. He was on his feet, bloodied and tottering. Powell backed into him, and Narrow Eyes wrapped his arms around him and they swayed like two dancers.

"Let go of me," Powell shouted. "What monster has me?"

Then, with a final burst of strength, Narrow Eyes drove Powell forward and into the bonfire. Both men disappeared in the flames. The fire roared as if in approval.

Indy held Deirdre close to him, hardly believing what he'd seen. "It's over. All over."

But then suddenly Powell reeled into view at the

edge of the blaze. His skin was blackened and in flames, but he still held the Omphalos. For an instant, Indy thought that Powell was going to lunge for them. But with a final piercing cry of terror, he collapsed back into the inferno.

25

APOLLO'S ARROW

A wisp of smoke curled from the ash-strewn debris where the bonfire had blazed. Deirdre watched in the early morning light as Indy and Shannon picked their way toward her. She'd wanted no part of their search. She wasn't going any closer to the gruesome remains. She'd experienced enough horror, and only wanted to sleep now. A long, deep sleep. She wanted to forget. That was all.

Indy was carrying a cloth bag, and from its shape it looked as if he'd been successful at recovering the Omphalos. "I guess you got it," she said.

"Yeah, it had sunk into his rib cage, and one end of it—"

She waved a hand. "Don't tell me about it. I don't want to know."

"There's something else we found, though, that you're going to want to know about," Shannon said.

"What?"

He held up a charred glob of yellow metal. "It's the gold scroll. What's left of it."

"Oh, no!"

"I'm afraid so," Indy said. "Powell must have had it in a pocket of his robe. It was a hot fire."

"It's still hot," Shannon said. "Look at this." He lifted up his foot; the bottom of his boot was smoking.

"Is it reparable?" she asked.

"The boot?"

"No, Jack, not your boot."

"The writing's all gone," Indy answered. "It's just a piece of gold now, a couple of ounces at least."

Shannon handed it to her. "Here, it's yours. You found it."

"What am I going to do with it?"

"You could throw a big wedding party and hire a jazz band and pay them real well. I just happen to have one in mind."

She laughed, and glanced at Indy, then looked away. After what she'd been through, she felt changed somehow, a different person, not at all like the one who had been excited about the prospect of returning to London and getting married. She felt uncertain; she needed time to think, to heal, to cleanse herself of the past.

Right now she needed sleep. Maybe after she was rested it would all work out as they'd planned. She looked at the remains of the gold scroll, and shrugged. "Well, I guess there's nothing more here for us. Can we leave now? I'm ready to drop."

Indy slipped his arm around Deirdre's shoulder. "So am I. Let's go."

"What about the fake Omphalos?" Shannon asked.

"Let's leave it," Indy said. "It's a nice symbolic gesture of the return of the Omphalos."

Shannon shrugged. "Don't suppose it would matter which of the two were planted there anyway, would it?"

Indy looked at Shannon, who had never held the Omphalos. "Naw, I suppose not."

They should have felt relieved and excited, looking to the future, but something had changed between him and Deirdre, shifted like the ground during an earthquake, Indy thought. They seemed like two different people. Yet, he knew that more than one person who had survived a life-threatening situation had felt an inexplicable letdown when the danger was over. The feeling would pass, he was sure, and they would come back together. At least, that's the way he hoped it would work.

He slipped his arm off of Deirdre's shoulder, and took one more look at the stone formations. He noticed that the bluestones, which formed a horseshoe within the five trilithons at the center of the ruins, were conical like the Omphalos. The cone and the parallelogram were the two shapes of stones considered most sacred by the ancient Greeks, and both shapes were present at Stonehenge. But Stonehenge was conceived and built even before the ancient Greeks had risen to prominence. He thought of the gold scroll with Merlin's story, and the odd vision of the tall man in the gray cloak. Stonehenge, he decided, was a place where myth and fact merged, and the truth was maybe as strange as any of it.

They passed through one of the trilithons and Indy stopped as he spotted his Webley lying at the base of it. He picked it up, then looked at the massive block of stone and ran his hands over it. "What are you doing?" Shannon asked.

"Just taking a look. I really haven't had the chance since we got here."

"A stone's a stone, Indy, no matter how big it is," Shannon said.

"And all jazz sounds alike."

Shannon rubbed his neck, grinned. "All right. I get it. Every stone has a different story to tell."

"Come on, you two. Let's go," Deirdre said. The carriage was waiting for them. Randy had taken his father back to the village at dawn and then had returned for them. He knew Deirdre was anxious to leave.

Indy started to turn away, but then he saw something. A few feet above his head on the block of stone was a carving. It was a dagger about a foot long and pointing downward. Its hilt looked identical to carvings of Aegean daggers he'd studied that dated back to the second century B.C.

"Now what are you doing?" Deirdre asked.

He pointed to the dagger. "Do you see it?"

Deirdre stepped closer to the stone. "It looks like an arrow."

He shrugged. "I suppose you could call it that. Maybe it's Apollo's Arrow."

"What's that?" Shannon asked.

"Apollo gave an arrow to the magician Abaris who traveled over the earth on it."

"Why would he have stopped here?" Shannon asked. Indy turned away, and gazed across the vast, desolate plain. He thought about the tales of Apollo and Merlin and wondered. "Who knows? Maybe Apollo sent him here to pick up something he'd buried a long time ago."

ABOUT THE AUTHOR

ROB MacGREGOR is an Edgar-winning author who has been on the *New York Times* bestseller list. He is the author of seventeen novels, ten nonfiction books, and numerous magazine and newspaper articles. In addition to writing his own novels, he has teamed with George Lucas, Peter Benchley, and Billy Dee Williams.

The story of the early years in the life of Indiana Jones
continues in the jungles of Guatemala with

INDIANA JONES™

and the

SEVEN
VEILS

Read an exciting preview of the next novel in the
series, starting on the next page....

PROLOGUE

August 14, 1925

I'm anxious to get moving. My bruises and sores are healed and I have new hope. The canoe is stocked with supplies: rifles, ammunition, clothing, and food. The amounts of the latter are meager, but the fish in the river are plentiful and when we take to the land, we will hunt game.

Now I'm waiting in the canoe for my two companions. They're not the pair I'd choose as my travel mates, but there is little choice at this juncture. Harry Walters is the name of one of them. He seems to survive on rum, but he claims to know this treacherous jungle like the back of his hand. We'll see.

The other is a woman, Maria.

Most of my colleagues would scoff at the very idea of taking a woman into the jungle. I can hear them now: She'll get in the way. She won't have the courage, will, or determination of a man. Women are trouble, a distraction, prone to faintness of heart and physical weakness. Maybe true. But they don't know Maria.

From my observations of this woman these past few weeks, she knows nothing of the expected weakness of her sex—not the physical, nor the mental, nor the emotional. She's a levelheaded gal if there ever was one. She's extremely patient, honorable, and trustworthy. I'm not sure yet that I can say the same for Walters.

Maria and I have taken walks together, and by God she's more of a man than half the men I've met in my day. I am particularly impressed by her familiarity with and knowledge of the jungle, as well as her fleetness of foot. But I am most enthralled by something that she has only hinted at: the place where she came from. She is my guide, after all, and her former home is where we are headed.

But I am getting ahead of myself. Let me backtrack, for I did not arrive at this point without great effort and considerable discomfort. The jungle, I should begin, is no place to venture alone, and after months of trekking through this harsh land, which conspires daily to kill anyone who would dare challenge it, I was indeed desperate and alone. My son, lame from a bad ankle and feverish from malaria, turned back some weeks ago and I sent our last guide with him. God save them.

I followed a river upstream for several days, but saw it was veering from the direction I was headed. I left it and marched directly north toward uncharted territory. On the third day I ran out of water, and for the next two or three days my only source of liquid was the dew I licked from leaves. How I questioned myself over and over about my decision to go on alone. I called myself a fool, an idiot, a madman, and more names than I care to mention. I wandered aimlessly and soon found myself talking to old friends and even animals that appeared and vanished. Finally, I could walk no farther, and I crawled. Insects chewed on me. I desperately needed water, and knew I had but hours to live. I fought against death, and refused to give up. But I must have lost consciousness.

When I awoke I found myself in a mission outpost on the Rio Tocantins. Maria had found me and dragged me through the jungle. She nursed me back to health, so I can say nothing against her.

Indeed, she is clearly a most unique individual. She

claims that she knew that I was coming and needed help, and that she had gone out to search for me. Under normal conditions, I would say her comments were just so much poppycock. However, I am beginning to understand that survival in the jungle requires a certain sharpness of the senses that we citizens of the civilized world have disposed of in favor of logic and analysis.

Now about Walters. He's an Englishman like myself, but he has lived in and out of the jungle for years. From what I gather, he is charged with locating Indians for the missionaries. He gives the heathens pots and pans, trinkets, and clothing, and prepares them for their eventual submission and conversion.

I was surprised to learn from Walters that he is something of a religious mercenary. Within a few miles of one another are Protestant and Catholic missions, and Walters works for both of them. Besides laying the groundwork for the missionaries, he also spies for each of them, gathering information about the competition's activities and progress. This I find rather humorous, but Walters considers it to be normal jungle communication between rival clergies. Oddly enough, this foulmouthed drunk is the missionaries' most important link to the outside world. Since money isn't much good in the jungle, the missionaries pay him mostly in rum, which they obtain from traders.

One day, a few months ago, Walters showed up at the Catholic mission with a young woman who was not from any tribe anyone had ever seen. He isn't the sort who scares easily, but he confessed to me that he was extremely frightened the day he encountered her. He had almost finished a bottle of rum when the woman suddenly appeared in his camp. He was sure he was seeing things. Her skin was white, and her long chestnut hair reflected a reddish tinge in the firelight. When he reached for his gun, she swiftly vanished as strangely as she had appeared.

Walters thought he must have encountered the jungle spirit, Yaro, guardian of jungle beasts. According to the

Indian legend, she lures men into the jungle at night where she kills them and feeds their body parts to her animal children. Walters vowed to stay awake all night, but eventually he dozed off. When he awoke at the first light, she was standing over him. He saw that she was no spirit, but he didn't know what she was. Without a word, he packed his gear and returned to the mission. She followed him.

The woman, of course, is the one I mentioned, Maria. That is the name the missionaries gave her when they baptized her. I had been recovering at the mission for a couple of weeks when I heard Walters's tale. I was fascinated and uplifted, because I knew immediately where she had come from, the place that had been my destination all along. My destiny.

I speak, of course, of the lost city known as Z.

—*From the journal of Colonel Percy Fawcett*

ANCIENT MARINERS

The room was crowded with penguins, a typical opening night for a museum exhibition. No, maybe not so typical. There were more than the usual number of newspapermen; they stood out because they never played the penguin game, and several wore hats with press cards.

Indy tugged at his starched collar, swiveled his neck uncomfortably, then adjusted his black bow tie. He didn't much care for wearing a tux, especially with his arm in a sling. But when he'd arrived in New York a week ago, he'd promised Marcus Brody he would show up, at least for a while. So here he was, a winged penguin attending "New Evidence of Ancient Forays to the Americas," an exhibition that was probably going to turn out to be a major embarrassment.

He wandered about lost in thought, only pretending to look at the exhibits. Things had not gone well since he'd taken his leave from teaching. His fieldwork at Tikal had been cut short after the nearly disastrous encounter with the band of *huaqueros*. Although the grave robbers had been caught, the Guatemalan army had moved in and confiscated all the artifacts.

If that wasn't bad enough, Bernard had blamed Indy for everything. Indy had been responsible for hiring the Mayan workers, and had taken on a man who was associated with the *huaqueros*. There were a dozen responses he could make to that accusation, but Indy knew it wouldn't do any good. It would only get him into even hotter water.

To top it off, he hadn't seen Deirdre since they'd arrived in New York. She was staying with a friend who was attending Columbia University, and every time he called or stopped by the Greenwich Village apartment, she was out. He knew she was avoiding him, but he couldn't say why. He'd thought everything had been cleared up between them. Then on the train trip to New York, she had gotten cooler and cooler toward him by the hour, until at Grand Central Station she'd told him that she didn't want to see him for a while.

Just as his thoughts touched on Deirdre, he saw a woman with long red hair that fell over her royal blue dress. She was studying an inscription on a triangular stone. He moved toward her, and with each step his anticipation grew. Deirdre had come to the opening knowing he'd be here. Things were going to work out. She sensed his presence as he stopped behind her. She turned, and he realized he was mistaken. Even though her trim figure matched Deirdre's, the woman was at least ten years older than Deirdre and didn't look anything like her.

Indy looked down at the stone, embarrassed by his mistake. "Excuse me."

"Do you think the Phoenicians were in Iowa twenty-five hundred years ago?" the woman asked. "That's when they say this stone plaque was made."

"Maybe the Indians gave them the plaque as an award," Indy said as he started to move away.

The woman gave him a puzzled look. "But seriously,

do you think it's possible? I mean it is a Punic text and it was found in Iowa."

"Anything's possible, but don't count on it," Indy said, and excused himself. He meandered through the crowd, then saw a hand raised in greeting.

"There you are, Indy. Glad you could make it."

"Evening, Marcus."

They shook hands and Brody clasped the younger man's shoulder. He was a kindly man who had always treated Indy like a son. "How are you feeling?"

"Fine. The sling comes off in a couple of days. Just a minor flesh wound."

"You were lucky. I had a long chat with your father yesterday. I told him what happened."

"You did?" Indy wished he hadn't. "What did he say?"

A pained look crossed Brody's face. He shrugged. "You know how he is."

Yeah. Indy knew. It wasn't worth talking about.

"By the way, he knows Victor Bernard and he doesn't think much of him." Brody brightened as if the comment was some consolation for Indy's nonexistent relationship with his father. "I understand that Victor is not being very sensible about the unfortunate affair in Tikal."

"So I've heard." Indy didn't feel like talking about his father or Bernard. He turned and looked at a collection of Roman coins from the fourth century that had been found on the coast of Massachusetts. "I bet they couldn't buy much with those coins back then."

"But don't you think it's all very interesting, Indy? Look over here." Brody pointed to a stone inscribed with glyphs. "This is a reproduction of one of the Libyan inscriptions from California. It dates back to around 232 B.C. to the time of the pharaoh Ptolemy the Third, and was found on the outskirts of the Mojave Desert. It says: 'All men, Take care, Take care. Great desert.' We've also got photographs and replicas of inscriptions in Nordic runes, Phoenician, and Iberian-Celtic. Some date back as far as 500 B.C. and they're from all over the Americas, from Vermont to Brazil. It's truly amazing."

Brody sounded awed, and with good reason. The exhibition was a visual display of virtually every anomalous artifact that had been discovered in the Americas in the past hundred years. Placed together, they were a bold attempt to virtually rewrite American history. But not many scientists were buying it. For the past week, detractors had been condemning the exhibition before it even opened, and Brody was probably going to end up looking like a fool by the time the press was through with him.

"Marcus, you know these Libyan inscriptions could be Zuni," Indy said in a gentle voice. "Their writing was a lot alike."

"Oh, I know. It's interesting that you point it out, because the Zuni Indians may well have learned their written language from Libyan explorers and colonists."

Indy nodded. He hoped Brody's reputation wouldn't be too greatly damaged. "Well, you've got quite a turnout tonight. That must please you."

"Yes, indeed. It's going to be quite controversial, you know. Some of your colleagues are not so pleased with me."

"Really?"

"You wouldn't believe it. But I don't pay them any heed. I'm convinced that these inscriptions deserve attention. I did quite a bit of work pulling all of this together. It took me two years."

"You did a good job, Marcus. Who knows, maybe you'll be remembered as the man who redefined American history. World history, for that matter."

Brody reddened. "Well, I just see it as an educational service," he said modestly. He gazed past Indy a moment, fixing his attention across the room. "I've got to start the press conference now, but there's something I need to talk to you about. Can you see me before you leave? It's a confidential matter."

Indy nodded, wondering what Brody was up to now. "Of course."

He moved over to a replica of a six-foot-tall statue from San Agustin, Colombia. On the headdress was carved a series of glyphs resembling Viking runes. Maybe it was someone's idea of a joke. Next to it was a table containing two figurines that had been discovered in a Mound Builder burial site in Iowa. They wore the high-crowned hats, called *hennins,* worn by Phoenicians during rituals and celebrations. Also on the table was a comparison between the alphabets used by Phoenician colonists in Spain and the script found in Davenport, Iowa in 1874, the one the redhead had been so curious about. Indy had to admit the resemblance was remarkable, but then so was the resemblance between the redhead and Deirdre until he'd taken a closer look.

Indy examined a series of photographs of underground stone-slab chambers from Mystery Hill, New Hampshire. They reminded him of Celtic *dunans,* "little fortresses" found in Scotland. Next to the photos was a report dated September 18, 1917, by Harold W. Krueger. It explained that while archaeologists had labeled the cellars less than a century old, the stones had been penetrated by the roots of a tree purported to date from A.D. 1690, plus or minus ninety years. An addendum added to the report said that other evidence suggested that the megalithic chambers were Celtic in origin and dated back to the second millennium B.C.

Nearby was a pedestal on which rested a stone lintel found at one of the cellars. On it were inscribed a series of short lines, tilting back and forth and poorly spaced, with a single horizontal line running through the marks. It was purportedly ogham Celtic letters.

Suddenly, Indy's interest was piqued. He ran his finger over the inscription. To the casual viewer, ogham didn't look much like an alphabet. But Indy readily identified the script and slowly translated the letters. He took out a pad and pen and wrote them down. During the past year, while teaching a class in Celtic archaeology, he had become fascinated with ogham. What he saw was an Iberian form of Celtic that included no vowels. They had to be added for the writing to make sense.

When he was finished, the letters read: PY HD T BL, HS Y S TH SN. Indy played with the sentence, adding and removing vowels until words were formed. Now it read: "Pay heed to Bel, his eye is the sun." He looked over at the translation written on a card next to the lintel. It said the same thing, adding that Bel was the Celtic sun god, sometimes equated with Apollo.

While Indy had once thought that his linguistics background had served only to delay his entrance into archaeology, he had come to realize that the years he'd spent studying ancient written languages were now invaluable. In fact, his specialization was epigraphy, the study of ancient inscriptions. He refused to call himself an epigraphist, though. The word sounded too much like the study of a certain farm animal.

But what was ogham script doing on a stone found in New Hampshire? Maybe Brody actually was onto something significant.

"Hello, Indy."

He spun on his heels at the sound of the familiar voice. "Deirdre!"

"How are you, Indy?"

"Better. I've been trying to see you."

She was wearing a powder blue gown that fell off her shoulders, and he thought she looked great. She ran a hand through her auburn mane. "I know. I've needed time to think."

"About what?"

"About us, and I've made a decision."

"Yeah?"

She nodded. "I just wanted to say good-bye."

"What are you talking about?"

"It's over, Indy. Our lives are going in different directions."

"What do you mean? What are you going to do?"

She shrugged. "I don't know. Maybe I'll drop out of the university and stay here in New York and get a job. I don't want any more adventures. I don't think I could survive another one."

"Deirdre, I know you're mad about what happened with Katherine, but it really wasn't my fault."

"Don't even mention her name around me," she snapped.

Indy kept his voice low and spoke rapidly. "It just happened. I'm sorry about it. How many times do I have to apologize?"

"I'm sorry too, Indy. But it's not just that. It's a lot of things. It's too late."

With that, she walked away. Indy was about to go after her when he felt a hand on his shoulder. "Jones, I didn't expect to see you here."

"Dr. Bernard, uh..." Indy looked after Deirdre, but she'd disappeared in the crowd. "I didn't expect to see you, either."

Bernard laughed. "I just wanted to see how far Marcus Brody has gone in his fantasy."

"I guess you don't agree with what he's doing here," Indy said, wondering how he was going to straighten things out with Deirdre.

"This ogham stuff is pure nonsense. The lines were probably made by a plow or a tree root."

"No, I don't think so. That's ogham."

Bernard smiled benignly. "I suppose if one tries hard enough it's possible to read anything into those lines. But you'd have to be a palm reader." He laughed again and made an expansive gesture with his hand to take in the entire exhibition. "No, Jones, I'd say what we have here is a mixture of blatant fraud, shoddy hoax, and inexcusable misinterpretation."

Indy didn't like the way Bernard so easily dismissed the entire exhibit, and felt compelled to defend Brody. "I think Marcus Brody has done us all a service. We should look carefully at what he's presented. Some of it might be valid."

Bernard clasped a hand on his shoulder. "I know all this may look intriguing to a young mind, but don't get misled by it. That's the problem with an exhibition like this. It's wild speculation, and it just confuses people. The Americas have been my specialty for thirty years, and I'll stake my reputation that neither Egyptians, Libyans, Phoenicians, nor Celts took tours here two thousand years ago."

Indy saw Brody mounting a podium across the room as camera bulbs flashed. Above his head a banner read: ANCIENT FORAYS. "I think I'll go hear what he has to say," Indy said.

"Wait a minute," Bernard said. "Do you want to go back to Guatemala? I'm restarting the excavation of the pyramid. I'm sure there's more to be uncovered."

"I'm sure there is, but don't you think it's a bit dangerous just now?"

"This time we'll have armed guards."

"I'm surprised you're asking me to join you. I had the impression that—"

Bernard waved a hand. "Don't worry about it." He reached into a pocket on the inside of his jacket and pulled out a sheet of paper. "I just want you to sign a petition I have here."

"What is it?"

"It's for the board of directors of this museum. It condemns this exhibition, requests it be closed immediately, and demands the removal of Marcus Brody from his position."

"Brody is an old friend of mine. I can't sign anything like that. Besides, I already told you, I think it's a worthwhile exhibition."

"Then I don't think you're going back to Tikal with me, Jones."

"I don't see what Tikal has to do with your petition."

"It has everything to do with it. A committee has been formed, of which I am the chairman, and any archaeologist who refuses to sign it will no longer be doing field-work for any of the major American, British, or European universities."

"You can't do that."

"Jones, you don't understand power and influence. If you did, you would put your name on this list right now."

"I'm not impressed," Indy said, and he walked away.

Indy approached the crowd surrounding the podium where Brody was speaking, and listened as he tried to calm his anger. Brody began by saying that the exhibition was dedicated to a woman he'd met many years ago while teaching a class in Nordic mythology at a Midwestern university. The woman later became his wife and source of inspiration for his study of Nordic heritage in the Americas. Indy knew she had died of pneumonia a few years after their marriage.

"But as I studied the subject, I discovered that the Norse sailors were only one of a number of early explorers who ventured to the Americas, and some of them apparently arrived here long before the Vikings."

Brody spoke enthusiastically about the evidence he'd gathered. He spoke with utmost confidence that what he presented was true, in spite of the critics.

"Not only do we have evidence in stone of Egyptian, Libyan, Celtic, and Norse adventures in both North and South America, but there are also legends from the time of the conquest about a tribe of white Indians living in the Amazon. Could these have been descendants of any early colony? An intriguing thought, and even as I speak a great British explorer, Colonel Percy Fawcett, is seeking such a lost city in an unexplored region of the Amazon. Just imagine what we could learn from such a tribe if we found it still in existence today."

A reporter called out to Brody. "If we forget about legends and just look at the hard evidence, are you saying that there is enough here to prove that our history books are wrong, that we've been misled? And my second question is: Isn't this exhibition a slap in the face to Christopher Columbus?"

Brody patted his forehead with a handkerchief, and took a sip of water. "Well, sir, we have not been consciously misled. At least, I hope not. What we are talking about goes beyond known American history into the realms of archaeology, the study of prehistoric culture. As always has been the case, when new evidence comes to light, the old theories fall away. And no, this exhibition is not an insult to Columbus. The fact is, he never claimed to be the first to sail across the Atlantic, and if he were with us today, I'm sure he'd find this exhibition an interesting one."

"This is utter nonsense," Bernard piped. Heads turned as the bearlike man moved through the crowd toward the podium. "What you see here is not scientific proof of anything. It's simply speculation, supported by highly questionable evidence. Granted, some of these markings may actually be man-made. But believe me, they are simply meaningless scratches made by primitive Indians to amuse themselves."

The pop of a flashgun accented Bernard's comment as a photographer snapped his picture. Bernard's eyes were like ice, not blue, but almost transparent. He seemed ill at ease in his penguin suit. "There's good reason our history books begin with Columbus. Libyans didn't go to California. Phoenicians didn't colonize Iowa. Celts went from Spain to the British Isles, but not to New England or South America. And Vikings didn't go to Minnesota or Oklahoma, much less Argentina and Brazil. A tribe of white Indians in the Amazon?" He smiled indulgently. "It's rubbish. Legendary lies."

"Now wait a minute, Dr. Bernard," Brody sputtered. "This is not a debate; this is an opening of an exhibition. You were not invited here to—"

"I understand that, Marcus. But we have a large contingent of the press here this evening, and I want them to understand that there is no record of cross-Atlantic trips by ancient mariners. The Vikings made it as far as Greenland. That is all. The Egyptians, Celts, and Libyans left no record of journeys across South America."

"Thank you, Dr. Bernard," Brody said, taking a new tack. "I'm sure your opinion will be duly reported. Now, I hope that all of you let your curiosity wander and seriously consider what you see here. Please enjoy yourselves, and thank you for coming." With that he stepped down from the podium.

Indy headed toward Brody, but several reporters and photographers immediately clustered around the museum director, while others peppered Bernard with questions. Indy decided he'd seen enough for tonight. Besides, he'd already promised Marcus that he'd meet him, and he had the feeling that the confidential matter was somehow going to be related to the exhibition.

As he stepped through the door and moved out into the Manhattan night, he had an urge to stop by the apartment where Deirdre was staying. He wasn't giving up on her so easily. But then he decided he'd give her a night to think it over.

He'd see her first thing tomorrow, and they'd work out their problems as they'd done before. He'd take her to Brody's office with him and then they'd have lunch and everything would be okay. It would be just fine.